AWAKENING
The Regonia Chronicles: Book One

By Elexis Bell

Eager to stay up to date on the latest dark fiction from Elexis Bell?

Sign up for her newsletter here.

To my family:
I'm sorry for the role I played in our destruction. And I forgive you for yours.
We are but humans, after all. Self-righteous and short-sighted, doing what we think best without ever truly knowing.

Prologue
Termana
3006 C.E.

Reginald

An errant creak in the night pricks at my ears. Eva and I look up from the documents and graphs displayed across the screen of our dining room table, and my eyes struggle to adjust to the darkness of the room, lit only by the eerie glow of our work.

"Olivia?" I whisper, but if she stirs in her room, she doesn't answer.

Eva shrugs and stretches to pull her bedroom door shut without rising from her chair.

I hastily type equations into the net, fingers never slowing. We settle back into our research, working on a new, improved defense program, testing its viability, desperate for anything to keep the Drennar out.

I pause to stretch my hands and glance out the window at my back. I look past darkened homes, letting all those little metal boxes fade into the background. The ceiling of our metal orb looms far above, hidden in the pitch black of simulated night on our terraformed asteroid.

Turning forward, I reach for a lemon cookie, sending a shadow of my arm to caress the ceiling. The package crinkles, almost masking the pop as the metal of the living room floor flexes.

My breathing quickens. I meet Eva's beautiful brown eyes, normally clear and sweet, now edged with concern. Swallowing, I turn to gaze into the dark living room, because even our relatively safe neighborhood isn't safe with aliens sneaking onto our space stations, sneaking onto Termana, to steal people away.

I set my cookie down, uneaten, and rise to my full height, hoping they haven't come for us this time. My mind whirls, trying desperately to think of something, anything, I could do to keep Eva and Olivia safe if they have.

But what chance do I have against a Drennar?

My limitations flash through my mind, and I swallow back the fear writhing within me, trying to claw its way out.

I have to try.

My Link shines a soft shade of amber, glowing from where it's implanted in my wrist, an indicator of increased stress levels, elevated heartbeat, and rate of breathing. Sweat beads on my forehead.

"Go to Olivia," I whisper, hoping the low volume keeps my nerves from my voice.

She nods and opens our daughter's bedroom door. Darkness welcomes her into its concealing embrace as she slips beyond the reach of our glowing table screen.

The floor in the living room flexes once more as our visitor takes another step. Panicking, I calculate the weight of the Drennar in the living room. I figure up the characteristics of the metal, using my Link to access the net and find the schematics of my own home.

Roughly 200 kilograms.

I gulp down a rough breath, uncertain as to what to do next. With a thought, I command my Link to turn on the living room lights. Relief washes over me.

Everything looks... normal.

Empty.

The little burgundy couch, the wooden table, quite a commodity so far from Earth, and the two chairs all sit just as they were when we tucked Olivia in. The windows are as black as the world beyond.

Though the front door is open just a crack, no Drennar looms over me waiting to steal me or Eva or Olivia away.

A sigh rushes from my lips. I chuckle.

Maybe the metal just flexed naturally.

But a little voice in the back of my head reminds me just how unlikely that is. And the door wasn't open when we sat down to work.

The floor flexes again, extinguishing every ember of hope.

I turn, seeking out the cause of the sound. Off to my left, a mere meter and a half from me, the air seems to shimmer and bend.

Furrowing my brows, I take a step forward, reaching out. My heart gallops in my throat.

Soft fabric meets my fingers, and I gasp. There shouldn't be anything there, but the strange, invisible fabric clings to a solid form, a waist, the size of a tree trunk.

A Drennar.

They've come for us.

The blood drains from my face, and dread pools in the pit of my stomach. My fingers move of their own accord, clutching a metal belt, pressing a button I've been told rests at its center. A mechanism whirs within it, and the air before me shimmers.

In an instant, the belt retracts within the center buckle, and my nightmare stands in my living room.

He looms over me, a full meter taller than I am. Electric blue lines mar his dark, grey skin, move within green irises, connecting his modifications to the brain concealed behind the plate that covers most of his skull.

I freeze, mind as blank as his expressionless eyes.

He's here to take us away.

That one thought fills me, reverberating through my mind. There's no other explanation. He's tailored for this one job. An extra set of arms to carry a prisoner. Dark wings, some strange combination of metal and skin, to haul his victim up from the surface of Termana.

My jaw drops as I wonder what other modifications he possesses, hidden within him, altering his senses, shaping his very makeup. My blood runs cold at the thought.

The belt buckle falls from my hand, landing with a solid thud. The button at its heart glows a soft blue.

All the academic curiosity I once held, all the times I wondered what it would be like to see one, sours in my gut. Regret floods me, and I wish I could go back to the days of not knowing, not understanding. Panic surges through my veins, and I try to come up with a plan.

But the Drennar reaches out one arm and sweeps me aside faster than I can blink. I slam head-first into the metal wall with a loud thud. Pain explodes through me, and I crumple to the floor.

In the next room, Olivia shrieks groggily. I can just hear Eva shushing her.

But it doesn't matter.

"What was that? Mom?" Olivia cries. "Where's Dad? Is it them?"

Dazed, I stare at Olivia's doorway. The world tips, and dark spots flicker over my vision. Everything slowly swims into focus as the Drennar moves gracefully through my home, toward Eva and Olivia.

"No," I mumble, trying to push myself up, trying to stand, but the world tilts and sways beneath me.

A thud from the next room. Eva screams, and Olivia cries out.

Rage builds within me, and my head clears, just a bit, just enough. I push myself to my feet. The floor tries to dodge my foot with every step, but I drag myself across the room. I bump the table, still lit up with our work, work it's seen now, work that's been rendered useless.

The Drennar ducks out of Olivia's door, and my hands curl into fists. Two of his arms pin her to his chest. Her tiny arms flail, and she kicks him as hard as she can, screaming all the while. She opens wide, clamping teeth on his arm and biting down.

But it's no use.

He holds fast to her small frame, undaunted by the measly assault one Human girl can offer. This beast steps toward me, pushes me aside, and I nearly fall over again.

My dazed mind races, spurred on by panic. I need an idea, any idea, to stop this thing, because I know damn well force won't work.

Behind it, Eva attacks, screaming, pummeling it with useless fists. "No!" she yells. "Give me back my baby!" Her voice rises in pitch, and she screams, "You monster!" Her voice breaks entirely, venturing into the realm of rage-induced gibberish.

But it's useless.

I can't beat this thing. I can't kill it, can't even wound it.

I need something else.

A desperate plea pops into my mind, and I speak it while I have the chance. "Take me, instead," I say. Quiet desperation fills my words.

The Drennar stops in the doorway to the living room, head bent low to slip through. Turning slowly, it straightens and stares down at me.

Eva and Olivia scream and kick and punch, though it must hurt them to do so. But it was my words that stopped him, insignificant as I may be.

A thin band of blue light emanates from the Drennar's eyes, and I freeze. It sweeps over me, scanning me. A chill dances down my spine, and my heart pounds behind my ears like a battle drum.

Olivia stills, but Eva continues her assault on the creature's back, missing the eerie alien technology completely.

The blue lines in its eyes move and shift, and I can almost see the calculations whirring through its mind.

"I won't fight you," I say, desperate to entice the creature before me. "I'll do whatever you want. I'll give you no trouble, just... Take me instead."

Another scan, this time two separate fans of blue light sweep over me. They move up and down my body, and I shudder, unused to such vulnerability. My heart lurches, and my palms sweat. I swallow back excess saliva.

Finally, Eva stills, exhausted. She falls to the floor, sobbing into her hands. Leaning against the Drennar's leg, she begs him to release Olivia.

And though I know she couldn't have heard me over her screaming, a small twinge of pain surges through me that she might sacrifice me without hesitation.

But for Olivia...

Would I sacrifice Eva for her? Would I give up Olivia for Eva?

My heart twists, and I know I couldn't make that choice.

Here's to hoping I'll never have to find out.

Here's to hoping I can save them both right now.

The Drennar speaks, and my cochlear implant translates what it can, given the limited samples we have of their language.

"...do anything?"

"Anything," I answer.

I don't need to know what else he said. It doesn't matter, as long as this works.

"I'll do anything you want. If you want us for experiments, if you want to study humans, if you want me to fight in some sick games, I don't care," I say, the words tumbling from my lips in a flurry of sound. "I'll do whatever you want. Just take me instead. Please. Leave them alone, and I won't fight you."

Eva and Olivia stare at me, open-mouthed.

Eva whispers in disbelief, "What?"

Another fan of blue light sweeps over me, and this time, I feel it, tingling just beneath my skin.

The Drennar speaks, and my implant translates, "Acceptable."

The Drennar turns and drops Olivia, practically on top of Eva. My heart leaps into my throat when it comes for me, but I nod. I don't fight as he reaches for me. I don't make a sound as he hauls me up, presses me against his chest with ease despite my 100 kilograms.

My head bounces against his shoulder as he walks to the front door. I find Olivia, Eva. They weep on the floor, watching me go. Olivia struggles in her mother's arms, trying to get to me, but Eva holds her back.

Voice thick with emotion, I say, "I love you."

"I'll get you back!" Eva whispers furiously. "If it's the last thing I do, I'll get you back."

My heart breaks, and pain lances my chest.

Tears fill Olivia's beautiful hazel eyes, and she cries out, "Don't leave me! Please, Daddy, don't leave me!"

I suck in a breath, heart lurching and twisting. Tears prick at the corners of my eyes.

"Don't take my dad!" Olivia screams at the Drennar.

But he only ducks out our front door.

I grit my teeth, scrunching my eyes closed now that Olivia and Eva have been stolen from my view. Tears streak down my cheeks, dripping onto the Drennar's shoulder, but he pays me no mind.

His wings unfurl, and he rockets upward. My head slams against the monster's shoulder, hard enough to make my world spin, and darkness creeps in at the edges of my vision. Everything fades away, and Eva and Olivia's cries drift out of earshot. Unconsciousness overtakes me before I can even see how the Drennar got past our security.

Chapter 1
Ulysses Space Research Station
12 years later, 3018 C. E.

Krona

For two days, I scream. My voice crashes over my Human guards in waves, undulating between rage and unbearable suffering. Fury burns its way out of my body, riding on my words, and they flinch as if punched.

But when I stop screaming, when I sing, they truly wish to flee. They gird themselves against my rage, but the sorrow in my songs pierces their armor.

I hope it burrows into their hearts and fills their dreams. I hope it haunts them, follows them, nips at their heels. I hope it sticks to their clothes like burrs.

Just as it does to me.

My heart twists, and my voice rises. The guards flinch as I sing, my voice soft and tragic, breaking over the words I commit to her, to Tenna.

To my lost love.

The guards shrink against the walls, huddling against cold stone as though it could protect them. Their armor, so rigid compared to mine, clanks discordantly on the rocks.

But I'll mourn her. I'll mourn the only way I know, the way *my people* mourn.

I find my own song, piecing it together bit by bit because this type of loss has never been mourned in Daen Tribe before.

How could she go to him? How could she betray me, betray our people?

My heart twists, and I shudder.

How could I...

I can't finish the thought, can't face what they say I've done.

She's alive. She has to be.

Her heart yet beats. It must.

So, I sing:

"Hoo kai voo mai." *You are my sound.*

"Coomli hoo vay tarn voo minay," *Without your name on my lips,*

"Voo mai kai tur." *My voice is empty.*

"Ulla minay ark voo sar voo reinlar," *Whose lips will find me when I'm gone,*

"Ahn rahn hoo?" *If not yours?*

The star-sickness, the thing they put in my head, translates the words into the Human language, destroying the melody. With a thought, I turn it off, denying their influence over my agony. A wave of bitterness rushes through me.

They've robbed me of my love. Why should they also rob me of the beauty of music?

But... Was it them who stole her from me?

My head drops, and unwashed black hair slumps into my face. I fall to my knees in my cell.

Staring down at my hands, I doubt myself. Pale, grey skin stretches over strong, nimble fingers, more than capable of all they say I've done.

There's a reason no one raised a challenge when Tenna chose me as her partner, as King. Swift and deadly, I'd already climbed through the ranks of Daen Tribe Warriors, earning an honorable position.

Now, these pitiful Humans claim she's dead, murdered by my hand.

My heart twists.

It's there, buried in the back of my mind. I can see it. But it doesn't feel real.

No!

It's not real! It's false. It feels *false.*

I grit my teeth as fresh agony washes through me.

I couldn't. I wouldn't *kill her.*

But I close my eyes, and there she is, face an ashen blue rather than her normal dusky gray. My hands squeeze tighter, wrapping around her throat, and horror shines in her beautiful, moss-green eyes.

I can feel her thrashing, feel her fighting, growing weak beneath me.

Her eyes lose focus, and all the life fades from her.

I open my eyes before the other lies the Humans told spring up again. My Tribe left broken without a leader. Tenna beneath another man, betraying me in body just as they say she betrayed our Tribe in spirit, leaving me for the enemy, the Chief of Roon Tribe.

My mind fills with images of Human ambassadors, rushing in to drag me away from a slew of bodies, from the killing rage they say I devolved into.

But it doesn't make sense.

I dig my hands into my hair.

It couldn't happen as they say, it wouldn't. She wouldn't betray me like that.

I couldn't kill her, couldn't kill our people, even if she...

My throat tightens at the thought. But it can't be. I feel it in every cell of my body, *know* I couldn't do it.

But then why do I remember it?

And yet, the memories aren't quite... right. My mind whirls, trying to analyze them. Something about the memories is strange, incomplete. The feelings they should hold are diluted, disconnected. Details about the Humans and their arrival on Regonia are missing entirely.

And how could they subdue me when so many of my kind failed?

All these details are just... missing.

I focus on this strange mystery, desperate for the distraction it holds.

They could never subdue me. Humans are... squishy.

Already, I've injured a few of them just taking my food tray with a bit too much fervor.

I stare out at them, peering between the bars of my cell. These strange creatures barely reach my chest, and even the soldiers are weaker than I. My brows furrow, because I know that no amount of training could have made them a match for me.

Their bodies just aren't made of strong enough materials. They couldn't stand up to someone from Regonia, let alone a renowned Warrior King supposedly dead set on destruction.

It doesn't make sense.

For a moment, I consider the glaring gap in my memory, the dark space between that false memory of Tenna and my waking in this prison with star-sickness in my arm and in my head.

The translator helps the doctors tell me what they'll do to me, but I shudder at the thought of it, of this thing buried so deep in my flesh I could never hope to get it out.

I stare at the thing in my arm, at the blood crusting the edges where I tried to tear it out. The little thing they call a "Link" stares up at me, determined to remain a part of me, and I grimace.

One of the guards sets his Link to play music, and the name of the song flashes on the little thing in my arm. "The Flame Deluge by Thrice. 2007."

The volume rises, and I know they're trying to drown me out. For a moment, I listen, feeling the song in my bones.

It isn't bad...

A grudging admission.

The screen on my arm flashes: Song Downloaded.

Fury burns through me at my own weakness, but what's one more moment of weakness after what I've done?

What they say *I've done.*

Tenna fills my mind, her betrayal and her death assaulting my frail sanity. Again, I see her lying beneath Chief Mourgam, sighing as he moved over her. I grit my teeth, trying to push the image away.

And still, I sing, letting it all fall from my lips, altering my words to fit the tune of the song.

"Is hoo arklar" Or have you found

"Visne mai," Another sound,

"Vay ris visne" The name of another

"Bin hoo minay?" On your lips?

"Mai ris hoo" The notes of you

"Traenboorlar" Exhaled

"Bin bisve cra?" On rival breath?

Even just thinking those words, let alone singing them, feels like a betrayal. It feels wrong to doubt her, despite the strange memories.

My eyes trace my tattoos, three simple blue rings encircling my wrist, pierced by an open circle on the top and the underside of my forearm. The mark of Daen Tribe.

My people fill my mind, batter at my conscience. Worry seeps into my gut.

Are they safe?

My eyes drift upward, sliding along the line that connects the Daen Tribe mark to that of my position as their leader, their defender. Their killer. Three rings circle my forearm, piercing open circles. I trace the line to its end in a circle on top of my hand.

I wouldn't betray this mark... Would I?

Tenna bears matching marks, bears the mark of our partnering ceremony. I finger the band at the base of my neck, etched into my skin. I trace the rays that emanate from it, branching onto my chest.

I couldn't betray her.

I couldn't kill *her.*

Crooning softly, gently, I raise my voice with the song, but no words come. Only sound. Only a sorrowful harmony.

A guard yells, but I don't want to understand his words, don't want to hear his pleas. Their suffering is insubstantial next to this.

Slowly, the fight leaves me, and all I can do is murmur her name, over and over. A lament.

A eulogy.

I slump in the middle of my cell, unmoving. My eyes drift closed, and I crumple into a ball, lying on my side. Exhaustion tugs at me, and I can't resist.

For the first time in two days, I drift into unconsciousness, welcoming the darkness that wraps around me.

Chapter 2
Odyssey Space Research Station
3018 C. E.

Tenna

Blinding light assaults my eyes. I slam them shut once more, blocking out smooth white walls and glaring, unnatural lights. Confusion settles over me, and my heart races.

Where am I?

I open my eyes again, seeking answers, but unfamiliar faces stare down at me. One says my name. The voice comes out small and kind, but the words around my name make no sense. I've never heard the language.

A disconcerting voice pipes up within my mind, offering what I can only assume to be a translation.

"Tenna, can you hear me?" the voice that shouldn't be there says.

The skin above my left ear tingles. Reaching up to touch the side of my head, I wince in pain. On my left arm, something sits, rooted into my dark, gray skin between bright blue tattoos.

A throat clears, drawing my attention back to the short beings around the bed. Their skin hovers around a mid-tone brown. Their ears are stubby, rounded things, rather than the elegant points of my own. One of the men smiles, showing fangs considerably smaller than mine.

What kind of people are these?

That eerie voice in my head supplies a word. "Humans."

"I'm Doctor Antar," the woman who spoke my name says.

I turn my head, raking my gaze over her short frame.

Is she even half my height?

Dark brown hair hangs around her face, unnatural and unsettling.

Where's the blue? The black or white?

I find crisp blue in her eyes, where a shade of green should be. Draped all in white, she nearly blends in with the sterile room around her.

Again, the weird, alien language grates over my ears, followed by the even weirder voice in my head, putting it into my language. "It's a pleasure to meet you."

I scrunch my brows, turning, looking for some source outside of me.

"That voice you hear," the Doctor says, and the voice in question translates it, "is your cochlear implant. It translates anything you hear into the language you're most comfortable with. We took the liberty of installing it while you were unconscious so that you might understand us when you woke."

Looking at my arm, I wonder at the function of the *thing* they put there. I don't know how I know it, but it isn't supposed to be there.

Doctor Antar says, "Yes, we installed that, as well." A small smile crosses her face. "That's your Link. It monitors all your vital functions. Temperature, heart rate, breathing, blood pressure, etcetera. If any of those reach unsafe levels, it emits a shrill beeping sound. You can change that later, if you'd like."

Somewhat apologetically, she adds, "Now, we are still learning about your physiology, so if you start feeling ill, or think anything's out of sorts, let us know. We'll help you and adjust the parameters accordingly."

I stare at her, nodding, but so much of what she says seems like nonsense. My heart races, yet the thing doesn't beep. I almost tell her, but she speaks.

"It can also be used to display a map of the station here, to set event reminders, and to contact anyone you wish to reach, either sending a message or setting up an audio or visual link. You can connect to the net with it and look up any information for which you have clearance. It can be used to interact with nearly everything on the station, or you can use it to play and gather music or videos. That's the most common use for these things."

But... What does that even mean?

What are vidos? Videos?

So many of her words have no translation, and the thing cobbles together lengthy substitutes that can't be possible.

Another tentative smile, and she continues, "We all have them here."

"Where is here?" I ask, voice too high. I speak the words in my own language, but horror moves over in cold waves.

What is my language?

After her implant presumably translates my words, Antar says, "You're on Odyssey Space Station." Yet another pause, and concern etches itself across the doctor's face. "You don't remember, do you?"

I cast my mind back, trying to find something, anything. But there's nothing.

My jaw drops.

A gaping black abyss waits within my mind, and all I have is this, waking here in this room with these... Humans.

I glance at the other two near my bed, raking my eyes over them, desperate to see some similarity, to feel like I belong.

They're male, taller than Antar, but nowhere near my height. One has slightly darker skin than the doctor, but the other matches her almost perfectly. The slightly darker one has darker hair, nearly black, with brown eyes. The other has yellow hair and brown eyes.

Yellow hair? What is this?

Panic grips me, and my breaths come fast.

I don't know them.

Have I ever known them?

I shake my head, uncertain. Nothing feels right. My feet stick out past the end of the bed I'm on, and I know it wasn't meant for me, wasn't meant for my species.

But what am I?

Why am I here?

Sitting up, my eyes catch on another bed to my right. Someone like me slumbers peacefully, unmoving. Gray skin, blue hair, some of the same tattoos. On my other side, three more beds hold three more of my kind.

My panic ebbs, just a little. The sharp edge of my fear dulls.

I'm not alone.

"What happened?" I ask.

"Oh, honey," Antar begins softly. "Your planet, your people..." She shakes her head, trailing off.

"What? What is it?" I demand.

One of the men answers, "They're gone. They're all gone."

Tears form and fall, cascading down my cheeks. A hollow pit opens within me, threatening to devour me whole. "How?"

The same male says, "A massive solar flare shot out and burned most of the planet. We were somewhat close and knew the flare was coming. We'd been studying that star. We happened to scan the planet for life..." He swallows hard, throat bobbing. "We got as many of your people off-planet as we could before the flare hit, but... we didn't have enough time or resources to make a second trip."

Antar whispers, "Most of those that we pulled off-planet didn't survive the trip back here. It seems that your bodies weren't prepared for a trip through space. We don't really know what happened yet, but we're looking into it. The five of you," she gestures to the beds, "are all that's left."

The remaining doctor, silent until now, says, "Your partner, Dremer, was conscious for a bit when we got him here. He told us your name, before he..."

The name Dremer strikes a false note in my mind. I am, indeed, partnered. But the name doesn't sound familiar. "Before he what?"

The first male doctor says, "Before he died. His heart gave out."

The world shifts beneath me, but it isn't the loss of Dremer that I feel.

There's someone... someone that I miss...
And he's gone.
But who is he?

My heart twists with the loss, made deeper by the darkness where my memories of him should be.

I shake my head, brows furrowed. Lying back on my bed, I close my eyes, turning away from the strange Humans. Tears fall over my cheeks as I claw at the black walls inside my head, desperate to remember him.

To remember anything.

***

The rest of the day passes in a blur of invasive tests. My nerves fray as the Humans break several needles on my skin before managing to pull blood from my body.

My muscles tie themselves into knots as they calibrate some machine, over and over, adjusting it to account for the differences between my skin and theirs. I tense as they use the strange device to take pictures of my insides, flinching at the wrongness of such an act.

"We'll need to compare everything with the tests we did while you were unconscious," Doctor Antar says, and I shudder.

What did they do to me while I was asleep?

But the healer doesn't notice my fear. She keeps talking.

"We'll compare those to the tests from your friends and see if we can figure out what brought you out of it."

Eventually, Doctor Antar pronounces a diagnosis of trauma-induced amnesia. With a smile that just doesn't feel real, she says, "I'm sure your memories will return with time."

The woman begins more tests, but I barely notice. I drift through it all, mind elsewhere.

I don't care what they're measuring. I want my home. I want my partner.

I want my memories.

Internally, I wander through the darkness, begging my mind to release its grip on my past, to show me where I came from.

And who I lost.

Crawling back into my bed for the evening, I sleep fitfully. My dreams are a vague mass of anxiety and unease, but they take no shape. Or if they do, I wake with no memory of the shapes they held.

As I lie in bed, waiting for the healer to tell me something, anything, another of these strange creatures appears. Antar brings her over to me, introducing her as Olivia.

I let my eyes drift over her, from her smooth black hair to her warm brown skin to her strange eyes. Shades of blue, green, and grey mingle within her gaze, but she looks upon me with compassion and unbridled curiosity.

"Hi," she says, a Human greeting. "We'll be working together, so they figured I could show you around. Want to go for a walk?"

The prospect of stretching my legs has me nodding, throwing my legs over the side of the bed. "Definitely."

"You know where to find me if you need anything," Antar says.

Olivia crosses the room, drawing up next to my bed. She holds out a stack of clothing. "Here you go. I'll show you where you can change out of that hospital gown."

I throw back the blanket, practically jumping out of bed, and accept the proffered clothing. It feels soft in my hands. Simple linen trousers, a cotton shirt, socks, underwear, and something... else. Two flimsy cup-like things on straps.

I stare at the strange thing.

Is it from before?

Are these mine?

"Alright, come with me," Olivia says, brusque but not unkind.

I follow her past the occupied beds, all the way to the end of the room. A single door leads to the bathroom they showed me yesterday.

I hold up the thing with fabric cups. "What is this?'

"A bra," Olivia says.

She explains its purpose, and I disappear into the bathroom to change. But the clothes hang strangely on my body, unlike anything I've worn before.

But what am I used to wearing?

On exiting the bathroom, I find Olivia smiling up at me. She holds out a pair of well-worn leather boots, and I return her smile.

I know these boots.

Every tug of the laces feels like it could pull a memory from the depths of my mind. I've worn these before, and those days hover just beyond my grasp, almost stepping forward.

But the darkness in my mind hides them too well.

The Human woman leads me around, and I try to keep my mind on her words. This stairwell leads to the labs. That one leads to the defense section. A hallway leads to a bar and the cafeteria.

So many circular halls, so many pale grey metal walls, such low ceilings... I walk in the center of the hallway to avoid hitting my head.

Olivia's Link begins playing a song, and I look down at the one stuck in my own wrist, wondering how the thing works.

Human words flash on the screen, followed by a translation. "Crash and Burn by Angus and Julia Stone. 2014."

Olivia stares at symbols on her Link, Human words, and I listen, letting it flow over me in this alien place. The music unties the knots within me. Something about it calls to me, resonating in my bones despite the strange language.

It's beautiful.

New words flash on my Link. "Song downloaded."

Downloaded?

What does that...

"Coming?" Olivia says, cutting off my thoughts. She stares at me with amusement dancing in her eyes.

I nod.

As we set off, I follow closer, pay more attention. But my mind drifts, regardless. We turn down one grey hall after another, pass beneath unnatural lights. They beat down on me, glaring and unbearable.

Up ahead, a dark square in the wall breaks up the monotony of the place. Our footsteps ring out, echoing through empty halls as we approach the window.

My jaw drops as I stare out. The night sky waits on the other side, unending darkness punctuated by tiny dots of light, all so much closer than it should be. A trickle of fear runs down my spine, but I can't place it, can't fathom why the sky should strike panic into my bones.

I touch the thick glass, startled by how cold it is. Beside me, Olivia whispers, "It's breathtaking, isn't it?"

I don't answer, and she doesn't seem to mind.

"It gets me every time," she says.

Is home out there somewhere?

My stomach lurches.

I guess not. Not anymore.

A wave of sadness washes over me, and I drag myself from the window to follow in the Human girl's wake.

No, she's not a girl. She's a woman.

The strange electronic voice in my head tells me that Olivia is indeed a woman of 24 summers. I shudder at the invasiveness of their technology.

Eventually, we find ourselves in a large room packed with boxes and bottles. I stare at them, trying to understand their meaning, but the names on the bottles are just that. Names. They don't tell me their purpose.

"Now," Olivia begins, lowering the volume of her music. "It isn't exactly glamorous, but for now, you'll be employed with the cleaning crew. Everyone here has to work, no exceptions. I'll show you the ropes tomorrow morning, just show up here at 9:00."

She takes my hand in hers, holding it up. Olivia taps the screen of my Link a few times, then releases my hand.

"There you go. I set an alarm for you and marked this spot on your map."

"That was quick," I say, surprised.

"Let's just say... I'm good with tech." She laughs. "I marked your room, the cafeteria, and the bar on there, too." Olivia winks as she mentions the bar, for some reason.

Why do I need to find a bar? And what's it made of?

Raising an eyebrow, I look at the display. "How do I use it?"

"Basically, just think of what you want it to show you. Or what you want it to do. Same with the translator. You can have it translate specific words or phrases whenever you want."

With a shrug, she begins walking again, waving for me to follow. "Now, I'll walk you to your room. It's on your map, but I want to show you, just in case you have any questions."

"Thank you."

"It's nothing," she says.

More long metal tubes, walking down the center to avoid ducking. We pass windows every now and again, and I force myself to keep walking, telling myself not to try to find my home among the stars.

Because it isn't there anymore.

Olivia walks on, unaware of my shattering heart.

As we approach the living quarters, we find more Humans. Most look pretty similar. Skin tones in varying shades of tan or rich browns. Brown and black hair. Dark eyes. A shock of yellow or red hair stands out here or there.

But one Human, in particular, stands out.

Clear, pale green eyes smile at me, pulling at my memories. The color feels *right*.

I know that color.

My heart twists painfully, and my mind screams at the agony of not understanding. That color, those eyes, reach into me, into my past. They're there, somewhere.

I can feel them.

Someone else has eyes like that, I know it.

Olivia's quick steps pull me onward, but I look over my shoulder at the man with the pale green eyes, refusing to lose that small scrap of familiarity. Finally, the curve of the hallway steals him from my view, and that perfect color, that tenuous link to my past, disappears.

I lock it into my mind, holding tightly to it, vowing to bring it out into the light when I finally have some time to myself.

I face forward, eyes tracing the doors lining either side of the curved hall. Every so often, hallways shoot off to the left, pointing inward, as though this place were a disc and this was the outermost layer. Halfway to the next hall, we stop at a door on the outward-facing side.

"This is it," Olivia says. She reaches up, holding her Link near the doorframe. "That keeps track of who comes and goes. You can use your Link to lock it or to program it to allow certain people in. Theft isn't usually a problem, though. Then again, this might be why."

With the rough grating of metal on metal, the door slides away, disappearing within the wall and revealing... another metal room. My heart sinks, but what did I expect?

I duck in and stare up at the ceiling, just barely high enough to accommodate my frame. Only the window offers any sort of relief from the crushing space.

A Human-sized bed rests on one side, and I dread curling in on myself to sleep there. With furrowed brows, I assess the rest of the room. A small table near the bed holds a light and a strange black sphere. The other side of the room holds a wardrobe and a doorway leading to another, smaller room.

"The shower, sink, and toilet can be controlled using the Link," Olivia says. "Just think, 'Turn on the shower,' or, 'Turn on the sink,' or, 'Flush,' and the Link takes care of it."

She says something about the Link auto-connecting to everything in the room. I look around, wondering what auto-connect means and gaping at how much they rely on these things.

When Olivia explains that the little black sphere is a projector for movies or browsing something called the net, also controlled by the Link, I sigh. It blocks the outside world, turning the window opaque and ruining the only relief I have from this claustrophobic nightmare.

The window means open space, terrifying as it may be. It means freedom. No metal walls, no ceiling looming just overhead.

A bench waits beneath the window, ready for me to sit, to dream of home.

No, that 'movie' thing won't be used.

Even now, the cold steel around me seems to suck the life from my body. I want to run, to feel a breeze on my face and in my hair. I want long grass whispering across my legs. I want the joyful laughter of one much loved close at my side.

The color Humans call mint springs to mind, the color of those eyes, and a lance of pain shoots through my heart.

Olivia's song trails off, leaving me far behind and taking that half-memory with it.

Turning from the window, I find Olivia standing in the doorway.

"This little thing also plays music," the Human says.

A spark of joy bursts within me.

Maybe I'll use it after all.

Olivia smiles and says, "I hope you don't mind, but I took the liberty of downloading some for you." Dipping her head to the side, she adds, "And by some, I mean all the free stuff."

My heart dances.

I have music.

Somehow, that makes things, maybe not better, but more tolerable.

"How do I use it?" I hold up my arm and glance at the Link. "With this?"

Olivia nods.

"You have a lot on there. Any music that's over a thousand years old is completely free, so anything released in 2018 or before. Stuff that's over five hundred years old is one credit for five hundred songs. The newer it gets, the more it costs. Until you start working, you won't have any credits of your own, so just free stuff for now."

I don't know how much I have, don't know what credits are, but I don't care. Not right now.

I'll worry about that later.

"Can I play all of it on here," I gesture to my Link, "when I leave my room? Like you did with yours."

"I can fix it that way," Olivia answers, grinning.

"Yes, please," I say, stomach fluttering. "I want music. I *need* music."

Those words ring true, resonating with every fiber of my being, and I'm glad that *this* need can be easily remedied.

Olivia taps my Link a couple of times, then shows it to me. "Songs downloaded." flashes across the screen. And though I still don't know what 'downloaded' means, relief floods me. I sigh contentedly.

"Just tell it what kind of music you want, or what you're feeling, and it'll choose accordingly. Once you listen to some and get some favorites, you can pick specific songs. You can also specify if you want anyone else to hear it, or to listen personally."

Sad music.

Personally.

A glance at the screen shows me strange alien symbols, "Think of Me by David O'Dowda and Rachel Wood. 2016."

I walk to the window, gazing out at the vast nothingness before me. Closing my eyes, I think of mint, and all it once meant to me.

Love. Joy.

Passion and strength.

Tenderness.

The concepts are there, but nothing concrete. No complete images, just mint, soft heather-gray, and strands of ink, all blurred out of focus. I push, but something in my mind pushes back. I can't break through, and frustration bubbles to the surface.

How can it all be lost so easily, wiped away in an instant?

How long will it take for it to come back?

I open my eyes, staring out at space for a while. I search for my home, heart aching as my eyes move from one star to another.

Can this just be a dream?

But I know I never would've thought any of this possible in my previous life. I know we didn't have this 'tech' Olivia speaks of, and I long for the life I once had, for the simplicity I know it held.

The metal around me seems to reach for me, moving closer, suffocating me.

From the doorway, Olivia says, "Shall we go eat? It's about lunchtime."

Reluctantly, I silence the music with a thought. Nodding, I follow the little Human woman into the hall. The door to my room shuts on its own behind us.

Chapter 3

Novay

Twelve years before, 3006 C. E.

Reginald

I lie in a bed too big for me, drowning in so much space. All my life, my beds, my clothes, my shoes have all been too small. I've always banged my knees on too-short tables, fell into chairs that sat just a little too low. I've always had to alter things to fit my tall frame.

Not now.

Now, I'm too small for the things around me, too insignificant. Everything dwarfs me here, and somehow, that makes it all worse, adding to the loss that fills me. So much distance when all I want is someone close.

I roll onto my side.

Don't let it bother you.

It's just another experiment.

I close my eyes, and my mind drifts back to my last day with them. I rack my brain for something else, anything else, that could have saved Olivia and left me with them.

But no perfect solutions present themselves, even now, even without the frenzy of the moment or the head trauma.

And I know I'd do it again.

Sighing, I play back a recording of Olivia's last birthday, letting the screen on the back of my eyelids show me the life I left behind.

She smiles warmly, looking so much like her mother that it breaks my heart twice over.

A cake from Olivia's favorite bakery sat on the table, decorated with my brother's candles, the same ones we use for every birthday. The little stubs were almost beyond redemption.

Have they replaced them yet?

Can Eva afford new candles now that it's just them? They're not exactly easy to come by.

Will Olivia even want candles for her next birthday?

My insides twist at the thought because I won't know who she becomes. I won't see what kind of woman she grows into.

The memory plays on, and I watch her blow the candles out quickly, not wanting to waste them. She and Eva laugh as my nephew cuts the cake lopsided, making extra cuts and curves, just for their smiles.

Plates and forks settle as people finish their slices, and I watch Eva approach, placing a hand on mine.

My heart leaps as I fetch Olivia's present, the only one this year given the cost. But we knew she wouldn't mind.

She sees my careful handling and unwraps it gently.

The dust cover shines brilliantly in the light, despite its age. A gleaming silver circle outlines a beautiful green iris in a woman's eye on the cover. Over a millennia old, and the book looks nearly perfect.

Olivia stares down at her favorite book, The Host by Stephanie Meyer, eyes shimmering in a sea of tears. She settles it softly on the table and rushes around to hug us.

My breath catches, and tears slip between my closed eyelids. I can almost feel her arms around my waist.

Rolling onto my back, I wipe the tears away and stare up at the ceiling. I can't watch her get her gloves to handle the book, can't watch her smile at me, can't watch Eva thank me for suggesting the book.

A chasm opens within me, threatening to swallow me whole.

Forty-five days have done nothing to lessen the pain.

***

I return to my room for lunch, following behind a Drennar, but I can still feel the small, circular pad they put on my inner elbow, the circlet they placed atop my head. I almost didn't notice the prick of the needle in the center of the pad, and I can't find a hole or a drop of blood.

My guard, a short Drennar, closer to my height, locks me into my room without a word. I don't try to ask her anything, don't speak any pleasantries. They never answer.

With a sigh, I approach my strange little nightstand. A single clear square waits on a white plate.

"Tasty..." I whisper, raising one eyebrow.

I pick the flimsy thing up and settle it on my tongue, wishing, just once, they'd put some sort of flavor into these things. But there's nothing. It dissolves quickly, leaving me wanting.

I yearn for real food, damn the nutritional value of these weird little squares. Damn the fact that I feel healthier.

I want my cookies.

I want the taste, the texture.

I want to chew something for God's sake.

The plate disappears into the depths of the nightstand of its own accord, and two orbs replace it. I pop one into my mouth, breaking the membrane with my teeth and swallowing the water that floods out. The membrane dissolves instantly, and I pop the other one in.

The tiny platter they rested on disappears into the nightstand as well, leaving the surface completely flush. No seam. No line. No ripples.

For the millionth time, I run my hand over the smooth, grey surface, trying to figure it out. For the millionth time, I find no answers.

The more I see of this world, of the Drennar, the more I realize that we're at their mercy.

We're completely outclassed.

Chapter 4
Ulysses Space Research Station
3018 C. E.

Krona

I wake on my bed, stiff and unrested.

And confused.

I fell asleep on the floor. I know I did.

I run my hands over my face, groggy.

I must have moved in the night. It's not like they'd move me. They can't be stupid enough to step into the cell with me.

I sit up slowly, mind a foggy mess. Dim as the light may be, it stings my eyes. My head aches with it.

"Ugh…" I groan.

The strange pain echoes in my past. After Chief Mourgam had his Tribe dam the river and our primary water source ran dry for far too long, after we lead our people against Roon Tribe and dismantled his precious dam with our bare hands, we celebrated our victory.

The river swelled, and we danced along its banks, raising our voices to the sky.

But the next day, Tenna and I spoke with the families of the Lost Ones. We mourned them with marks on flesh and voices raised to find their sounds.

Though we hadn't cut down anyone who hadn't raised a blade to us, though we lost fewer than Roon Tribe did...

We lost many.

And that night... I couldn't sleep. Though I had no clue what the normal dosage would be, though I ate far too many, Bellona flowers helped.

But the aching in my head the following morning, the fuzzy feeling in my thoughts, was the same as it is now.

Did they give me Bellona flowers?

I shake my head.

No. I wouldn't have eaten them if they'd offered.

But maybe it was in my food?

Closing my eyes, I turn onto my side, facing the wall. My mind drifts to the night after the battle, before the day of mourning. Tenna's smile flashes through my thoughts.

And just like that... I'm there again.

"You nearly cut his arm off," I say, wrapping her in my embrace.

"Bastard deserved that and more," she answers. "I don't think he'll order another dam built anytime soon."

A devilish glint shines in her eyes, and she takes a step forward, pushing me to our bed, taking me down upon it. Our lips meet, and I roll her to her back, staring into brilliant green eyes, so much brighter than usual next to our dark red bedding.

Her breath comes fast and hot, burning against my skin like wildfire. I grip her thighs, so strong but so soft. She kisses me, hunger driving her to take the lead, to push me back and climb atop me.

But another image rises to claim my thoughts, sending rivers of ice through my veins.

Tenna kissing the naked, ash-colored skin of Mourgam's flesh, lips moving to his neck, his shoulder, and finally to the scar she left on him in battle, almost apologetic.

"NO!" I roar, sitting straight up.

My guards jump, shrinking back into the wall.

Rage fills me, and my hands rise to the sides of my face, pressing on my temples as if to shove the thoughts out.

She was proud of that scar! She wouldn't apologize for it.

But something strikes me.

I didn't remember that yesterday. That bit of the memory wasn't there.

I shake my head again, rocking back and forth.

Am I sick?

Is my mind hiding things? Inventing *things?*

"WHAT IS THIS?" I shout.

The guards panic.

Gritting my teeth, I push my hands harder against my temples.

Maybe it's the translator, the star-sickness. Maybe it's messing with my mind.

I need it out. I have to get the star-sickness out.

For half a heartbeat, I claw at the skin above my ear, the little shaved patch where my hair should be, where a scar sits instead.

Or maybe they did something else when they drugged me.

Blinding clarity settles over me, and my eyes dart to the creatures on the other side of the bars.

That must be it. Nothing else makes sense.

On my feet in an instant, I turn and lift my bed. I fling it against the far wall of my cell, sending splinters and chunks flying.

I clear the distance to the bars in two steps, then rattle them in their stone footings. Hot, violent fury courses through me, and I scream, "What did you do to me?!"

My grip tightens on the bars, and I shake them again. Dust falls around me as the bars beat and bruise their way free of the stone ceiling, the rock floor.

Half the guards sprint out of the room, darting upstairs. A door flies open, and unnatural light pours through, too cleanly white.

I shut my eyes against it, ignoring the aching in my head at the blinding light.

"WHERE IS SHE?" I demand.

The light disappears, and my eyelids quit glowing with it. I open my eyes in time to see the two remaining guards catch small bottles, thrown down the stairs by those who fled. They open them, and a sickly-sweet gas erupts.

It smells of Bellona flowers, hundreds of them, an entire field.

The world slants, and my eyelids grow heavy. My body begs to slump down into the earthen floor. My hands slip down the bars. My knees bend. The floor rushes up to meet me, and the world turns out the lights.

The Humans walk to the bars, careful and slow. One of them, a female with red hair, speaks, and the strange voice of my translator says, "Holy shit."

I drift away, thinking of the absurdity of that phrase.

Why, after all, would anyone worship such a foul substance?

Stupid Humans.

***

I wake on the floor, staring at my shattered bed. Small pits ring the bars of my cell, and I reach out, letting one finger brush the metal. It shifts, still loose.

The guards, now numbering six rather than four, turn to face me. Every hip bears a holster, armed with Bellona gas.

Overkill.

A single bottle could knock me out for days. Those two might have done just that.

I close my eyes, regretting my outburst for a single breath.

No.

I shake my head.

Let them think me barbaric.

If they can look upon me and see anything other than a man at the end of his rope, then I'll use that against them.

My head screams at me to be still, to sleep, to shove the light away. The world swirls as I roll onto my back, groaning.

They really need to learn the dosage on that stuff.

I close my eyes, giving my head a reprieve from the blinding light streaming in from upstairs.

"How long was I out?" I ask.

After the delay of the translator, the guard closest to the bars says, "All day. You're just in time for lights out."

They blow out most of the candles and torches but leave the hearth lit. Someone treks up to close the door at the top of the stairs.

Stupid Humans.

I shake my head, letting my eyes roam over them in the near-darkness, seeing every detail. The pain in my head stops screaming, and I watch them fumble in the darkness, uncertain even with the light of the fireplace.

They can't see in the dark like we can.

My brows furrow as I consider this. It explains that glaring light. But how heavily do they rely on that? They light up the things in their arms, using them to find things on the table in the corner as if in answer to my question.

I'll take any advantage they afford me.

With that Bellona gas so close at hand, getting out might take some effort. Or at least, a few attempts.

I'll loosen the bars slowly. They'll dispatch those bottles quickly, so I'll have to make sure they can't get to them.

There will be a lot of blood.

My mind races, fitting pieces together, and I know I can kill them without regret.

They did something to my head, trying to convince me that I...

I take a deep breath, fending off the memories that just don't make sense, the images that just aren't whole.

No. They took me from Tenna.

They dishonor her with their accusations. They dishonor me with accusations of murder.

Though I can't fathom a way for them to do it, a way for them to get these things into my head, I know they have. I feel it in my bones.

The Bellona gas, the translator, the thing in my wrist that looks so much like theirs...

In all the stories of our Drennar ancestors, their mutations were different. This isn't star-sickness.

And Tenna isn't dead.

I know it.

She's alive, and so are our people.

I'll kill them to get to her, to get to our Tribe.

A deep resolve soaks through me, teasing the tension from my muscles. My hands curl into fists, and I let myself imagine the crush of their bones, the way it'll feel to get out of here, to find her.

Because I *will* find her.

Or unlikely as it may seem, I'll die trying.

When morning comes and I sing my torment, my words are different. They're tortured and full of longing, but gone is the insecurity, the doubt.

She was faithful, but they took her. Hatred fuses with sadness, and the guards shrink into the walls, hiding from my songs as well as they can without deserting their posts.

They previously thought they could hate this room no more.

They were wrong.

Chapter 5
Odyssey Space Research Station

Tenna

Just across the hall, we step into Olivia's room, and I breathe easier. Music begins to play immediately, and my Link flashes, "Crack Baby by Mitski. 2016." It whispers, low and soothing, slipping through the air around me.

Olivia moves around her room, bustling from one shelf to another, interacting with strange Human things that I don't yet understand. And I merely stand, arms hanging at my sides, letting the lyrics of the song flow through me. The singer laments something known but unknown, remarks upon horses, and something about it resonates with me.

Did I ride a lot... before?

"I had to dress nice for Doctor Antar," Olivia mumbles.

But I hadn't noticed her clothes, the khaki pants and her pale blue shirt with too many buttons seemed normal for these people. They closely match my own.

Even now, I barely notice her words as I stare in awe at the room she calls hers. No window offers relief, but the room breathes with a life of its own, cushioned and alive, transcending the mere metal box that it is.

Shelves and draperies cover every wall. Books and odd little bits and pieces fill the shelves, and I stare at them, unable to name a single trinket.

Gone is the harsh, stark white light of the rest of this place. A soft, amber glow fills the room, so close to the candlelight and firelight I'm used to.

I'm used to candles and fires?

I try to push at the walls in my mind, try to let this light lead me further into my past.

But I get nowhere.

"Have a seat," Olivia says, drawing my attention. She smiles at me. "I'll be out soon."

With that, she disappears into her bathroom with a bundle of clothes in her arms, pilfered from the wardrobe I hadn't even noticed yet.

There's just so much to see in here.

I wander closer to the shelves, eyeing the books. The words on the spines are unrecognizable Human symbols. But maybe the Link could help me understand them.

I stare at the objects on the shelves, stacked in front of and on top of the books. Statues of animals I've never seen. A dial with four evenly spaced letters around the outer edge and a needle pointing idly between two of them, 'N' and 'E.' I lift it, and the needle moves when I tip it sideways, falling under its own weight, though that can't be its true function.

Before the song ends, Olivia emerges from her bathroom in tight black pants and heavy black boots. Her tight black shirt bears a deep neckline and no sleeves. No tattoos mark her skin, and it sends a wave of sadness through me.

But she must have some place in society...

I stare down at the marks on my arms, turning my hands over to look at the underside of my wrists.

Is that what these are? My place?

With a sigh, I marvel that they haven't disappeared along with my world.

"Much better," Olivia says with a smile. "Now, I can relax, and they won't take this away from me." She takes a deep breath, shaking out her shoulders. "So. Food?"

My stomach growls, and I nod. We set off, leaving the brief respite of colors, sound, and softness behind for harsh, unfeeling tubes of metal.

A few hallways in, we find a wide, tall room packed with table after table after table. Humans fill most of the chairs, all turning to stare when we enter. Olivia might have been able to slip in unnoticed on her own, but I tower over everyone. They cock their heads back to look at me.

But it feels... normal.

How often did I command the attention of a room?

I furrow my brows, considering the thought as Olivia leads me to a line of people. They shuffle forward along a wall where basins of food wait on counters. The first few have some sort of soup. The next group of basins holds lumps of bread, and the last group has vegetables of some sort.

Olivia says, "The food on stations isn't great, but it eats just the same."

We load our trays, and Olivia holds her Link up to a little panel on the wall. I step forward, intending to copy her action and see what happens.

"Not yet," she says.

I pull my arm back, eyeing the panel.

"You don't have credits yet," she says. "I got it."

I thank her, then follow her to an empty table.

"I'll introduce you to a few people at dinner. Probably best not to overwhelm you right off the bat," Olivia says, voice light and teasing, as if feeling me out.

But it soothes my nerves.

"Probably." Taking on a similar tone, I say, "You're really smart. You should be a healer."

Chuckling, Olivia says, "Sarcasm. You'll fit right in."

But she grows serious as we tuck into our food.

"The whole doctor thing isn't for me. Too tedious. Being cramped in the hospital wing or the labs, all day, every day. Running the same tests on the same things. Treating the same vitamin deficiencies, depression, and insomnia…" She shakes her head. "No, thank you."

After a pause and a bite of food, I say, "But surely there are jobs better suited for you than cleaning and showing me around."

Her apparent discomfort in the clothes she wore for the doctors and the change in her demeanor when out of their view flashes through my mind.

Something you wouldn't feel the need to change yourself for, perhaps.

"Eh. I guess so. The tests the Coalition runs on everyone said I was suited for something like that. I just couldn't stand the idea of it." She shakes her head gently. "Really pissed off the Coalition when I refused. We compromised, though."

I tilt my head to the side, raising a brow, and she goes on.

"I don't just clean. I'm also a pilot, one of two on this station. We mostly just do supply runs down to Termana, which is why I have stuff in my room that you can't get up here. It takes both of us for those trips." She slurps a scoop of soup. "But it only takes one of us on a smaller ship for trips between stations. Between trips, I clean."

She shrugs, biting off a hunk of bread.

"And show me around, apparently."

"Actually, I volunteered for that."

"Why?" I ask.

"It gets boring here. Someone new to talk to, new stories to hear... once you get your memory back anyway. I couldn't pass that up." Looking down at her food, Olivia says, "I felt bad about it once I learned why, but I was really excited when I heard they were bringing aliens here. No offense."

I smile, despite everything. "None taken."

I shrug off the word 'alien.' To me, that means these Humans, but it really is just a matter of perspective.

"So, this Coalition..." I say. "They're in charge?"

"Have been ever since just before our ancestors trashed Earth." She looks up from her food and says, "Yep. Ruined a whole planet. I guess I should explain that."

I shake my head, incredulous.

How do you ruin a planet?

I stare at this little Human girl, apparently more dangerous than I'd previously thought.

"Alright," she says, settling her spoon into her empty bowl. "I guess you get to learn about Humans now.

We're not really all that great as a whole. Actually," she considers her words, "we're pretty terrible."

I stare at her, open-mouthed.

She explains that, for most of their civilized history, they paid no mind to the effects of their own actions. Only when the pollution was so heavy that entire cities couldn't breathe without filters strapped to their faces and entire species started dying out thanks to Human toxins did people notice.

"Even then," she says, "most didn't care."

How?

How could they not care?

"Around 2300 C.E., a couple supervolcanoes erupted, putting even more dust and ash into the air. Millions died, and Earth *started* dying. For fifty years, they just fought over what was left."

Olivia shakes her head, and shock sweeps through me at the thought of such a callous group of people.

"Anyway, in 2354, they formed the Survival Coalition. One supreme authority. One goal. Survival at any cost."

She goes on to talk about clean energy, but it goes over my head. Not that it matters. It apparently didn't work, something about too little, too late.

"So," she continues, "they scraped by until they could find a new planet. They chose a few asteroids that had ice and all the minerals we'd need, Termana among them, and made new planets."

"They *made* planets?"

"Well, they started to," she says. "Then, 2812 happened."

"The fourth largest nuclear power plant in the world melted down. It spit so much radioactive waste into the air that the atmosphere just…" She trails off, going quiet for a moment.

"They ordered an emergency evacuation," she eventually says. "But Termana was the only asteroid far enough along to support life in any permanent way. It wasn't perfect, but there were farms, already functioning, and enough resources to sustain the amount of people they could save on such short notice. Mostly just the ones that were already in transit."

She stares at the room beyond, at the people around us. "Billions were abandoned."

Horror settles on my shoulders, and ice moves through my veins.

"They left them? What about survival?"

"By the time the ships would have gotten back, they would've all been dead." Olivia meets my gaze, eyes filled with sadness. "The people on the other asteroids, just little outposts, nothing permanent or sustainable yet, were abandoned to fend for themselves, but... they didn't make it."

We sit in silence for a moment, and I stare down at the food before me. My stomach roils at the loss, at the echoes it holds with the lost planet the Humans saved me from.

"Now, we're here," Olivia says. "A few hundred years later, and still struggling to come back from it. We might go back someday, if the planet recovers, but that could take another few centuries."

My heart breaks. So many lives gone. So much wasted. And for Humans, it didn't have to go that way.

Their ancestors really do sound terrible.

But that doesn't lessen their final suffering.

"The Coalition does what they can, but mostly we just need time to repopulate, now," Olivia says. "And someone to keep us from destroying this place too."

I sit quietly, forcing myself to eat despite the sick feeling in the pit of my stomach as I consider rulers that would abandon so many and the guilt that must have followed.

Eventually, Olivia says, "Anyway, once the Coalition gets a better feel for what you can do, they'll probably move you from the cleaning crew. It's one of the easiest jobs here, and who knows what you're good at. For now, though," she raises one eyebrow, "you're stuck with me."

A laugh slips through my lips. I consider her and find that I don't mind being stuck with this strange, little Human woman.

We finish our food, all the while discussing music, and then set off through the barren metal halls to the outer ring, the residential section. Briefly, I wonder if I was a navigator, having pieced together my surroundings so quickly. But shadows wrap around my past, hiding it all from me.

"I wanted to show you something," Olivia says. "It isn't the greatest thing, but I bored you with our history. Figured you might want to see what we have left."

We approach a window, a little alcove between two bedrooms. Chairs and a table sit facing the vast expanse of space. But something blocks the view.

A huge metal ball, punctuated by massive panes of glass consumes the sky. At regularly spaced intervals, things Olivia calls airlocks perch on the metal shell, waiting to allow ships to dock.

"They always remind me of the portholes on old-school submarines or ships," Olivia says.

My Link provides images to show me what she means, but I stare at the planet before me, wondering if something so alien could even be called a planet.

"Why does it look like that?" I ask.

"Well, the old Coalition, way back around 2400, thought that was a good idea. They cased the whole asteroid in." She shrugs, pursing her lips. "That was the best they could come up with on short notice. I guess they couldn't figure out the whole atmosphere thing, and there were plenty of nearby asteroids to mine for the metal."

Pointing off to the sides, I ask about the smaller hunks of metal surrounding Termana, all shaped like large spheres with rings around them. "And those? The other Stations?"

"Yep." Olivia says. "Research Labs, mostly, but they're outfitted for Defense, as well."

"Are there more species out there?"

"Yeah. The universe is a big place." Tension lines Olivia's eyes for a second, but she says no more. Another shrug, then a pat on the arm. "Alright, well, I have to get you back to the hospital wing for the afternoon."

I tense, unwilling to leave the freedom offered by the window. But my people might have woken in my absence, alone as I was when I first woke.

"Relax," Olivia says. "Doctor Antar just wanted to check in and run a few tests. You won't be staying there, anymore."

The little Human woman walks me to the hospital entrance, promises to come back at dinner, and vanishes down the hall.

Disappointment settles in my gut when I see all the beds occupied, all the remnants of my planet still unconscious. With a sigh, I find the doctor and settle into the bed she indicates. The doctor draws blood, breaking several needles on my skin.

"Have you remembered anything yet?" Doctor Antar asks.

But I have next to nothing to report. "I'm drawn to music," I offer. "I miss someone, probably my partner. All I remember of him are mint-colored eyes."

My face falls.

How could it all be gone?

"Nothing to worry about," the doctor says.

But her tone pricks at my ears. A strange paranoia settles into the spaces between her sentences. Some extra sense, hovering in the back of my mind, tingles with the things she isn't saying.

She's just trying to reassure me. She wants me to believe it'll come back in time.

But doubt still plagues me.

The doctor pokes and prods, with needles and words. Olivia arrives just before dinner time, only to find me somber. She walks quietly at my side all the way to the cafeteria.

"You know," she says, "I can introduce you to my friends tomorrow, if you'd like. I know it's been a long day."

I nod, thanking her. We eat quietly at a table for two, and I wander through the darkness inside my head. I push at the walls, screaming internally.

I latch onto the soft, pale green color, trying desperately to remember more of him.

But nothing reveals itself.

With a sigh, I finish my food. Insisting that I can find my way with the map, I set off for my room.

"See you at work in the morning," Olivia says, rising to join her friends.

I wander toward my room, letting my Link play music through the cochlear implant they installed inside my head. The soft musings of "Kanata by Mono. 2014." call to me, despite the lack of lyrics.

I take refuge in my room, shutting the lights off and sitting on the bench beneath my window. Only then, staring out at the vastness of space, do I set my music to play through the speakers.

The sound fills the place, nearly blocking out the thoughts swirling violently through my head, threatening to topple my precarious hold on the strange metal world around me.

But my mind allows me no peace.

It's all gone.

Everyone I knew, everyone I loved...

And I can't even remember their names.

Tears prick at the corners of my eyes, and my throat grows tight.

Friends and family, people I never thought could be taken from me, people I never thought I'd forget... All gone.

Thick, black walls hold me in the center of my mind. All my memories, my entire life, wait on the other side.

I try to think of my home, my planet.

Did my partner and I have children? Were my parents yet living or had they passed years before, spared the tragedy of losing everything? Or were they lost to the solar flare, as well?

My heart wrenches, and my stomach twists in agony. My mind settles on one word, "Gone," sending it spiraling through my head, over and again.

For a long time, I don't move. I just listen. I just feel.

And I remember those eyes.

When I finally move, heaving myself up from the bench, I dance a slow, sad dance, and I know I've done it before. My feet move through the familiar pattern all on their own, requiring no real thought, just muscle memory, the only memory I still have.

One leg crosses behind the other, and I sway a few gentle steps to the left. Tears slip over my cheek as I cross my left leg behind the right and drift in the other direction. A sob breaks through me as I spin, a sensual swirl.

One arm reaches out for something, someone.

But no one reaches back.

Chapter 6
Ulysses Space Research Station

Krona

My guards pace restlessly near the door to the stairwell when I wake, lying on my side on the stone floor. Last night, they shied away from me, from the bitter songs and furious shouts I filled the air with.

But I don't pity them.

Not with what I know they must be doing to me when they use the Bellona gas.

May their sounds never be found when they pass.

I reach for the bars, testing them gently, inconspicuously. They slide in their footings, a product of a long, slow day of concentrated pressure.

I itch to wrench them free, to break them down. But I'll only get the gas if I do. I have to move slowly and hope that Tenna and our people have time, that *I* have time.

My mind wanders, trying to figure out what they could be doing, why they haven't killed me yet, why they're messing with my mind.

How they're messing with my mind.

If these strange memories that can't be memories are their doing, what are they doing to Tenna?

Horror slides through me, and my gut churns at the thought of her suffering.

Images of her with Chief Mourgam, of her dying by my hand, rise from the dark corners of my mind, and I shove them away.

She can't be dead.

She wouldn't betray me, and I wouldn't betray her. I wouldn't kill her.

I shove those thoughts away too, accepting the implausibility of these Humans tampering with my mind over the impossibility of her death. It explains things that these memories don't.

It explains the gaps.

I close my eyes, concentrating on Tenna, and I could swear I can feel her heart beating, somewhere beyond these walls. I know she's alive.

I'll get to you.

I grasp the bars, ready to begin my silent vigil, ready to relax my body and focus all my strength on the gradual shifting of metal, the slow cracking of stone. My mind fills with all the songs I might sing today, inflicting the words upon my captors with a vengeance.

But one of them speaks.

"Why do you sing so much?" he asks.

My eyes snap open, and I stare at him. It's such a simple question, but the implications astound me.

He knows nothing about us.

They had no ambassadors. If they had, they would know the answer to that question.

The fire inside me grows. Something is very *very* wrong here.

Even if he weren't an ambassador himself, even if he'd never met another Regonian, this guard should have been told that we sing.

Either the Humans tell their soldiers nothing... Or I'm right, and things are not as they would have me believe.

An ember of hope burns just a bit brighter within me.

I sit up straight, taking stock of the man on the other side of the bars. Unlike his companions, all cowering near the door, this man stands just out of my reach. Perceptive amber eyes sweep over me, set in tawny skin. With his long, curly black hair swept back into a tight tie, he holds himself upright. The posture of a confident warrior.

But not arrogant or foolish.

He knows his limits, knows not to get close enough for me to overpower him, knows I *could* overpower him.

Any warrior needs to know their limits. Overconfidence can be deadly, for self and others.

I raise a brow, considering him at eye level though I sit and he stands. But he's giving me an opportunity, even if he doesn't realize it. I can learn what he knows.

Or doesn't know.

So, I say, "Singing is our way. It's how we show respect to our ancestors and each other. It's how we rejoice and how we mourn. It's how we remember."

Long strands of black hair fall in oily clumps in front of my eyes, and I wonder if I look like a monster to them.

Almost certainly.

The amber-eyed guard nods slowly, but he says nothing more. With one last glance my way, he walks to the wall, still just out of my reach. He leans against the tan stone, utterly at ease.

Peculiar.

I lean my head against the bars, watching the strange man relax near the hearth. He watches me, and we pass a few moments in silence.

Certain that I was right, that these guards know nothing of Daen Tribe, that the doctors here have tampered with my mind, I close my eyes. As the day passes, I use the things they've implanted within me to learn their language.

The translator fills my mind with their words, and I commit them to memory. It couldn't hurt to learn it.

Maybe it'll even provide an advantage later. But for now, it keeps my thoughts from wandering as I pull the bars gradually apart.

Brilliant white light spears the earthen room, spilling down the stairs in an instant. Everyone turns to face it.

Even without the Bellona flower hanging onto my system, it unsettles me. Where the firelight offers a gentle caress, that light beats itself against the stonework.

Footsteps sound on the stairs, and I draw myself up to my full height. A man descends, garbed in white from head to toe. The cloth hangs from him, starched and stiff, but he wears no armor.

Dark eyes peer at me with an odd mixture of curiosity and menace. Short brown hair and olive skin make him unremarkable next to the guards.

"Bring him," he says, and the thing in my head translates.

One of the guards near the stairs, a woman with strange red hair, reaches for her can of Bellona gas, and I shout, "Wait."

Amazingly, she does. Her hand pauses on the bottle, just about to lift it free of its holster. Curiosity sparks within her eyes, chasing her fear and anxiety away, if only for a moment.

"Where are you taking me? What's happening?" I force my voice to remain calm, though my heart pounds in my chest.

The man in white speaks, voice smooth. The amber-eyed guard tips his head to the side, brows furrowing at the man's words.

But I haven't learned enough of their language yet, and the delay spares me for half a heartbeat. My translator does little to soften the blow as it whispers, "It's time for your Queen's funeral."

My shoulders droop, and my world shatters, falling away to nothing. I slump to the ground, all my certainty evaporating in an instant.

The guard sprays a gust of Bellona gas toward me.

As my eyes close and I fall to my side, I whimper, "Tenna…"

***

I lie on the cold stone floor, face pressed into rough rocks. Thoughts drag through my mind, slow and heavy. The light from the candles and the hearth burns my eyes. The light from the stairwell threatens to blind me.

I slam my eyes shut.

What happened?

And then, I remember.

Tenna's funeral.

My heart plummets, and my stomach roils as it all washes through me in slow motion, my head still groggy from the Bellona.

The remainder of Daen Tribe stands solemn. Tenna's brother and sister lead our people in song, neither bearing the marks of monarch just yet.

And I stand chained, too far away to see Tenna very well.

But it's her.

Even from a distance, I'd know her.

I've kissed that dusky skin countless times, ran my fingers through her luscious blue-black hair. I know the waves that fall around her face, know the way the wind plays with them.

Tears prick at the corners of my eyes as I stare at her body in my mind, arranged in a small boat with flowers and logs.

As her parents light her boat on fire and set her adrift, the voices of our people rise in tribute.

My Human guards stand watch over me. Flimsy chains tie me to the ground, but the weight of grief is my true restraint. My throat constricts as I recall singing the words of her loss, but I force them out again, mourning her the only way I know how.

The burden of acceptance threatens to crush me.

I sing louder, voice breaking with guilt and sorrow. The image of her body, floating, burning, sears itself into my mind.

The guards play music as loudly as they can, but I sing on, resenting them for thinking that their annoyance could ever outweigh my agony.

Another scrap of memory floats out of the darkness, and I see Tenna explaining herself, explaining her betrayal with the Roon Chieftain.

"It was the only way to repair the rift between the tribes, to stop Mourgam from building another dam," she says in my mind, voice firm and eyes ardent.

But the words aren't like her.

She'd rally for a battle if Mourgam built another dam. She'd lead us to war, just as she did the first time.

And her expressions feel... off.

I shake my head, struck by the wrongness of it all. It's so close but doesn't quite fit.

But I can't hold onto the oddity for long.

The funeral flashes through my mind yet again, ripping at my heart. Again, I see her flesh consumed by flame, see her ashes float into the sky to become a brand-new sound, see the shining metallic remnants of her bones, melted across the boat.

I choke back a sob as a chasm expands within me and ice moves through my veins.

I vow to find the sound that embodies her, keeping her alive with my voice, just as our Drennar ancestors wished us to do for all our Lost Ones. I sing and scream until my throat goes raw, voice cracking over the words and sounds.

A man with skin slightly paler than the rest pulls out his canister, spraying Bellona gas into the air, and I scream louder. The sweet smell drifts through me, and I drift into unconsciousness. The funeral sinks its teeth into me again, but this time, I see what I missed before.

The Marks.

No one had the fresh black tattoos that would mark Tenna's death. No Memory Markers perched on white sheets near the river, hands busy at their work.

And they would be busy, for days to come.

Everyone of appropriate age would receive a mark. A thick black, horizontal line on top of their forearm, butted up against the Daen Tribe tattoo. The death of a Queen or King demands it, as it affects the entire tribe.

But there were none.

***

Hope simmers beneath the drowsy edges of the Bellona. That seductive gas lingers within me, sending plumes of smoke drifting through my mind, trying to keep me from waking.

But I know.

She's alive.

A funeral without Marks would never happen.

Even if the Humans tried to prevent it for some unfathomable reason, they'd fail. Even if she *had* betrayed our Tribe, the Mark would have been altered, but it would've been there.

Our Queen's death would have been Marked.

I dig deeper into that horrendous vision, not even bothering to call it a memory anymore. I listen to the words of those nearest me in the crowd.

Vile defamations spew from their lips. They denounce me as a lousy King, calling Tenna's actions right and just. They toy with the idea of joining forces with Roon Tribe, following in her footsteps.

I stare at the stone ceiling, shaken by the thought. False or not, their words claw at my insides.

Again, the terrible light from upstairs assaults my eyes. I slam them shut, wishing I could shut out the world along with the light. I ache to be free of this dingy cell, of these terrible Humans. I burn to hold Tenna, to sing and dance into the night with her and our Tribe.

But the Humans stand in my way.

Bitterness rises like bile, and I sing for vengeance.

"Hoo mai kain," *Your essence remains,*

"Ense," *Unchanged,*

"Loom daet isvene," *Despite the will,*

"Ban daet svensen ris voo mai." *Which seeks the bending of my spirit.*

"Voo taesei joom hoo." *I'll come for you.*

"Daet Pargal loo carnum," *The Mark that they've forgotten,*

"Taekai loo sohyve." *Will be their own undoing.*

My voice shifts between a caress and a hoarse war cry, then back again, lending an eerie quality to the song.

The amber-eyed guard leans against the wall, close but not within reach. He tucks his hands into his pockets, relaxed despite the bitter giant threatening revenge so close at hand.

His expression softens as I sing another refrain, but the other guards eye me warily from across the room. My voice rises, reverberating through the stone walls as I sing from the floor.

And one of the guards begins to crack.

He paces, and beads of sweat roll down his temples. Music blares through the room, an attempt to drown me out.

My Link flashes. "The Best of Me by The Used. 2009."

The guard jams his fists against his ears, trying to ignore me, but I sing louder, extolling the tortures of questioning my own mind.

Amber-eyes stares at me intently.

"Daet isnebauns hoo avekyrlar," *The stories which you've planted,*

"Avelar sove," *Have grown up rotten,*

"Lar artur." *Long since falling short.*

"Wal hoo ol," *Try as you might,*

"Daet rak hoo sua," *The yield you desire,*

"Kai vud gaur yen hoo al hoo." *Is out of reach for you and yours.*

"Joo emi kai jinow," *Our trust is freely given,*

"Valn rahn o svefraetow." *But not so easily broken as this.*

"Valn daet altuns," *Yet the images,*

"Loo vuarn rein fei." *They never go away.*

"Voo srone sval loom voo," *My own mind works against me,*

"Daet svarisoorta ris hoo bar." *The handiwork of your craft.*

Face turning red with rage, the splintering guard screams incoherently, running at the cell. His hands fly out, grasping the bars, shaking with all his might. His puny Human arms almost rattle them.

"Shut up!" he screams, eyes tight with rage. "Stop singing! I'll cut your tongue out myself! Just shut up!"

Rage burns in my belly, sweeps through me like a wildfire. Slowly, smoothly, I rise to my full height, staring him down. I take even, measured steps to the bars, hiding the hurricane of fury roiling just beneath the surface as I approach.

Realization dawns, bright and fearful, on the face of my prey. The guard attempts to back away, but I'm so close and so much faster.

My arms lash out, and I grasp his wrists. With one swift pull, I jerk his arms through the bars, slamming him into them.

Cold fury burns through my veins as I stare down at him, pulling all the while, relishing the feeling of his shoulders sliding out of their sockets.

"Do you know the weight of your threat?" I ask, voice even despite the fire within me.

The guards by the door stand immobilized by fear, but Amber-eyes watches, curious, as every muscle in my body tenses, begging me for vengeance.

I grit my teeth, staring down into wide eyes.

Don't kill him.

Don't do it.

He can't know what his threat means.

"While I have you here, why don't I tell you a little about myself," I say.

I smile coldly as his face presses against the bars. He winces, barely biting back a scream as his shoulders finally pop out of place.

"When our ancestors, the Drennar," I begin, glancing quickly at Amber-eyes when his brows shoot up, "brought us to Regonia, it was in hopes that we could live on in their place. They ventured too far into space, exploring places they shouldn't have. They found a strange sickness that slowly killed them, mutating their flesh. They realized it too late to save their planet."

I pull harder on his arms. Frail Human elbows begin their migration, sliding free. The guard's face goes pale.

"The next generation of their race was in some sort of cryo-storage, awaiting maturity, untouched by disease. Undistorted." Beads of sweat roll down the guard's face. "They brought their young to this planet, used strange machines to shield them from the sickness while they taught them what they could before the last Drennar died."

The guard's elbows dislocate with a satisfying pop-pop. I slide my grip to his hands, working on his wrists, pulling them far behind my own back.

"Their last words to us before they boarded their ship one last time were to live within the means of our planet, to honor them with our strength, and to find them within the beauty of our own voices."

I stare down at him, gaze boring into him as his wrists begin to give way.

"We sing to pay tribute to those who came before us. The Drennar ancestors who, in death, gave us life. The Regonians we've since descended from, who forged a home for us on this planet. We sing to keep their memories alive long after they've passed, striving to find a sound that perfectly embodies each and every one. We sing to honor the triumphs and sacrifices of the living. We sing in joy and in pain."

The guard's eyes flutter closed as unconsciousness begins to claim him. I jerk my hands, fully dislocating his wrists. The jolt of pain brings him back just long enough.

"If I ever wake to find my tongue gone, I will level this wretched place."

Then, in the language of the Humans, I add, "Do you really think I'm here because these flimsy bars and the four of *you* are keeping *me* here?"

I shove the man back, and the red-headed woman catches him before he hits the floor. My hands shake with rage as I turn from the bars, pacing the length of my cell.

He's lucky he uttered that insult to me. Any other Regonian would've ripped him to shreds.

My mind whirls with the fear of never finding a loved one's sound, of truly losing them forever.

Unconsciousness claims the guard, and his music stops. Silence falls over the room, heavy and tense.

I lean against the wall, trying desperately to calm myself.

He didn't know.

He couldn't possibly know what he was saying, couldn't know the severity of such a threat.

I look up to find the amber-eyed guard staring at me, eyes probing. His brows furrow as if he's trying to figure something out.

But what?

Chapter 7
Ulysses Space Research Station

Ricardo

I sit on the bench in Francis' quarters, peering out the window at the black expanse of space. I pull my leg up underneath me as she plops onto her bed. My eyes focus on her reflection for an instant, drawn to the flash of her red hair, but I return my gaze to the stars.

After working some magic on her Link to loop camera and recorder feeds from her room, she says, "Okay. We're good. Now, what's wrong?"

I turn to face her, stomach in knots.

"Something isn't right," I say.

And everything pours out.

The details that just don't line up. All my questions about the prisoner, Krona. The oddity of his behavior.

"He doesn't act like a Drennar. Hell, he said they're his ancestors, that they're dead." Sighing, I run a weary hand over my face. "I don't know if it's a trick, if he's toying with us, or what, but he doesn't act like them. He's... emotional. When he sings, I *feel* it. We all do, that's why Garcia cracked. It was too much for him."

Francis stares at me, uncertain, but she says, "He's probably just trying to trick us."

I shake my head. "I don't know. If it was just the story about them dying off, maybe, but it isn't. He's different. He's not one of them."

Realizing the words that just crossed my lips, I rush to add, "Or... he might not be. I don't know."

"I think you might be reading into it a little too much," Francis says, but her tone does little to back her words.

She's perceptive. She must have questions.

"Then, explain the emotion? Explain the woman he's clearly mourning, or the doubt in his words. The translator can't be adding too much to that. Hell, it doesn't have to add anything to it. Even in his language, I feel it. He's mad and upset, and I don't know why. But Drennar don't feel. If they do, they don't express it. You've seen the footage of them just as well as I have."

Francis' brows reach for each other, carving lines in her face, and a deep breath puffs out her chest for an instant. She purses her lips as my words sink in.

So, I forge ahead.

"All the times the Drennar came for us, did they ever sing? Even once?" I shake my head, answering my question for her. "If he's one of them, why the weird renovations to his cell? Why a stone cell? He's strong enough to get out. He showed Garcia that pretty clearly today."

Recalling his words earlier, I ask, "What's really keeping him in there? Because it sure as hell isn't us."

Giving in just a bit, Francis leans forward, propping her arms on her thighs. "Suppose you're right, and he is something else. What are we supposed to do about it? What does that change? He's a prisoner. We're Guards. It's simple. And why would they lie to us? If he's not a Drennar, why would they *say* he is?"

"I don't know," I say. My stomach turns, and I look out the window again. "I don't know what to do."

But I do.

Defeated, I take a deep breath. "I need some answers. Something doesn't add up."

Shaking her head, Francis says, "I don't like the sound of that."

And if I'm being honest with myself, I don't either. My gut tells me something's wrong here, and it's never steered me wrong.

But it has steered me straight into trouble, many times.

***

My feet carry me through the halls, and my mind fills with the memory of Krona, motionless on the floor of his cell, knocked out by the gas. My stomach sours.

He only intentionally hurt someone once. Today. And if everything he said was true, his actions were justified.

If what he said was true.

My mind whirls, wavering between believing the strange alien and believing my superiors.

Believe my gut or stick my head in the sand.

Regonian...

I test the word in my mind as I approach the labs. Everything about Krona's behavior fits with the story he told today while dislocating Garcia's arms.

He doesn't act like he knows much about tech, which Drennar certainly do.

Crisp white halls wrap around me, cold and unfeeling compared to the stone and firelight of Krona's prison cell. My pace slows as I try to figure things out, try to avoid what I'm about to do.

He's definitely strong enough to get out, but something is keeping him here. The gas is all we have that can stop him, and he didn't know about it at first.

So, what stopped him then?

He was more depressed the first few days. Maybe that stopped him?

But Drennar don't get depressed.

The man's songs fill my head, haunt my steps, and I try to make sense of them. Why would he wonder if he'd been betrayed? Why would he think someone was messing with his head?

And why would he say they become sounds? It was almost religious. Drennar aren't religious.

The lab door comes into view, and butterflies erupt in my stomach. My heart pounds.

A message comes in, blinking on my Link. A glance at the screen embedded in my wrist reveals a message from Francis.

"Are you sure about this?" she asks for the millionth time.

But I need to know.

I swallow hard and scan my Link at the lab door. A hint of guilt swirls through me, but I know anyone reviewing the Link scans will only see a Guard on rounds.

The door unlatches, and I push it open. The metal chills my skin, and I find myself wishing for the stone walls of the cell.

As I step into the lab, emptied of all personnel hours ago, I marvel yet again at the renovations they did.

Why stone, candles, and a hearth?

And then, I remember more of what Krona said. He spoke of Regonia, some planet, as if he were there. I stop in my tracks, shoulders falling.

He doesn't know we're on a space station.

If he's a Drennar, it might be a trick to make him think himself beyond assistance. The Drennar they had on Bolivia Station hacked everything, slaughtered people, and escaped.

But he sees our Links, even has his own for some reason.

A Drennar would have used that by now.

And why was the Coalition so adamant about not using the same station they used last time?

My eyes roam over the terminals, and I force myself to move, skipping past them. My Link has no clearance for those. My amber eyes stare back at me, reflected on their screens, and another realization hits me.

Krona spoke of the Drennar as if they've been dead for a couple thousand years. He doesn't even realize they're still alive.

The phrasing of my thought stops me in my tracks.

Holy shit...

I believe him.

I push the thought away for the moment and push myself forward to open a file cabinet. A quick perusal of the documents inside reveals nothing. I move to the next and again, find nothing related to Krona. The next two also turn up nothing of interest.

Strange chemical recipes. Employee information. Nothing I need.

But the fifth is conspicuously locked.

My breath catches.

I don't bother to scan my Link, knowing I don't have clearance. Instead, I retrieve a pin from my pocket and seek out the manual lock, a holdover from older times just in case a scanner goes out.

After a few attempts and several broken pins, the lock gives. I sift through documents, lifting the first one that holds more than equations and chemical compositions.

My gaze sweeps over the words, the lists of tests and subjects, and my eyes widen. Ice runs through my veins, filling me with dread.

"No…" I whisper, shaking my head.

I put the paper back, then retrieve another, taking pictures of each one with my retinal cameras. Each document digs the hole a little deeper, opening it like a great ravine before me.

"What have we done?"

The answers spread out before me, but they're too horrible, too much.

I send a private message to Francis. "It's so much worse than I thought."

Chapter 8

Novay

Nine years ago, 3009 C. E.

Reginald

I lie awake long after returning to my room for the evening. My fingers move idly over my scalp, moving short, brown hair around, trying to work out the nervous energy. I tap the nearest corner of my little grey nightstand, summoning forth a water globe from depths unknown.

After three years, I barely think about the oddity of it, barely care where the water comes from or what makes up the strange membrane that holds it together. The sensation of drinking from a glass is lost to memory, the idea of it cumbersome at best.

I roll onto my back and drop the globe into my mouth. The membrane dissolves, and water bursts through my mouth.

For the first time in ages, I consider the strange things, the material that contains the water. I wonder whether it possesses any nutritional value, marvel that it clearly isn't harmful, try not to think of how they developed it to work so perfectly with the human form.

But the distraction is short-lived.

The dull ache that resides in the back of my mind throughout every day built to an all-consuming agony this morning. Despite all my attempts to ignore it, it's only grown sharper.

September 21st.

Our 15th wedding anniversary.

My mind fills with Eva and the celebration we should be having, with Olivia and the smile she should be sharing with us.

My heart twists.

I knew today would be a hard day. I've known it, been dreading it for weeks.

But for the Drennar to have made it worse...

I close my eyes, rubbing my hands over my face.

Did they know?

Did they know it would be a hard day?

Sighing, I laugh at myself.

Of course, they knew.

They've studied us for years. They know that anniversaries carry weight with us.

And that's why, instead of the normal tests of strength and endurance, of stretching my mind, of exploring my ability to learn, today...

They hurt me.

They showed me Eva and Olivia.

In my mind, I'm back in my testing room, sitting in the center of that dull, grey space beneath the watchful stares of four Drennar, still and cold as statues. The memory plays over the tiny screens on the backs of my eyelids, showing me what became of my life.

Eva moves between desks and tables in the lab on Termana. An old favorite plays on the speakers, "Espana Piano by Pistol Annies of the West. 2013."

The song we almost chose for our first dance at our wedding. The song she listened to a few days ago, apparently, thinking of me.

Was she dreading our anniversary too?

A lump forms in my throat as she bends over a terminal, comparing figures with those on her Link.

Wrinkles edge her eyes, far too early in life. Only 43, a year younger than me, but these past three years have aged her a decade. Gray streaks shoot through her dark hair, pulled taut in an efficient ponytail.

But she's still beautiful.

My breath catches, and I hardly notice the other researchers buzzing around her like bees.

All I see is her.

The rich chocolate of her eyes, the wonder of seeing her after so long…

But a researcher, a man, eager with the youth of his early 30s, comes up to her, and my attention splits. He waits patiently, quiet until she addresses him.

He says something about water treatment tablets for Bolivia Station being ready for testing, but I don't catch the details. I wait with bated breath for him to say it again, to call her Minister.

It's only been three years... How did she rise to Minister of Medical Research and Scientific Development so quickly?

She's on the damned Coalition.

But I can't wrap my head around it. Either she sucked up to everyone she could, which I know she wouldn't do, or she spent nearly every second in the lab.

It means Olivia has been alone all this time, basically orphaned, by choice.

My hand clutches at my shirt, and I try to stop my heart from shattering, all to no avail. I splinter beneath the weight of this revelation.

My baby girl... deserted.
Does she blame me?
Does she blame Eva?

My chest collapses beneath the weight of freshly awoken grief, and I choke on it. A small part of me wishes Eva were the type to kiss ass to get what she wants, just to know that Olivia hadn't been alone all this time, but I know better.

I wouldn't have fallen in love with Eva, over and over, if that were the case.

But now, her drive, her passion for her work, reaches into my chest and wrings my heart out like a wet rag, twisting and squeezing. The very thing I loved so much about her has ruined Olivia's hopes at a normal childhood.

But the memory continues playing, and I hear her voice. In my older memories, she sounds sweet and warm, but now, a cold brusqueness coats her terrible words.

She shakes her head at the man and says, "Administer them."

Two words, heavy as lead. Only two words, but they spoke volumes of the woman she is now.

"And if there are side effects?" the researcher asks.

She doesn't bat an eye, doesn't flinch, as she says, "We'll deal with that later. This is the test."

Again, a chill sweeps over my spine.

Untested drugs going into the water supply of an entire station, so off-handedly, as if it were nothing.

But it's certainly something.

The Drennar explained them, told me the dissolving tablets hold chemicals to alter DNA. The petite

Drennar with black wings didn't blink as she said it, as she explained the results Eva was hoping for.

But I heard nothing more.

Untested.

Without consent.

Where did her heart go?

I stare up at the grey ceiling, heart twisting in my chest, mourning the woman I love even though she lives and breathes.

She went into this field to help make the human race better, not to risk lives so needlessly.

What happened?

My gorge rises, and I fight back disgust at what my wife is doing.

She isn't the same person. She isn't the woman I remember.

But then, neither is Olivia.

My memory moves forward, and again, the screen shifts to show me my daughter. Clad all in black, she sits in a chair in her room with heavily booted feet propped on her bed. A book lies open in her lap, and "Sky Burial by Avatar. 2016." seeps through the air. Dark hair hangs limp in her face, unwashed for days.

My breath catches at the sight of her, letting herself go, one basic hygienic task at a time.

Heavy black make-up lines her eyes, failing to cover the dark circles beneath. She turns a page with a long, black fingernail, finishes it, and marks her place.

She closes the book but doesn't set it aside, doesn't rise. It sits in her lap, a lead weight, as she stares into space. She doesn't move, barely breathes.

And all I can do is watch.

Watch the crushing weight of depression bury her, a pain I've known all too well.

Watch her suffer, unable to help her.

The light that used to dance in her magnificent hazel eyes is gone, and she sits, as if in the grip of that terrible numbness that plagues the darkest depths.

My heart drops.

Eventually, she looks at her Link, mumbles, "Time for school." But her voice comes out flat.

She rolls her eyes, rises to her feet, and drops the book on her bed. I clutch at my shirt as she drags herself out the door, so unenthused about the coming day.

But she used to love learning.

She loved solving intense math prompts and working through philosophical debates and writing computer codes.

She used to love life.

Staring into my dark, empty room, I whisper, "What happened to my family?"

Chapter 9
Odyssey Space Research Station

Tenna

I drop into a chair in the cafeteria after a stunningly boring day of cleaning. Thanks to Olivia, I now know where everything is and how to use every bit of tech I encountered through the course of the day. I paired my Link with nearly everything, despite my limited access.

We never left the public access areas, cleaning hallways, the cafeteria, bathrooms, schoolrooms, and the bar. And all day, Olivia remarked upon my capabilities, certain that the Coalition would tire of such caution when they see what I'm truly capable of and move me off the cleaning crew.

And though I hate the tedium of cleaning, though I hope for something else, I don't want to lose this strange Human woman's company.

A sigh slips through me. The speculation of Olivia's friends at lunch time floats through my mind. Maybe repair work since I'm strong. Maybe a position in the lab since I'm apparently smarter than the average Human.

"It'll probably depend on what you did before," one of them said, a woman with long, dark hair. "Once you remember, they'll want to use those skills."

A pang of grief twists my heart, just as it did then. Because I don't know myself.

I have no place here.

I have no place anywhere.

My heart shrivels in my chest. Every move I make seems off, just shy of the mark. Every thought is empty, lacking memories to ground them.

All around, Humans sit together, enjoying their meals at their tables. Their strange words fill my mind, swirling in incomprehensible patterns, bordering on gibberish despite the translator buzzing away in my ear, despite my burgeoning grasp of their common language. The noise washes over me as they talk about their lives, their perfectly orderly lives that they remember without issue.

I close my eyes, filling my lungs. I blow the breath out, pushing my resentment out with it.

These people did nothing wrong.

It isn't their fault I can't remember anything.

I pinch the bridge of my nose, then release it and open my eyes.

Olivia settles into the chair next to me, full tray of food before her. A stocky man named Lachlan sits across from her. His khaki skin makes him the palest I've seen yet, a fact that's highlighted by the jet-black hair that hangs loose around his ears and his strikingly dark eyes.

He's... the mechanic.

He watches Olivia, smiling when she does. I wonder briefly if he wishes to partner her or if I can trust my judgement when it comes to these Humans.

But I can't even trust my judgement of myself.

He and Olivia discuss her ship, and I pay their words little mind. The tech they speak of makes no sense to me.

Matteo fills out the chair across from me, plump and shorter than Lachlan. His wife, Maria, sits beside him, shapely yet thin, with long flowing brown curls reaching halfway down her back. High cheekbones and kind eyes draw the stares of multiple men throughout the cafeteria.

I test myself, sifting through my memories of the afternoon for the name of the place they run here, something called a bar.

The Little Elephant.

The name comes easily, showing me once again that only my past is gone.

I drop my gaze to my food, eating slowly. But a man comes to sit beside me. A man with warm brown skin and hair three shades darker.

Nico.

The man with the eyes that haunt me. That perfect pale green tugs at my heart.

Why couldn't he have sat across from me instead of Matteo?

I need to see his eyes, need them to pry the memories out of me. That color shakes me to my core. That color was everything in my past life.

I look around the cafeteria, suddenly claustrophobic in the dead metal shell. Music plays softly, echoing off the walls, humming beneath the cacophony of voices. "Estemos by E. S. Posthumus. 2001." flashes across my Link.

I glance at Nico, at the smile in his beautiful green gaze. And when I turn forward, when I close my eyes, I see that perfect color still, see the eyes I miss, framed by thick lashes.

And a little bit comes back.

The ghost of long, blue-green grass slips over my calves as I run through an open field. Behind me, someone runs with me, laughs with me though I no longer remember why. His laughter sends my heart skipping frantically. It pulses, low and full, from somewhere deep.

In the distance, horses, or our equivalent, graze atop a small hill. Our Tribe's horses.

The massive beasts stand proud and majestic, larger and stronger than any horses the Humans have ever known. I focus on them in my memory, on the tails like those of furry dogs, the broad flat antlers like those of the Humans' moose.

My footsteps slow, and those behind approach. Strong arms slip suddenly around my waist and a body I know as well as my own presses against my back. But he's moving too quickly. Our impact sends us to the ground, and my skin tingles at his touch. Warmth spreads through me, and I turn in his arms, facing him as we fall.

All I see is those eyes, and then my mind goes blank, once more.

Heart faltering, I open my eyes to find the cafeteria now completely full of Humans, and I swallow hard.

Olivia and Lachlan argue amiably over a new piece of tech for the spaceships. Something about being lighter and faster, which Olivia loves, but harder to work on when it breaks, much to Lachlan's disapproval.

A hint of anxiety slips through me at the mention of travelling through space. And though their words wash over me, that strange, nervous tension piques my curiosity.

It feels almost like… fear.

Was I afraid of space travel?

I furrow my brows, trying to listen closer, to stir something from my memory. But Nico joins their conversation, making fun at every turn, desperate to keep the tone light. I stare at him, only to realize he dislikes arguments.

Not that he need bother splitting them up. Any argument is cut short by Lachlan's awkward attempts to impress and please Olivia.

Maybe I'm a better judge of Human character than I thought...

Maybe reading people was important to me before?

My attention falls upon Nico once more, grasping at straws. I watch his mannerisms, analyze how he interacts with the others. But it doesn't fit with the man of my memories, the man who shares those eyes.

Vague bits and pieces float through a crack in the walls of my mind. I feel that mesmerizing laugh slip through me once more, the laughter from the field. But his eyes looked sincere, not desperate to smooth tension like Nico.

What was his name?

I sift through my mind, feeling out the edges of the walls, peering into that internal darkness, but I find not even a scrap. And the name Doctor Antar gave me, Dremer, doesn't feel right.

I test it in my mind, feel the weight of it, roll the shape of it over my tongue. And though I know almost nothing about myself or my life or even my partner, that name feels false.

Frustration bubbles up within me, turning my stomach. I force myself to finish eating, though the food seems to spoil the second it touches my tongue.

When everyone finishes their meals, Maria and Matteo call for attention.

"As you know," Maria begins, patting her husband's arm, "Matteo and I have wanted to start a family for a while now."

The Humans around me lean in, waiting for more. Excitement rolls off them in waves.

"My beautiful Maria is pregnant!" Matteo exclaims. "The doctors say it's twins!"

The table erupts in cheers and congratulations. A few people at neighboring tables jump to their feet, offering happy wishes. I play my part, wishing them well and clasping their hands gently in my own.

But with every word of joy that flutters around my ears, my life seems farther and farther away.

"Lucky," Nico says, teasing. "You get a bigger room now."

Everyone laughs, but I stare on, confused.

Olivia leans forward, looking past me and saying, "Yes, because moving to the family section is the *only* reason to have kids."

Giggling and mocking agreement follow, and the news spreads through the cafeteria. The mood shifts around us, lifting and effervescing. As people file out, heading to work or their rooms or the bar, they stop by, whispering congratulations, patting Matteo or Maria on the arm.

Eventually, Olivia and I rise, wandering out of the cafeteria.

"Pregnancies are big news," she says. "We're still technically recovering from near extinction. Even a couple hundred years into life on and around Termana, there are only about 100,000 people here. Pitiful next to the billions that lived on Earth."

"So," she says, "when a woman is pregnant, especially with twins, it's fantastic news. It gives us a bit of hope. Especially with the Dre—" Olivia halts midsentence but recovers quickly. "With the dramatic struggles of rebuilding."

I glance at her for a single heartbeat, trying to figure out what she was really going to say. Twice now, she's held back, and considering how open she is with everything else, I can't help but think it related.

But when I look at her, only concern hides in the shadows of her eyes.

Concern for me?

I swallow, wondering what else could possibly go wrong. But for now, I don't ask, content to give her time to tell me.

At the door to my room, Olivia says, "I'm going to the bar soon since we don't work tomorrow. Just need to freshen up a bit. Want to come with?"

"No, thank you." I let out a deep breath. "I just... want to be by myself." My brows scrunch together. "Besides, I have to go to the hospital for more tests in the morning," I add, already dreading the prospect.

"Okay," Olivia says, unperturbed. "Well, I'll see you in the cafeteria for lunch tomorrow?"

I nod, slipping quietly into my room as Olivia turns for her own. Immediately, I start some music. I don't know any songs yet, so I give the Link my swirling thoughts.

It takes them literally and plays, "Green Eyes by Dark Moor. 2005."

Those beautiful eyes fill my mind, tug at my heart. Undressing quickly, I fold myself into the tiny shower. Hot water falls over me but does little to ease the chill inside.

The Humans have hope. They were prepared for the end of their planet.

But I have nothing.

Something inside me cracks, and bitter tears cascade over my cheeks, lost in the water that pours over me.

He can't be dead. He can't just be floating around space somewhere.

The thought sends a shiver through me, and sobs wrack my body.

He can't be dead.

My thoughts whirl, and the world falls out from under me. With my heart in my throat, I choke on the life I don't have anymore.

The other five of my kind, still slumbering in the hospital wing, spring to mind, and I wonder if they're partnered.

Could they rebuild our species? Or are they too few?

I count myself out, knowing that I couldn't find another, even without my memories of him. He was my one. And though I know nothing else, I know he was my partner, my only partner.

Tears fall faster, and my breath hitches. Hope deserts me.

What do I even do now?

If I can't remember them... How do I mourn them?

But the thought of mourning them, all of them, the thought of mourning *him*, claws at my heart. A hole opens within me, all-consuming.

I force myself to wash, to finish my shower, but the tears never stop flowing. I dress in things the Humans call pajamas, specially printed for me while I slept in the hospital.

Resentment builds within me, and I wonder why I can't have my old clothes. Maybe they'd help me remember, but all I have are my boots.

Standing in the middle of my room, I stop the music, head full of a tune from my life. I hum it quietly, and it eases the tension within.

My feet move, leading me through the dance from last night, the dance I know from my past. I drift one direction, then the other. I spin briefly, arms rising, reaching.

And this time, I know what I'm reaching for.

I'm reaching for him.

***

Morning finds me wide awake, dreading my trip to the hospital wing. With no exact time to arrive, I turn to face the wall, putting an arm over my head.

It's still dark out. I can sleep a while longer.

Realization dawns on me.

It's always dark outside here.

A morbid laugh bursts from me, and I sigh. A glance at my Link reveals it to be 7:34. Somewhat early by Human standards.

I pull myself out of the scrunched position the too-small bed forces me to sleep in and dress quickly. The Human clothes feel strange, unnatural and somehow dainty.

I move through the station easily, having learned the layout of the place while cleaning. The Station passes by me in a blur, a mass of Humans milling about, staring as I pass.

Some offer kind smiles.

The hospital wing looms ahead, tucked into the heart of the Station. The open door greets me, but I hesitate, nerves tingling. Something I can't quite put my finger on tugs at my senses, tells me this place is wrong.

My stomach flips uncomfortably, staring at the people sleeping in the beds, the people like me.

I'm just anxious. That's all.

This place is just a reminder that I remember nothing, that I'm failing the people I left behind.

I stop in my tracks as a slip of memory wafts through a crack in the walls of my mind, ethereal and serene. A glimpse of a smile, a hint of beautiful pale green eyes.

But who is he?

The memory slips behind the wall before I can get anything more.

A nurse steps out of a back room, smiling brightly. "I'll just go get the doctor," the tiny woman says, then bustles off.

They return together, and Doctor Antar approaches. "How are you feeling today?"

My face falls. "I suppose I'm alright. I still don't remember much of anything, though."

"That's to be expected, dear," Antar says, but the concern in her voice rings false. "Are you remembering anything?"

"Barely."

Antar escorts me to a small room beyond the beds, bidding me sit on a chair made for my frame. She moves to the counter beside me, eyeing the medical instruments atop it.

"So, what *do* you remember?" Again, her tone pricks at my nerves.

The woman wraps a cuff of strange fabric around my upper arm. She watches her Link as it inflates, deflates, and attempts to prick my skin. The tiny needle breaks off, lying flat beneath the cuff.

Drawing a deep breath, I finally answer the doctor's question.

"I remember the color you call mint," I tell her. I open my mouth to relay the rest of the memory, the field and the man with mint eyes running and laughing behind me.

But the doctor's head tips to the side, her eyes narrowed, almost imperceptibly.

So instead, I say, "And I'm really drawn to music." Though I know it isn't quite true, I add, "Maybe I was a musician."

Doctor Antar's shoulders fall as she lets out a little breath, and she speaks. As the translator gathers her words to relay them to me, I stare at her.

Relief.

She's relieved.

"That's very likely," the translator says. "I can't imagine any other reason for that to be one of the first things to come back."

My brows draw together as I consider her words, and my stomach drops.

Something is wrong.

I wait as the doctor pulls the cuff off and retrieves a peculiar white needle. The strange material tugs at a memory, pricking at my past as it pierces my skin.

It shouldn't be used for this.

I consider the little white needle, trying to remember what it should be used for, but nothing comes to me.

My blood seeps through it, deep burgundy flowing into a handful of clear tubes. Antar withdraws the needle, and my skin closes over instantly without even a lost droplet.

It takes a great deal more than that to make me bleed any significant amount.

But why do I know that?

The Human doctor asks how I'm adjusting and administers a few more tests. She calls them routine, but they're too invasive.

"Alright," Doctor Antar says. "That's all for today. You're free to go."

I push myself up from the chair and step out into the main rooms of the hospital. But I don't go far.

My compatriots lie unconscious, each with a tube and needle running into their arms. My heart twists seeing them so weak, so helpless.

This is wrong.

An older female lies nearest to me, with black hair shot through with streaks of grey fanned out around her. I take her hand, smoothing my thumb over lustrous, blue-black skin.

My eyes trace the bright blue of her tattoos, some of which match my own. Bracelets pierce open circles on the tops and bottoms of her wrists, but she doesn't have a matching mark near her elbows, doesn't have the line that attaches the two sets of rings.

Black circles outlined by blue and struck through with a blue line dot the top of her hand, and my heart clenches at the sight of these.

I turn her hand over, exploring her Marks, wishing I knew what they mean.

Because they mean something, I know they do.

Four unfilled circles of vivid blue form a line on the underside of her wrist. I stare at her arm, then at my own.

I shake my head at the smooth, unblemished skin of the inside of my own wrists. My throat grows tight, and I realize I have no children.

A spike of sadness shoots through me at the hopes for our species, but maybe it's best I don't have any. No children seem to have survived the solar flare.

Swallowing, I take in the Marks on the others. None of them have the ones that I have by my elbows. Two of them have the band around the base of their neck, including the old woman, and somehow, that makes my heart clench.

Loss and pain flood me, and I touch the band at my collar. The man with mint-colored eyes fills my mind, and lost details taunt me, biting into my flesh.

Because they're things I should know. His name, the shape of his face, the feel of his skin, the warmth of his lips...

I should know.

The morning passes me by, but I never leave these people. They're the only links I have to my life, the only links I have to him. I cling to them, desperate for any clues, but nothing comes to me.

At lunch with Olivia, I push my food around my plate, picking at a bite or two every now and then. But today, Olivia doesn't seem to mind the quiet.

She holds her head, saying, "It hurts something fierce."

I almost laugh at the strange phrase.

Almost.

Have I laughed since I woke up here?

Another thing I can't remember. I search my brain, sifting through the recent memories, trying to recall a joke or a conversation with any of these Humans that might have made me laugh.

But I hope I haven't.

The people I've lost deserve better than for me to forget them, to have fun, to laugh.

They deserve to be mourned.

Slowly, the other Humans disperse for their afternoon tasks.

Olivia rises, holding a fist to her mouth and closing her eyes as she does. Eventually, she says, "I'm going to go sleep this off."

I nod, though her words make no sense. I finish my food alone, ears full of the Human language. People mill about, noisy and unconcerned.

Pushing myself to my feet, I return my dishes to the counter and step free of the cafeteria. My eyes drift to the hall that'll take me to my room, to the window and the view of space.

But my feet lead me back to the hospital, to the people lying there unconscious.

***

Frustration simmers in my gut as I drag myself to the cafeteria for dinner. My jaw clenches, but the emptiness in my mind persists.

The speakers in the cafeteria play, "Hurricane by 30 Seconds to Mars. 2009." I let it seep into me as I get my food. It resonates with the tension that coils in my muscles and the pent-up anger festering in my stomach.

I settle in at the table, and Olivia and her friends pepper me with questions, genuine in their desire for me to remember.

But my answers are short.

My culture, my people, and my life before slip further and further away as their questions show me just how little I know. The tension in my shoulders intensifies, and my brows knit together. In my mind, I reach out, arms stretching, fingers grasping, clawing at empty air as I falter for answers that *should* be easy.

"Does everyone look like you or was there anyone that looked more like us?"

I don't know.

"What kinds of tech did you have?"

I don't know.

"What was your religion like?"

I don't know.

Everything blurs together, and I hardly notice who asks what. I stare at them, eyes unfocused and heart elsewhere.

How long do your people live? What's your planet like? What does the ground feel like? Was it hard like the metal floors? Did you have pets? What do your tattoos mean? Why do all of you have them?

I don't know.

I don't know.

I don't know.

Their questions grow personal, but my answers barely improve.

"Were you married?"

"I think so."

"What was he like?"

I shake my head, eyes glued to my plate. "Nico's eyes remind me of him, but that's all I remember."

"Did you have kids?"

I shake my head.

"What was your job?"

I doubt the words as they cross my lips, but I say them regardless, desperate for an answer, *any* answer. "Maybe a musician."

With every question, my heart drops. I have nothing. Nothing for me, and certainly nothing to tell them.

Everything slips through my fingers, and I grasp at smoke, thin wisps of gray floating around closed hands.

Another question poises on the edges of Nico's lips, ready to pour out, but Olivia elbows him gently. Much to my relief, the discussion closes, but only after they assure me that they can't wait to hear more.

And then, they ask Maria about her pregnancy.

A near endless stream of words gushes from them, crashing around me, shattering like broken glass for me to step on. But I try. I lift my head. I listen.

And they don't seem to notice the false note beneath the happiness I show them.

Slowly, the conversation fades, and meals disappear from plates. Everyone disperses, and I drag myself along through cold halls in their wake. Their words crash against my ears, reverberate through my translator, but the meanings are lost.

At our rooms, Olivia touches my arm. "We're going to play cards. You want to come?"

I swallow, gaze drifting over them.

But I can't.

I can't keep filling my head with strange Human customs. I want to remember my own.

"Maybe another time," I say. "Thank you."

A sympathetic smile graces Olivia's soft features, and she nods.

I duck into my room, breathing a sigh of relief when the door slides shut. I don't bother with lights. My Link obeys my command, starting music and turning the volume up as loud as it'll go. It takes my desire literally, playing, "Help Me Lose My Mind by Disclosure. Mazde Remix. 2013."

Far more upbeat than I would have chosen, it pulses through the air. I tell the Link to play it over and again, not wanting to learn new songs. I drift on the alien notes, eyes closed and chest rumbling with the music.

Eventually, I step into the bathroom, disrobe, and climb into the shower. Hot water glides over my skin as I let the words of the song flow past my lips, phrasing it as a plea.

I don't want to think about how little I know about myself or my past.

I want to break something. I want to run, to do something to let everything loose.

But I can't.

I tense, hands curling into fists in my hair.

"I can't do anything," I say through gritted teeth. "Because I'm here. On an alien space station with no open space and no one to spar with. These Humans would snap like twigs if it came to a fight."

I freeze.

My hands fall away from my hair, and my breaths come fast.

I'm no musician.

I'm a warrior.

I shake my head, incredulous. But that isn't the whole of it. Even this revelation is incomplete, somehow.

I'm not just a warrior, I'm a warrior... something. There's more to it.

I grit my teeth, tap my fingers against the wall. Desperately, I try to find it, to figure it out. I push against the darkness in my mind.

And I am a sort of musician, that isn't completely wrong. Just incomplete.

Everything is incomplete.

But I have something now.

I pull in a deep breath, focusing on the small victory. I piece together clues that should've led me to this realization. My strong form, my quick reflexes, the way my eyes assess the people around me.

Being a warrior just makes sense.

My heart soars, embracing the new knowledge of my life, because this feels significant, it feels heavy and important. It's part of my culture, a *big* part of my culture.

I know it, feel it in my bones.

Singing with renewed fervor, my words become boisterous and full-bodied. I finish my shower and step out, dressing quickly.

But as I gaze out at the vastness of space, the glee slowly seeps out of me. The darkness reminds me just how much I've lost.

Scraps of memory won't bring my people back.

But maybe I'll remember how to mourn them.

Chapter 10
Ulysses Space Research Station

Krona

I wake on the floor, joints stiff and muscles sore. Sitting up, I stare at my guards.

But something is off.

My nerves wind tight as I watch them exchange pointed glances. Amber-eyes looks to the others, and his gaze seems to weigh the most. The other two fidget, leery of me, as usual, but also of him.

Amber-eyes peers down at the thing on his wrist, then at the other guards. They go still, clearly aiming for nonchalance.

But it sets me on edge. I freeze, watching, waiting for something to happen. I stare at them, brows furrowed.

Amber-eyes glances at his arm and says, "It's up."

The air in the room shifts as the guards sigh, filling the space with a discordant mixture of relief and anxiety. I watch through narrowed eyes.

It'll happen now… Whatever they're going to do, it'll happen now.

I tense.

Amber-eyes walks closer, careful not to step within my reach. "Time to talk," he says, then clears his throat. "My name is Ricardo. Yours is Krona, right?"

I nod, thankful that I only need the translator for a few of the words he speaks.

What could they possibly want to talk about?

"Before I get into it, I want to say... I'm sorry." Ricardo's features soften, eyes turning to liquid gold, and he shakes his head. "For everything."

My heart leaps into my throat, and fear trickles through me.

Is Tenna really dead?

I choke on the thought.

Is she okay? Are our people okay?

I pull myself to my feet, grasping the bars. My heart beats erratically as the world threatens to collapse beneath me.

Say something.

"Now, you're going to be angry, I know that. You have every right to be angry," Ricardo says, "but please know that if we knew the truth, we wouldn't have kept you here."

"Just tell me already," I say, voice gruff and hurried. I close my eyes, forcing myself to add, "Please. I need to know what's happening."

I look at him, take a deep breath to calm myself. I can't ruin this chance to get answers.

Ricardo stares at my hands, white-knuckled on the bars. He takes a step back, hesitant.

"Please," I say.

Blowing out a long, deep sigh, Ricardo says, "This Tenna, she's your wife?"

"By your words, yes. She's my partner. She's the Warrior Queen of Daen Tribe. She's *everything* to me." I lean my head against the bars, bowed by the weight of grief and uncertainty. My voice cracks as I ask, "Is she ok?"

"She's alive and healthy," Ricardo says.

My legs grow weak, and I fall to my knees, hands sliding down the bars. Whispered words of thanks seep from me, hoarse and shuddering on haggard breaths.

Relief washes through me so fiercely that I almost miss the small, "Ahem," from Ricardo.

"You were right, Krona. She didn't betray you or your people," Ricardo says, and now that he's started speaking, he barrels through it. "And you certainly didn't kill her, or any of your tribe members."

A sob breaks through me, and I shudder, shoulders heaving. My heart swells, and only now do I realize that I didn't trust myself, not fully.

But I finally have my chance for answers.

I force myself to speak. "Then what is this?"

"It's a pretty long story," Ricardo says, crouching to be closer to my crumpled height. "I guess I'll start with this. Those memories were fake. One of the doctors here implanted them."

My eyes snap up to his. Though I hoped that was the case, hoped beyond all reason, it makes no sense. "How?"

"I don't really understand the science behind it," Ricardo explains. "There's a reason I'm just a guard. Something about certain chemicals being injected into the brain while someone suggests whatever memory they want to form. I don't know."

He shrugs for effect.

I shake my head incredulously, and Ricardo continues. "Some of our leaders, a couple members of the Survival Coalition, kidnapped you and your tribe. They brought you back to our stations here around Termana to perform experiments on all of you."

My heart stutters.

The translator does its best, stringing words together to explain the concept of experimentation, but I barely hear that part.

"We're not on Regonia?" I ask, voice quiet.

Ricardo shakes his head, eyes full of pity.

We're in the Realm of Stars...

We'll fall to star-sickness.

My heart rattles in my chest, but I force myself to be calm.

The Humans are fine.

Anger sweeps through me, because I know they aren't fine. They're vile.

But they don't have star-sickness.

They have these things in their arms, in their heads, but nothing else. And they all have them, all exactly the same, not a ton of different mutations.

"What are they doing to us?" I demand. "And why?"

Ricardo opens his mouth, closes it. With a sigh, he says, "You aren't going to like this." He rakes a hand through his dark curls. "The Drennar are taking our people. They didn't die off, like they told you. They weren't even sick, unless you mean sick in the head." Ricardo's gaze drops to the ground, then rises to meet mine. "They made your people in some lab, plopped you down on that planet, and left, just watching over you all. And now they're taking Humans. We don't know why, just that the people who're taken... never come back."

My mind spins.

The Drennar are alive? And they've been watching us?

What would they want with Humans?

"I guess..." Ricardo continues, "Your people are pretty similar to them. Some of the Coalition members, two of them at least, Defense and Research, decided to take some of you to study, to learn about the Drennar in a roundabout way since we can't study them directly."

He casts a glance at the other two guards, then looks back to me. "They tried to study a Drennar once, on Bolivia Station." He pulls in a deep breath. "It didn't go well. The thing escaped, massacred everyone there."

Rage curls my hands into fists. I force myself not to shout as I say, "So, they're taking us to learn about the people taking them? That's stupid."

"I know." Ricardo holds his hands up, pleading. "I don't know what they told themselves to make it ok, but that's what they're doing."

Disgust writhes in my belly. I slam my hands against the bars, and the two guards near the door jump. Ricardo eyes the bars as they rattle in their footings.

"What are they doing to us?" I growl.

"In your case, they were trying to alter your memories, aiming to turn you against your partner and your people to see if it's possible to turn a Drennar later down the road." Ricardo shakes his head.

His face softens, and he says, "With Tenna, they've blocked her memories. They want to see how your kind learn, how you acclimate to new environments. She knows nothing of your land, your tribe, or herself."

My heart shatters, and my shoulders droop. The pieces fall from me, rolling across the floor.

I whisper, "Or of me?"

Ricardo's mouth moves wordlessly, and he shakes his head. "She…" He trails off, clears his throat, tries again. "She doesn't remember you."

I pull in a sharp breath, and my gaze drops to the stone floor. Ice flows through my veins, and the corners of my eyes prick.

"I searched everything I could find," Ricardo says, voice earnest. "I tried to find more about what they're doing with her, but there isn't much here. I only found the original plans for the operation as a whole, and since she's on a different station, there wasn't much about her."

Tears fall, and Ricardo flinches.

"They were worried she might start to remember," Ricardo says, offering some slim bit of hope. "Who knows how effective it was, after all. The stuff they did to you didn't go how they planned."

I nod, but only because there's nothing else to do. My eyes slip out of focus.

"What of our people?" I ask, voice flat.

A quiet sigh slips from Ricardo, and I close my eyes, bracing for the words that come next.

"They're split up on a few stations in chemically-induced comas. A select group of doctors are taking samples of blood, skin, and bones. They're studying them, but I don't know what they're looking for."

I slump forward, head resting against the bars. My hands fall to my lap, lying useless.

Ricardo shifts, boots scuffing the floor. "We've discussed it, me and the others here."

Their feet shuffle.

"We're going to do what we can to help you," Ricardo says.

I look up, bewildered. "Why? You're Human. Why would you help me?"

"Because what they're doing is wrong," Ricardo whispers. "They might think this is the best way to keep our species alive, but what good is it if we don't deserve to survive?"

The words resonate with me. I pull in a deep breath, searching the amber eyes before me for deceit, but I find only earnestness.

"It'll take some time to figure out a way to get you out, but we intend to try." Ricardo glances at the device on his arm, then says, "We're out of time. It'll be suspicious if we loop the footage for too long. One of us would move sooner or later, and we can't expect their surveillance team to believe we'd all sit still for much longer. Just know we're working on it."

Rising to his feet, Ricardo says, "Stand how you were before we started talking."

I do my best approximation, hoping it's close enough for whatever he's talking about, and the guards move into their positions. Ricardo glances at his arm, then gives a nearly imperceptible nod.

The rest of the day passes slowly, surrounding me with normal Human conversations, and my mind whirls.

Was that even real? Or is star-sickness warping my mind?

I shudder, but when I sing, my heart comes forward, filling my words with a need for revenge.

And I know that, deep down, I believe this strange Human with amber eyes.

Chapter 11
Ulysses Space Research Station

Ricardo

My heart hammers my ribs, and I feel every pulse in the gash I carefully cut into my arm. Yet, I smile at the techs in the lab.

Early morning rounds offer a convenient cover, and I slip quietly through, heading to the office. Screens go dark as I pass, guarded from prying eyes. I never thought anything of it before, just assuming they were trying to crack Drennar defenses. Now that I know what they're working on, it turns my stomach.

Maybe they don't know.

Over and again, I tell myself that they're as clueless as I was just days ago. More so, actually. They haven't seen Krona awake, haven't heard him sing, heard him speak.

To them, he's just a Drennar we managed to capture. He's a cold, unfeeling enemy that we're studying.

That's all they know.

But telling myself this doesn't quiet the dread within, doesn't quell the urge to shout at them that this is cruel and unjust. All that holds my tongue is the knowledge that yelling at them would help no one.

And I can't escape the fear that... maybe they do know. Maybe they don't care.

At the door to the main office, I knock and plaster on a look of ease, even going so far as to lean against the wall. But my insides are screaming.

Should I really be doing this?

I quail before the heat this could bring down on me. After all, this involves members of the Coalition. How many of them, I don't know, but it goes too high.

If they find out, I'll be jettisoned. They'll take me out.

Why wouldn't they?

If they're willing to experiment on six thousand innocent beings... What would stop them from killing someone getting in their way?

My heartbeat accelerates, and for the briefest second, I look back at the lab, at the doorway out of here. But I can't leave them to their fate.

I've never been good at looking out for myself and letting everyone else fall. My nerves wind tight, and suddenly, I'm just a little kid again, drawing my drunken father's attention, taking the beatings to spare my little brother, Ferdinand.

And just like then, I can't stand by and watch.

I can't let them hurt these people.

Pulling in a deep breath, I knock again. The door slides open beneath my hand, catching me off guard, and Dr. Sullivan appears before me. Relief floods through me, but only for an instant.

Behind him, Dr. Jackson sits, peering closely at the tilted screen of his desk. I grit my teeth at the sight of him, hating the fake smile that creeps over his face and the charm that pours out on a warm greeting.

I return it out of necessity, cringing inwardly all the while. Then, turning to Dr. Sullivan, I offer up a genuine smile. After all, he *doesn't* know. He's here for us, not for Krona.

I hold up my arm, showing the cut on the top of my forearm. "I could use a little help, if you have time," I say, keeping my tone light.

"Oh," Dr. Sullivan says, dark eyes softening with compassion. "Of course, I have time. Let me take a look."

Gently, he takes my arm in his hands, inspecting the cut. "It doesn't look too deep," he concludes. "Let's get it cleaned up, though."

He leads me to the treatment room. The bright lights reflect off his umber skin. As he bustles about, gathering all the necessary items to sterilize my tiny wound, I shut the door.

A quick message from Francis reads, "Ready."

"Doctor," I say.

He turns to face me with sterilizing wipes in one hand and a bandage in the other. "Yes?"

And I bring the world crashing down on him.

I tell him everything I've learned, confident that Francis has blacked out the surveillance in the room.

Chapter 12
Odyssey Space Research Station

Tenna

Silence follows me as I clean the public areas of the station, a hollow substitute for Olivia's presence. Off on a supply run to Termana, she won't return until after I've retired for the evening, and I'm stunned by how much I miss her.

I work as hard as I can, push myself as far as the work allows, telling myself to be grateful that I'm pulling my weight. But as I scrub toilets and wax floors, my muscles itch for something more.

Even the small gym here offers no hope of relief. The weights are too light, the track too short.

Tension coils in every fiber of my being, begging for relief, begging to run, to move, to truly push myself.

I close my eyes, returning my thoughts to the tables of the cafeteria. I concentrate on the movement of my arms as I clean one after another.

Be grateful.

They didn't have to rescue you.

But something about this doesn't feel like rescue. I chide myself, trying to chalk that up to mourning and loss, but my gut says otherwise.

My mind fills with the strange feeling I got when speaking with Doctor Antar, the idea that she was worried I *would* remember things.

My intuition always served me well as a warrior.

Not that I know why I know that.

Not that I can think of a single instance to back that up.

Again, I push against the walls in my mind, but the black bricks hold firm, keeping me from everything. I try to go around them, over them, but just like every other time, I fail.

There's just... nothing.

I grit my teeth and focus on this dull job.

***

In the supply room, I scan my Link at the end of the workday, and within minutes, my credits appear. I wander to the cafeteria, wondering if I can take another conversation about Maria's pregnancy or my own failure to remember anything.

Maybe I should sit at a different table...

But where would I sit? I don't know anyone else, and it's always too full to sit alone.

I claim my soup, bread, and vegetables, scan my Link to pay, and sit across from Nico. I want to look at his eyes, want to stare at them until they tell me what I've forgotten.

Maria, Matteo, and Lachlan settle in, smiling and greeting me warmly. A twinge of guilt slips through me for having thought to sit elsewhere. My eyes fall on Olivia's empty chair, and again, I wish she were here.

But her seat doesn't go empty for long.

Doctor Antar comes to join us, and a hush falls over our table. Surreptitious glances pass amongst my companions, brows raised almost imperceptibly.

Always eager to smooth things over, Nico recovers first. "How are you today, Doctor Antar?"

"Oh, please, call me Jessica," she begins with a smile. "I'm well, Nico. How are you?"

"I'm pretty good."

Stunted pleasantries make their way around the table, and silence descends once more.

She's never sat here before. Not once.

Utensils scrape and clink against bowls. Glasses settle onto the table, too loud in the quiet that hovers over our heads. All around us, voices rise and fall, far beyond our reach.

"So, Tenna," Doctor Antar begins. "Have you remembered anything else yet?"

Again, her tone just doesn't *feel* right. The hairs on the back of my neck stand up.

I shake my head, doing my best to look forlorn. "Unfortunately, no."

The tiny Human Doctor frowns, but relief shows in her eyes, in the way her breath flows easier. "Just hang in there," she says. "Perhaps you're focusing on it too much. Try not to think about it for a few days and see if anything comes back to you on its own."

My stomach turns, and I stare at the woman. "I'll give that a shot. Thank you," I say, quelling the anger that surges through me.

The doctor shifts the conversation to Maria's pregnancy, and true hope shines in her eyes. She lights up as she wishes the expectant parents good health for them and their family.

I shake my head, incredulous.

She really *doesn't want me to remember. It's not just in my head.*

Again, I find myself wishing for Olivia's company, suspecting that she'd notice this odd behavior too.

Maybe I can talk to her about it tomorrow?

Antar finishes her meal and quickly excuses herself. I sit, staring after her, eyes narrowed at her retreating form.

"Why did she sit with us?" Lachlan asks. "That was... odd."

"She's just being friendly," Nico says.

But Maria and Matteo look at each other, the former pursing her lips, and the latter raising a brow.

Turning to Nico, Matteo says, "Then why was she so awkward with Tenna?" He looks to me. "Is she always like that with you?"

I nod, still staring at the door that swallowed her little frame.

"She's probably just nervous," Nico assures us. "She's known us a lot longer than she's known Tenna."

I drop my gaze to the man before me, to those lovely pale green eyes. I tip my head to the side, brows furrowing as I wonder at the difference between him and the man I can't quite remember.

He would have seen the oddity, would have seen it for what it was.

Suspicious.

Nico's Link flashes with an incoming message. Within seconds, his face glows, firmly moving my concerns to the back of everyone else's minds.

"What is it?" Maria asks.

"They liked us!" Nico says. Tears glisten at the corners of his eyes.

I squint at him, every bit the outsider.

"Hans and I found a couple we like. Francis and Giselle. They like us!" He turns and throws his arms around his friends.

But it makes no sense to me.

"We can finally start a family. We'll have to move to Termana, of course. There aren't any communes available in the family section here or on Ulysses Station, but at this point... It'll be worth it."

Maria giggles excitedly, and congratulations abound.

But my spirits sink further.

"Oh!" Nico exclaims. "I forgot to tell you. You'll love this, Maria." He lifts his arm, showing her a picture on the screen of his Link. "This is them."

My eyes drift to the picture, tugged along by an odd shade of orange.

Maria's jaw falls open and her eyes sparkle. "Is that natural?"

"One hundred percent. She has a lot of Irish and Scottish in her blood, I guess. But can you believe it? Red hair!"

"I hope the baby gets her hair. Oh, and your eyes! That'd be beautiful. Or a baby with your eyes and Giselle's cheekbones. They could cut glass," Maria says.

Doubtful. These humans' bones are too fragile for anything of the sort.

"So," Lachlan asks. "What do they do? Are they on Termana already?"

"No. They're guards on Ulysses Station." Nico tucks his arm back down into his lap. "I'm a bit worried about them, actually."

"Why? There's almost no one there right now. That's probably the safest place they could be stationed. Besides, I'm sure they can handle themselves," Maria says, rubbing Nico's back.

"I wouldn't be so sure about that..."

My ears perk up.

What danger lurks on this other station?

Nico casts a quick glance around the cafeteria and leans forward, gesturing for us all to do the same. I duck forward, bowing as close as I can get without hunching and hurting my back.

"There's a reason they moved everyone out. There's only about twenty or thirty people there," he whispers. "They caught another Drennar. They don't want another massacre if the thing escapes, not after what happened on Bolivia Station."

Everyone at the table gasps. But my heart skips a beat.

Drennar?

The word feels familiar, somehow. It seems like a part of me, tugging at the memories locked behind the black walls in my mind, pulling at one through a crack.

"What's a Drennar?" I ask, quiet and reverent. The word seems to demand it.

"They're the aliens that have been taking our people for decades," Matteo says, then casts a sidelong glance at Nico. "The ones we weren't supposed to mention around Tenna, just in case it would freak her out."

"Shit," Nico mumbles. "Sorry."

"No, it's fine," I assure him. "I want to know. What do you mean they're taking your people?"

"Exactly that. They come here on ships that we can barely detect, they get past every security point, every airlock, and they take people. They never bring them back." Matteo's face falls.

"They've taken thousands," Maria adds. "I don't know if she'd want me to tell you, but I doubt she'll tell you herself. She doesn't really talk about it. They took Olivia's dad when she was a kid. I guess they came for her, but he went in her place. It really messed her up. Messed her mom up, too."

My brows furrow, and my heart lurches. My petty jealousies dissipate, replaced by a cold, impotent rage that one race could prey upon another like that. My hands curl into fists in my lap, and tension builds within me.

I force out an apology that I know doesn't fix anything and shovel in the rest of my food. Desperate for release, I clear my dishes and head for the gym. "Wolf by Highly Suspect. 2016." blares over the speakers.

I lift the heaviest weights I can find, but they aren't enough. The Humans around stare, open-mouthed, but I need more, need something heavier.

Casting a glance at the exercise machines, some dotted with Humans, I let out a frustrated sigh. None will accommodate my frame.

I run around the track, doing lap after lap, passing the Humans with ease. But the track isn't long enough, doesn't let me get up to speed.

I'm just running in a box.

A giant, floating, metal box.

The shape of the station comes to mind, and I remind myself that it's a sphere with a ring, but that doesn't help. My skin warms, and my muscles tense.

If only I could do laps around the residential ring without plowing into Humans.

I grit my teeth and blow out a long breath.

Giving up, I tell my Link to let the song follow me and return to my room. Defeated and tense, I move through the halls without truly seeing any of the people milling around me.

In the darkness of my room, I sprawl out on the floor, foregoing the tiny bed. The notes of instruments which have long since been destroyed on Earth wash over me. Grief tugs me down, pulling my spirits lower and lower.

A knock at the door reverberates through the room, and I grit my teeth.

Why would anyone visit me so late?

Reluctantly, I turn the volume down and push myself to my feet. I open the door, and Olivia smiles up at me, hand resting on the large box standing next to her. The dim lights of the hall cast shadows over her in a poor semblance of night.

Beaming, this strange Human asks, "Did you miss me?"

I chuckle, but my heart swells.

I did miss her.

"You mean you went somewhere?" I say.

Olivia feigns disappointment, but a smile tugs at her lips the whole time.

"Come on," she says, gesturing to her room. She pushes the box along the floor, leading me across the hall.

I follow, and my door slides shut behind me. We step into Olivia's room, and the door closes. It even locks with a solid thud, surprising me.

"Sit," Olivia says. She pushes the box toward me. "You said you thought you were a musician before. I thought you might like this."

I slide the box closer as Olivia bounces.

"Well," she says. "Open it!"

I do, and a wooden instrument waits inside. It stands upright, held carefully in velvet lining. Four strings run from the head down almost to the bottom of its body. It perches atop a long metal rod for height, and a stick with a flat fiber running its length rests beside it.

"It's a double bass." Olivia says. "These things have been around for ages. This one is about 300 years old, I think."

"Thank you," I stutter. "But why? Why did you get it for me?"

Olivia sits on her bed and says, "I thought it might help you remember if you took up music again." Her gaze drops to her hands. "I can't imagine how it must feel... to have it all washed away like that."

Olivia glances up at me, eyes shining. The warm light brings out the azure streaks in her gaze.

"I want to help. If I can," she offers.

Tears prick at the corners of my eyes. "Thank you..." I whisper, stunned.

Guilt sweeps through me for having told them I thought I was a musician now that I know I'm a warrior, but musician isn't wrong.

Not completely.

Was I both?

I nod.

I was both.

"How do I play this thing?"

Olivia smiles, pulling the long stick from the case. "Well, I haven't practiced, or anything, but the general principal is…"

She removes the bass from the package and the bow draws across the strings, demonstrating that the sound varies if you move your fingers over different parts of the neck.

"That sounded terrible," she says, laughing. "But that's the gist of it."

She hands it back to me, and I stare down at it. The bow looks so small in my hand, the bass miniscule next to me. I fumble with it, pulling sounds into the air.

The instrument itself doesn't feel familiar, not exactly, but my heart soars, elated to make music. I ache to sing. It seems like such a powerful thing to do. I part my lips, about to let words leap into the air.

But something in Olivia's eyes stops me.

"What is it?"

She shakes her head. "Nothing. I just hope it helps. And I hope you know I mean that."

I cock my head to the side, eyeing her with brows creased.

"I talked to Lachlan. He insisted that I let him know when I got back." Olivia rolls her eyes. "He said

Doctor Antar sat with you guys at dinner, said she was weird."

"That she was..." I tell her.

"He said it was like she didn't care if you remember..." Olivia says. Her lips fall into a frown. "But how could she not care?"

Oh, she cares. She doesn't want me to remember.

"Anyway," Olivia says. "I want to make sure you *know* that I care. I want you to remember." She laughs, adding, "And not just because I'm curious."

"I know," I say with a smile. "I can't tell you how much that means to me."

Words fill my mind, ready to leap out. I want to tell her what I really think of Antar and that I was a warrior.

But Olivia's mouth opens in a yawn. She tries to hide it, drawing her hand up to cover it, but dark circles hang under her eyes.

She was gone long before I woke for the day and only got back a little while ago.

She must be exhausted.

I bite back the words I want so badly to tell her, vowing to do so tomorrow.

"Sorry," Olivia says.

"It's okay," I assure her. "You've had a long day. I'll let you get some sleep."

"You sure? You looked like you were going to say something."

I nod, smiling. "I'll tell you tomorrow."

Nodding, Olivia yawns, yet again.

I pack the bass and bow back into the case, gentle but quick.

"Thank you, Olivia."

Her eyes soften, and she nods. "No problem."

Chapter 13
Novay
3018 C.E.

Rone

I walk away from the subject's room after escorting him back. His experiments today proved informative. Emotions hold more power over humans than we once thought.

Turning a corner, I wait as the wall parts to allow me passage and then step into the lock chamber. The air around me changes, growing heavier with the weight of the Alonarium.

How strange that the humans are so weak in the face of it that we must filter it from their air.

The wall before me opens, allowing me passage into the rest of the facility. Pale grey walls guide me to the center. My ears blink three times, syncing all my findings with the network. The subject's heartrate, the flicker of his eyelids measured down to the micrometer each time the screen changed, the constriction of his pupils, the firing rate of each synapse in his brain.

And it all comes down to these strange things called emotions.

I send out a request, syncing with the network, and quickly, another Drennar stands before me. I look up at him, staring into his eyes. With a thought, I scan him, letting fans of light emanate from my own eyes. I don't measure the firing rate of his synapses, knowing that the Human would never compare.

He maintains near perfect stillness, though I note a millimeter of sway in his stance. The Drennar man blinks, and I measure the time from one blink to another. His pupils maintain a steady dilation and his eyelids never flutter.

Setting his constant posture against that of the Human subject makes the contrast stand out even more. In the back of my mind, I run a scan over the Regonians, our only other real comparison to the Humans. I analyze their emotional patterns and the point in their evolution when emotion became a factor, noticeable enough to be weighed and measured.

This strange force seems to change beings drastically, altering their perception and reactions to everything.

It baffles me.

An idea forms, a new experiment, and I draft the request quickly and efficiently, including my willingness to act as prototype. The approval comes back instantly, and my individual ranking goes up 0.0007 percent.

Ceasing my scan, I send a release to the Drennar before me. He blinks, just in time to offer his eyes the exact amount of lubrication they need, and turns away.

Chapter 14
Ulysses Space Research Station

Krona

Doubt nips at my heels as I pace my cell. It plagues me as I sit on the floor. Silence rules as my guards switch off throughout the day.

They stare at me, watching as I wonder if Ricardo spoke the truth. I hope for one part of his story to be true, all the while, fearing it all.

It seems like nonsense.

Implanting and erasing memories?

My mind rejects the notion, but isn't that what I suspected? Isn't that what I already feared?

And how could they ever justify kidnapping us all?

My stomach turns, but if Ricardo spoke true, they're all alive. Tenna and our tribe still live.

We can rebuild. Tenna and I will find a way. We always do. Always.

When our crops started dying, we figured it out. When the river ran dry, we found Roon Tribe's dam, and we dealt with it. Each time the Vaerkin invaded, we fought them off. When disease struck down our livestock, we got through it. We quarantined. We found a cure.

We always find a way.

My heart twists in my chest.

We always found *a way.*

Now...

Now, she doesn't even remember me.

Icy fingers claw at my heart. I gasp at the loss of us, of all we had, all we wanted. I shake my head.

I'll make her remember.

Or I'll make whatever "doctor" did this to her reverse the process.

Doubt fills me, and I question the possibility of such a thing. But for people capable of travelling through the Realm of Stars, capable of erasing an entire life, surely restoring it is possible.

Somehow, she'll have herself back. She'll remember our life and our Tribe. She'll remember me.

When the guards douse the candles, I lie down with my stomach in knots. I toss and turn, muscles tense. My hands ball into fists.

Whoever did this will pay.

Chapter 15
Ulysses Space Research Station

Ricardo

On Francis' signal, I approach Dr. Sullivan's office, knowing he waits for me, stalling Dr. Jackson. My hands clench and unclench at my sides, but I push myself forward. The last lab tech leaves, offering up a shy smile as she slips past me. I incline my head, trying not to seem nervous.

But if she notices my nerves, she must attribute them to her own subtle advance. Warmth spreads over her tan cheeks, coloring them a soft pink.

Yet, I barely see her, don't even notice the color of her hair or eyes. The door to the office looms, a harbinger of change ruling my thoughts.

Once I go through this door, that's it.

Everything will change for me, one way or another. Whether we pull this off or not, my simple, peaceful life is about to vanish.

My stomach turns over, flipping uneasily as I reach up to knock. I hesitate, hand stilling in the air.

Because hasn't my life changed already?

I know myself well enough to know that peace will elude me until I do something.

So, I take a deep breath... and knock. The thudding matches the hammering of my heart, far too loud in the quiet room.

The door slides open, revealing the doctors at their respective desks. They both look up and smile, but the expression doesn't seem right on Dr. Jackson's face.

What memory is he crafting? How is he going to try to rewrite Krona's life next?

I smile back, gritting my teeth all the while.

He's not rewriting anything anymore.

Dr. Sullivan ushers me over to his desk, saying, "Ah, Mr. Bourdeau. How's your arm?"

"Healing up nicely," I say. "Thank you."

"Why don't we take a look at it, just in case," he says, rising to his feet.

His chair scoots across the cool metal floor, and he ushers for me to pass behind the desks. A small cabinet behind them holds a few basic medical supplies, and he waves me over, positioning me right behind Dr. Jackson.

Confident that his screen will automatically darken in my presence, he closes his eyes, working on the backs of his eyelids, instead. He doesn't even glance over his shoulder.

Dr. Sullivan digs in the cabinet, making a show of finding a bandage of just the right size to replace this one. Turning to face me, he removes my old bandage and peers closely at the cut. "I think that'll heal up very well," he says, voice calm and even.

But my heart slams against my ribs, rattling in its cage.

Carefully, he slides a syringe into my grasp, meeting my eyes for a second before applying a new bandage. His dark eyes shine with enough certainty to still my trembling hands. His inability to break his oath, to do harm even to such a terrible man as Dr. Jackson, fills me with relief.

Pulling in a deep breath, I steady myself. "Thanks, doc," I say with a smile.

"No problem," he answers. "Helping people is my job."

I hear the unspoken jab at Dr. Jackson, and a smile spreads over my face. Turning, I do as Dr. Sullivan instructed, driving the syringe into the base of Dr. Jackson's neck. I push the plunger down in an instant.

"What the fuck?" he exclaims, but the sedative works quickly. The words that follow come out garbled.

Dr. Sullivan rushes forward to catch the asshole's head before it slams down onto the desk. Our eyes meet over the unconscious man, and we nod.

Staring into those dark eyes, I see the compassion that stayed his hand from performing the injection himself and the compassion that pushed him to let me do so for the sake of the Regonians.

I pull the syringe free of Jackson's flesh, and Dr. Sullivan indicates a drawer in the wall labeled, "Sharps." I deposit the used syringe and take a breath.

I'm officially a criminal, now.

But even as I stare at the limp body before me, I don't feel guilty.

My mind fills with Krona and his songs, with the horrific things I found in that file cabinet, and I know I've done what I need to do.

Or at least, part of it.

There's so much left to do, but it has to start somewhere.

"Shall we get him to a bed?" I ask. "I have a few calls to make."

Dr. Sullivan pushes the sleeping scientist back in his chair, and I peek out at the lab. Empty desks and blank screens greet me, pristine white and grey glaring in the bright lights.

With the coast clear, I nod, and the good doctor wheels him into the lab.

Once near a bed in the treatment room, we heft Dr. Jackson up and out of his chair. We settle him onto a bed easily.

"Good thing you're not as small as he is," I say.

Dr. Sullivan laughs, and the sound rumbles through my chest.

Chapter 16
Ulysses Space Research Station

Krona

Blinding light streaming from the stairwell greets my weary eyes when I wake. Ricardo bounds down the steps, two at a time, amber eyes aglow and bulky Human armor clanging noisily.

Keys hang from his grip.

I sit up, swallowing nervously. My heart pounds in my chest, and my palms sweat.

"Before I let you out of here," Ricardo begins, "I have to know you won't hurt any of us. If you give me your word, I'll trust you."

I take a deep breath. "What of those who did this?

"Unconscious," Ricardo says. "We need him alive. We have to use his Link, so you can't hurt him either."

I raise an eyebrow, wondering how much this man has learned of me. He stands here, reasoning with a Warrior King, knowing that I won't harm innocents, that I'll listen to reason.

Blowing out a deep breath, I say, "You're sure we need him alive?"

"Very sure," Ricardo answers. He holds up his arm, gesturing to the screen there. "If he dies, his Link shuts off. That means we can't access any of his files. More importantly, it means his reports to the Minister of Research stop going out."

Ricardo shifts, taking a single step closer to the bars, still just out of reach. "As long as we have his Link, we can tell her whatever we want her to believe. We can tell her the experiments he was doing on you are going perfectly according to plan."

I close my eyes, pushing my rage down into a knot in my gut. With a sigh, I nod. "Okay. I won't harm him. Is it only the one man?"

"He's the only one here who knew you weren't a Drennar," Ricardo specifies. "Everyone else here thought the Defense Department captured another one. We've been running Ulysses with only essential personnel since just before they brought you here, and the head doctor is the only one who knew what you are... Or what was really being done to you."

My brows furrow, and I stare at Ricardo. The openness of Daen Tribe fills my mind, and I long for those simpler days.

"Such secrecy," I whisper.

"I guess they knew most people wouldn't be okay with what they're doing," Ricardo says. He jingles the key. "Now, do I have your word that you won't hurt anyone if I let you out?"

I size him up, see the worry lines creasing his eyes, the weight on his shoulders.

I nod. "I'll keep my anger in check. Those who didn't know are in no danger, and as you said, this doctor seems more useful alive. But once he outlives his usefulness…" I clench my jaw, considering my words carefully. "I can't speak for my actions then."

"That's fair," Ricardo says.

In an instant, he moves forward, setting upon the locks of my cell door. He doesn't even bat an eye at how much the bars move in their footings.

How much does he see?

The door swings open, and I rise to my feet. I swallow nervously, waiting for a trap, waiting for the gas. I take a single step through.

And nothing happens.

I turn to Ricardo, my unlikely ally, and say, "Thank you."

He shakes his head. "No need for that. This shouldn't have happened to begin with."

I take a deep breath, and my shoulders fall as I exhale. I look around the cell room, spinning to take in the hearth, the Humans surrounding me, the stairs that lead up into that terrible, blinding light.

I'm free.

But my heart splinters.

"Now what?" I ask.

If everything Ricardo says is true... We're in over our heads.

I face the amber-eyed guard and ask, "Can we find Tenna?"

"I'm still not sure where she is," Ricardo says, eyes softening. "She's on one of four space stations, but I don't know which one."

My heart sinks, and I close my eyes.

Ricardo rushes to say, "But there's someone that can help. She's a legend as far as hackers go, and she's made a habit of flaunting the authority of the Coalition."

My Link struggles to translate the word "hacker," but it doesn't matter.

"So, she'll help us find Tenna? And our Tribe?"

"Almost without a doubt," Ricardo says, excitedly. "She's pretty bold. And very rebellious."

His eyes sparkle with admiration, an oddity given his position as a guard. But I don't ask about his nonsensical adoration of a girl he doesn't even know. Instead, I grasp the only lifeline I have, desperate to find Tenna, to get her back.

"How do we find this woman?"

"She lives on Odyssey Station. Her name's Olivia." With a smile, Ricardo adds, "We leave this afternoon."

Reaching into a pocket, he withdraws a square of metal with a glowing blue button. He presses it, and a metal latch slides out of one side, slipping out where no opening existed. Metal scales follow, locking together and forming what looks like a flattened metal snake.

Ricardo holds it out, and I grasp the lightweight thing nervously. Flexible but strong, it seems to hum in my hands.

"It's a Belt. Put it on and press the button," Ricardo says. "It'll make you... basically invisible. We found it in the lab."

I furrow my brows, shake my head. Doubt creeps in, and I ask, "Why do I need to be invisible? If everyone here knows about me, why hide?"

"Cameras," Ricardo says.

My Link translates the single word into a long string of words, explaining that they're like fake eyes used to watch people, and my skin crawls at the thought.

"We can't do a loop on the whole Station or block every camera. It'd be too suspicious," Ricardo says. Tilting his head to one side, the strange man continues, "That's another thing we need Olivia's help with. She'll be able to figure out something to do with the cameras."

He turns, gesturing for me to follow, and makes his way up the stairs. I do as he says, putting the Belt on and pressing the button before trailing along after him.

I cast one glance at the cell, at the warm hearth, before climbing the stairs into another world. A metal hallway swathed in bright, white light swallows any scrap of familiarity, and my jaw drops. The bulky, unfeeling walls are too close, too cold.

My breathing grows ragged as I stare.

It's all true...

The doubts, the hopes... They all disperse. Because now, I know for sure.

Ricardo was telling the truth.

Tenna's alive.

But dread tinges my relief, because she and our entire Tribe have been kidnapped, and we're in the Realm of Stars. I follow Ricardo through cold, sleek halls on numb legs.

Chapter 17
Novay

Rone

After surgery, my eyes open to the blue-grey ceiling of my room, a sight I've seen many times. But today, it seems different. Somehow, it feels cold, though a scan of the room finds both the temperature of the room and my body temperature to be adequate. A strange sensation in my stomach begs for my attention, something like a knot drawn too tight.

Did something go wrong with the operation?

The unpleasant feeling intensifies as my mind fills with possible scenarios of failure. After all, any operation involving the brain has many ways to go wrong.

Was the modification not successful? Did they damage my brain?

Chills shiver over my spine in a way they never have before, and the knot inside pulls tighter.

Surely not.

Only the best are allowed to do such delicate procedures as this one. This must be a side effect of the experiment.

But... Do these things have side effects?

I comb through a million Human sayings, analyzing them anew. Through this frame of reference, humanity doesn't seem quite so hyperbolic as we thought. Centuries of poems and songs filter through my thoughts, packed to the brim with notions of a stomach in knots or a chill up the spine.

I lift my hand to touch the tiny line on the side of my head where they cut into me. I sit up on my bed, wondering if my chest will truly feel like it's collapsing someday, if my heart will race or flutter.

Surely not.

But the uncertainty, the curiosity building within me proves me wrong, elevating my heartrate and spreading my lips into a smile.

Glancing around my room, I compare it to the dwellings of Humans. Where their homes are packed with trinkets, things they keep due to something called sentimental value, my room houses only me and the necessary items for my survival and contribution to the Drennar pursuit.

Will my room soon overflow with useless objects or clothing I have long since outgrown?

I laugh at the prospect but don't dismiss it outright.

After all, I did just laugh, such a strange yet pleasant sensation.

My brows furrow, and I start my report, adding every odd reaction thus far.

Including the furrowed brows.

Chapter 18
Novay
3018 C. E.

Reginald

What will they test today?

I perch on the edge of my bed and stare with unfocused eyes at the dull grey room. I scratch my chest, trying to sort through the mind-numbing blur of my life. Every day, my guard marches me through cold grey halls. Every day, they put me through one test or another.

Every day, I care just a little bit less.

I used to marvel at what they have, what they know, what they can do. Now, I hardly notice when they turn a blank wall transparent or morph solid surfaces to allow objects passage or transform walls into touch screens. I no longer care what the things around me are made of.

The implants and genetic modifications of the Drennar used to consume my thoughts. They make us seem ordinary by comparison.

But now...

Even that has lost its ability to thrill me or spark even a hint of curiosity.

Maybe their lack of emotion is rubbing off on me.

I sigh, running a hand over my face.

Maybe it's from years spent basically living in solitude.

On a whim, I repeat the basic instructions they've spoken over the past week, amassing a whopping seven sentences. Nothing unnecessary. Nothing frivolous.

The wall slides open, and my guard stands in the hall, waiting. I push myself to my feet, not even bothering to tidy my blankets. The fog in my mind thickens, and a twinge of worry slips through me.

I should care...

It should matter what they're testing, whether I keep my room tidy.

This is my life.

It should matter.

But I don't know that it does. Not anymore.

Plodding along behind the same Drennar that escorts me to my testing room every day, I make a conscious effort to *see* her. My eyes roam over her, assessing, calculating.

Was she engineered to be shorter than most Drennar? What would be the point in that?

Is that why she was assigned to me, or was she merely available?

Vaguely, I wonder if she hates being the shortest person in the room when around her own kind. After all, she's only a few centimeters taller than me.

Shying away from unanswerable questions, I focus on her, taking in every detail. Anything to keep the numb haze from descending again.

Black, feathery wings burst from her skin, just inside her shoulder blades. An elegant knot rests between them, tying a strap attached to the collar and waist of her shirt. The back flutters open beneath her wings, letting peeks of pale grey skin greet me.

Folded comfortably against her back, those massive wings bring to mind a mixture of angels of old religions and the dragons of folklore.

Another bio-mod, of course.

I almost ask why she has them, what they were for, why others don't have them or have different wings. But the effort to speak seems gargantuan. And I've asked questions before, always with the same response.

Silence.

I trail along in her wake, watching.

Her short, silky black hair has been shorn off behind the left ear, but only recently. A thin line, less than five centimeters long, glistens on the clean-shaven skin. Their healing salve shines in the light, and a braid holds her hair away from the wound.

I try to figure up the original size of the cut, considering the speed of the salve and the wound's current size.

It had to have been done this morning.

Maybe a 15 centimeter cut?

My brows shoot up.

That's one hell of a surgery for them. For us, whatever they did probably wouldn't be possible.

Finally, the haze lifts. Curiosity pushes me through the fog that's descended over me of late, and I find myself wondering what she had done.

And why?

They experiment on themselves as much as they do on us, and all they seem to want is information. But what could this have been for?

I guess at the cause, the desired effect, over and again, filling my head with endless possibilities to keep the numbness away.

She leads me through sterile halls, and still, I watch her, trying to pick out anything different. For the first time in a long while, I wonder about her life.

After 12 years, I still don't even know her name.

Does she have a name?

How do they identify each other, with serial numbers?

She walks lightly thanks to her smaller stature, yet the sound bounces off the steel blue walls, echoing through the vacant hall. Every surface buzzes with energy, and the walls seem ready to close in on me now that I'm paying attention to the world around me.

I force myself to focus, using her to center my mind. Her tight, black jumpsuit ends in the openings of her shoes, strange sleek things which contour her feet, even outline her toes.

She stops, but I don't look up, don't need to. In seconds, a portion of the wall slides open, melting back inside itself. We pass through, and it closes seamlessly.

The testing room is barren. No desk awaits me, only a sleek chair in the middle of the room. The last time it looked like this, they showed me Olivia and Eva.

My heart pounds, twisting anxiously. My palms sweat, and my mind fills with the things I saw that day.

Olivia, young and depressed.

Eva neglecting her, working around the clock.

Am I ready to see them?

Can I go another day without *seeing them?*

Either way, I'll get no choice in the matter.

My breath catches. I force my eyes to rise, staring at the wall before me. The Drennar in the corners of the room stare at me, but there's one too many.

My guard doesn't take her post in the remaining corner because there *is* no empty corner. Instead, she moves to stand between my chair and the wall that will become a screen, angled to see both, and my stomach turns uneasily.

But I'm left no time to consider it. The wall transforms, glowing to life. Upon it, six screens light an otherwise dark room. Their glow lines the silhouette of Eva's face. Her tight bun pulls at the skin of her face, hair straining against its tie. Shot through with streaks of grey, it ages her. Wrinkles rim her magnificent eyes.

But it doesn't matter.

It's her.

My feet drag me to my chair, but my eyes never leave her beautiful face. In a daze, I sit, staring openmouthed at my wife.

She works with a man I don't recognize. They lean over the shoulders of a few Defense workers, watching those screens. Three scroll various data streams, and three are consumed by different views of a rocky landscape.

On those tiny screens, defense personnel, loaded down with weaponry the likes of which I've never seen, faces barely visible behind their helmets, are... picking flowers.

On the side of a mountain.

The absurdity of it sends my mind into a tailspin.

"Termana doesn't have mountains. Where the hell are they?" I mumble.

In the bottom left corner, a date tells me that the video is old. Nearly a year old.

I shake my head.

"Why are you showing me this? Why now?" I ask. Tearing my eyes from the screen, from my wife, I look to my guard.

My jaw falls open at the sight of her.

Emotion, *empathy*, shines in her pale green eyes, vibrating in those strange blue striations. She stares at me, eyebrows creased. The muscles around her eyes are tense and tight.

A voice reaches to me from the screen as the man with Eva asks the personnel before him if they weighed the flowers. My head jerks to the screen, and I resolve to sort out what's going on with my guard later.

"Yes, Minister," comes the reply.

I shake my head, confused.

"She's working with the Minister of Defense?" I mumble. "To pick flowers?"

And sure enough, the soldiers on the mountain toss heaps of small, white flowers into a bin labelled, "Bellona." The wind whips a few of them free from the bundles, and those blossoms, apparently lighter than feathers, drift on the breeze, fluttering over the edge of the cliff.

Behind the soldiers, the rest of the mountain rises from the plateau they stand upon, blocking half the landscape from view. But what I *can* see steals my breath away.

Blue-green fields of grass stretch out as far as the eye can see, broken only by a crisp blue river. Clouds idle along, serene in such a natural, wholesome place. The drifting white blossoms send the whole thing over the edge, taking it far past anything I can believe.

When the bin begins to overflow, the same woman who spoke from the mountain before says, "One kilogram, obtained. That makes five kilograms total. Let's get home."

"Good," Eva says, though the people on the fucking mountain can't possibly hear her. "We need those, asap." Her tone comes out clipped, nearly unrecognizable.

All the sweetness her voice once held is gone, replaced by a hardness that smacks me across the face. The screens she watches go blank once the defense personnel pile into their space craft, and she turns to the Minister of Defense.

The wall before me goes black before she speaks again. For half a breath, I sit in the darkness, stunned, thoughts every bit as scattered as those delicate little petals on that faraway mountainside.

It can't be real.

It has to be a trick, a fake video, something.

"There's no way they could've gone to a place with mountains just to pick some freaking daisies," I say. "Why would they waste the money, the time?"

I falter. Words desert me, and my jaw works uselessly, opening and closing simply to occupy itself.

Before I can make sense of anything, the wall glows to life again, and the air rushes from my lungs. My eyes glue themselves to it, searching the hangar bay it shows me, trying to figure out which space station it's on.

Eva enters, standing with impeccable posture as she watches the hatch of a massive ship open. The hiss of its hydraulics makes my hair stand on end. In the pit of my stomach, something dark and oily churns.

Suddenly, I'm afraid. Of her. Of what she's done.

Of what lies in the cargo bay of that ship.

I try to swallow, but my throat is too tight. This fear feels a lot like betrayal, like treason even, not that that makes any sense.

After all, she's the Minister of Medical Research and Scientific Development. She's part of the Survival Coalition. Surely, her actions are for the good of humanity.

And yet, deep down, despite all that, fear slithers through me, freezing my veins.

The ship's hatch touches the floor, forming a ramp and revealing rows of massive metal crates stacked four high. They reach into the darkness of the cargo bay, extending past my view.

Holes dot the sides of each crate, right next to a four-digit number. My brows furrow, and I shake my head. But somehow, the sight calms me.

What did I expect to see?

Someone with an industrial jack wheels the first stack of crates out and lowers the one marked "0001" from the top. Everyone in the cargo bay watches, but not a soul speaks.

Eva approaches, footsteps echoing loudly through the hangar, heels beating the polished floor into submission. She leans close to the box, holds her ear near it.

Realization washes over me in cold waves.

The holes in the crates...

They're air holes.

I strain my ears, and the soft, even sound of breathing whispers out of the crate. My heart pounds, and one of the Drennar raises the volume.

Slow, steady breathing fills the air.

My heart sinks, and dread pools in my gut.

"They're unconscious?" Eva asks, voice far too calm. But her fingers tremble as she reaches out to touch the lid of the crate, the *cage*.

"Yes, Minister," a nearby soldier answers. She forces a cool tone into her words even as she grips her gun with white knuckles. She even points it loosely in the direction of the crates, as if some monster might pop out at any moment.

But the monster stands beside that single crate, not within it.

My breath catches, and I lean forward in my chair.

Standing up straight, Eva glances at her Link. Her other hand reaches for the chain around her neck, fiddling with the wedding ring that dangles from it.

She nods, and the crate's metal lid rises on hydraulics and slides sideways on telescoping rails. A small gasp bursts from everyone present, save the ones disembarking from the ship.

Eva steps forward, eyeing her prize.

My gorge rises, and I swallow back bile. Pushing myself to my feet, I approach the wall for a closer look.

"No..." I choke out.

Tucked within, an alien man slumbers. Pale grey skin marked with vivid blue tattoos stretches over a muscular frame. Shaggy black hair reaches just far enough to tickle black leather armor.

Despite his massive frame and battle-scarred skin, he's helpless, lying there asleep. My stomach roils at the injustice of it.

A hose runs to his nose from a tank embedded in the crate. Its label reads, "Bellona."

The flowers they picked...

The planet they found...

His planet.

His sedative.

I gape at Eva, trying to hold back the bile that threatens to rise. She retrieves a pen light from her pocket and leans over the unconscious man. Lifting one eyelid, then the other, she shines the light into striking green eyes.

"Excellent," she says, though horror brings a hand to my mouth. "Leave crates 0001 through 0006 here. We'll transport this one to Ulysses ourselves. Get the rest to their respective stations."

I reach out, touching the wall where it shows the crate's opening. My mouth goes dry as I stare at the sleeping man. The lid hisses, moving back into position, and I shake my head.

What have you done, Eva?

I stare at the man before me until the lid closes, stealing him from view. My gaze darts to Eva's face, impassive as she glances at her Link, callously tapping away at it while hundreds, maybe thousands, of people lie in *boxes.*

Because of her.

She walks away as soldiers move the appointed crates off ship. My heart plummets, dropping further with every step she takes, deserting her responsibilities, her morals. She fingers her wedding ring the whole time, and I swallow, chest heaving.

A heavy metal door slams behind her.

I turn my gaze upon the thousands of lives she's tampering with. I watch, aghast, as soldiers shuffle crates carelessly, as if there aren't living beings in them.

With crates 0001 through 0006 removed from the hangar and all humans clear, the ship's hatch closes.

The screen goes dark, and my knees give out. I collapse, hands streaking down the cold, grey wall, squeaking loudly in the silent room. The world I thought I knew shatters in my mind, broken by the woman I love.

But how can I love her now?

She's become the monster she vowed twelve years ago to rescue me from.

My heart twists, contorting my chest. Pain lances through me, and I clutch my shirt. My mind splinters beneath the weight of her atrocity, and the pain in my chest grows worse until I fear it may actually kill me.

And maybe that would be better.

Some small part of me wishes for it, calling out for the reaper to take me away, just so I never have to see those crates in my memory again.

So I never have to see the cold eyes that now lurk in Eva's face.

Already, they flicker over the backs of my eyelids in a terrible strobe of anguish and horror. Eva's hard eyes. Thousands of victims, defenseless in cages. Her cold, assessing gaze.

Her fingers playing with her wedding ring.

Her kneeling in the floor of our home twelve years ago, cradling Olivia as she vows to get me back, no matter the cost.

But this price is far too high.

My head falls forward, thudding against the cool surface, and I whisper, "Eva... What have you done?"

Tears fall freely over my cheeks, splatter on the hard floor.

Behind me, someone sobs, a gut-wrenching sound, the kind that shakes shoulders and makes the chest feel like it may collapse.

I turn, startled, to find my guard, the primary researcher for my case, staring at me with tears pouring over her cheeks. Her blue and green eyes are red-rimmed, and her hand covers her mouth, trying so hard to hold in the wretched cries that escape as she watches me.

The other Drennar stand motionless.

Chapter 19
Odyssey Space Research Station

Tenna

I tear a chunk off my bread roll and pop it into my mouth, mind occupied by the bass. I work through the hand positions in my mind, reviewing what I practiced yesterday. Dexterous fingers and an ear for music served me well last night, and I smile, eager to pick it up again after dinner.

"You should come with me, tonight, Tenna," Olivia says, whining teasingly.

"What do you even do there?" I ask, uncertain about forsaking my plans to venture to the Little Elephant.

Matteo interjects, laughing deeply, "Well, Olivia mostly drinks until we cut her off."

Olivia tosses a wadded up napkin at him, feigning shock. "How could you say that?" Calmly, she adds, "I dance, too."

Everyone bursts into laughter, but I turn to face Olivia. "You dance there?"

"I thought that might get you..." Olivia says with a sly smile. "There's always music and dancing. It might just be your new favorite place."

"That it might," I whisper.

***

I tug at the hem of the tight white dress Olivia had made for me. With straps in place of sleeves, a scooping neckline, and thin construction, it offers no protection. It clings to me, almost restrictive, and my insides squirm.

The stark white fabric stands out against my dusky skin, but it feels like a color reserved for special things.

Not a night of dancing with drunken Humans.

I slip on the flimsy, strappy shoes, and stare down at my exposed feet, my bare legs. I long for something sturdy, shoes that could withstand a journey, clothes that might fend off a blow from an axe.

But I suppose that won't be necessary tonight.

Forcing a smile onto my face, I step out into the hall and meander to Olivia's door. She opens it before I knock, catching us both off guard.

Olivia wears a short black dress with a single strap and shoes with tall, spiked heels that bring her eyes even with my chest. Smoothing the fabric down over her hips, she beams up at me.

"You look amazing!" she says.

I thank her for the dress and shoes, but mainly for the fact that she's trying, that she cares.

Smiling wide, Olivia practically bounces. "Alright, let's go."

She walks quickly, leading me to the bar with eager chatter that I barely hear. All I can think about is music and dancing. I need it to swallow me up, to let me forget the mess I'm in, to remind me of the life I left behind.

Hope builds within me, some unnamed intuition making my heart swell in my chest. My pulse quickens, and I find myself moving faster.

"Oh, while we're there, if you see a little, tiny, itty-bitty statue of an elephant anywhere in the bar, tell me or Maria or Matteo," Olivia says.

"What?" I ask, turning to face her. The frantic hope, the need, of a moment ago lost to Olivia's strange instructions.

"If you don't plan on drinking any alcohol, just tell me," Olivia says with a laugh.

"...Why?"

"If anyone finds it, they drink free for a week," Olivia explains. "That's where they got the name for the bar."

I pull up a picture of an elephant, making a mental note of it and marveling at the strangeness of these Humans.

As we move through the halls, I strain my ears, hoping to hear the music I've been promised. I want to feel it, want the voices and instruments to drown out the empty chaos in my mind.

We leave the residential ring far behind, entering the circular hall held within the ball of the station.

And I hear it.

Pulsing words and sounds are indistinguishable at this distance, but it whispers, calling me closer. Each beat pulls me further down the hall. The music echoes in my chest, resonates in my blood, beguiling and wondrous.

It goes quiet as we draw near, switching to a new song, something I haven't heard yet. I glance at my Link for the name. "Stranger in a Strange Land by Thirty Seconds to Mars. 2009."

Long fingers of dark sound reach out, pulling me into the dimly lit space. A mass of Humans moves on the dance floor to the left. They writhe to the beat, thrashing and grinding together.

Lachlan and Nico look up, catching sight of me. They break from the pack, heading over toward us, garish clothes glowing faintly in the strange lights.

Lachlan's eyes widen when he sees Olivia. His gaze slides over her, but no one acknowledges it.

How long has he liked her? Have they addressed this already?

His arms twitch as if aching to reach out, to close the awkward distance between them. My brows furrow, but I get little time to consider the strange dynamic.

"Time for a drink?" Nico asks.

"Damn skippy," Olivia says with a laugh, and though I understand more of their language, this phrase eludes me. My translator strings together a rough translation that amounts to, "Yes."

She takes my hand, hauling me toward the bar that lines the wall opposite the dance floor. I fight the urge to dig in my heels, to go to the floor and dance.

Trailing behind, Lachlan asks, "Jumping right in?" His tone holds a hint of mockery.

Is that right? Is that what his voice holds?

Again, I question my ability to read these strange people, but I must have heard him right, heard the disappointment, the insult, buried in his words.

Olivia merely laughs. Glancing over her shoulder, she says, "Oh, go jet yourself."

Lachlan grimaces, only softening when Olivia smiles at him.

What does that mean, though?'

All around, lights flash in random, disorienting patterns. The music slows, and a male voice reaches out in an eerie caress. The crowd of dancers slows with the beat, and I long to join them.

But I force myself to the counter.

Maria stands on the other side, filling glasses with a dark, translucent liquid. Red and purple lights flash over her hair, pulled up in a bun, but her dark clothes don't glow like Lachlan and Nico's... or mine.

Just down the bar, Matteo serves another patron, casting soft glances at his wife. My heart warms. Olivia greets her friend, my friend, and Maria smiles at us, dark eyes sparkling in the flashing lights.

"Hey, guys," Maria says, handing drinks to a woman with a shaved head. She turns to us and asks, "What would you like? The usual for you, Olivia?"

Olivia nods.

Nearly shouting to be heard, Nico asks for something called a stalagmite, telling Lachlan he should try one. Lachlan nods to Maria.

"Finally loosening up?" Olivia says.

Everyone laughs... except Lachlan.

His face sours, and he turns to Maria, offering up his Link for a credit transfer.

Olivia and Nico follow, and Maria pulls out glasses, pouring various liquids of different colors and thicknesses into them. As she works, Olivia, Nico, and Lachlan lapse into conversation.

But Maria turns to me.

"Would you like anything?'

"Just water," I say, holding out my arm for the transfer.

My Link prompts me to confirm the single credit transaction, and I accept. But I have my opportunity for an answer now.

As Maria returns to her work, I lower my voice and ask, "What does 'go jet yourself' mean?"

Maria laughs, eyes dancing, "Where did you hear that?"

I glance at Olivia, then Lachlan. Maria laughs, a deep, throaty sound.

"Figures," she says. Then, somewhat more calmly, she explains, "When people die, we don't really have a place to bury them, like Humans always used to on Earth. We jettison the bodies into space after the funeral."

She shrugs, and continues, "So, 'go jet yourself,' comes from that."

I scrunch my face in horror at the image of a lifeless body soaring through space. Not to mention the morbid humor of mocking it with a trite phrase.

Maybe coming back from an apocalypse does that to a species.

Not that my species will ever find out.

I take my glass of water from Maria. She finishes the other three drinks, handing Olivia a tall glass of light brown liquid and a lot of ice.

Lachlan and Nico receive short glasses with dark liquid and a mass of cream shaped like a spike in the bottom. They throw the drinks back quickly, faces screwed up at the taste.

But Olivia seems to savor hers.

"Why did you get something gross?" I ask. "You should've asked for what Olivia got."

"Yeah, okay." Nico laughs, struggling for breath. "We can't handle what Olivia drinks."

"That's right," Olivia smiles, taking another sip. "I'm a Little Elephant veteran. Perrin Whiskey isn't for amateurs."

I drain my water and set the glass back down, trying to quell the queasiness that slithers through me as Lachlan grimaces at her. Something in his expression unsettles me like nothing else here has before.

But if he dislikes her habits so much, why does he like her?

I shake my head, convinced I've misread him. Especially since no one else acknowledges the look on his face.

The music swells around us, tugging at my hands, pulling me forward. I hold back, sticking close to the bar and my friends.

But another song begins, "Guilt by Nero. 2011."

And I give in.

Stepping casually through the crowd, I let the beat flow through me. My heart pulses alongside it, giddy and aching for movement. Excitement bubbles through me, effervescing in my veins.

On all sides, people crush against me, lost to the music and unaware of my presence. My eyes close, and I find my place on the floor. My hands reach for the sky, falling just short of the ceiling.

I start off with the only dance I remember from before. A few steps to one side, crossing one leg behind the other, then the same in the other direction. I spin, arms reaching out over the Humans around me.

People move back, giving me space to breathe, to feel the music. They watch me, but I don't care. The sea of people parts, leaving a circle for me to dance in.

Their eyes shine as they stare, whispers buzzing beneath the strange, alien music. It flows through me, and I stretch with it, reaching, turning, reveling in it.

The music drops away for a heartbeat, and I fall to my knees with it, hands still reaching. The beat pulses anew, and I move, perfectly synced with this song I've never heard. It rushes through my veins, surging then ebbing. My heart thrills at the steady rhythm, the heaviness of it.

When the beat rises and the singing stops, I jump to my feet in a single fluid move, spinning all the while. The people around me cry out, clapping. They cheer as my feet move, as I sway. They jump with the beat, hands pumping, urging me on.

The world, the frantic attempts to remember, the travesties and loss...

It all falls to the back of my mind, overrun by harsh, alien music and feminine notes. The flashing, spinning lights change colors, splashing a beautiful panorama across my closed eyelids.

Panic, fear, worry, it all falls from my shoulders, chased away by the music. Freedom rushes through me, promising me that I can be okay.

I stretch out, finally able to really push myself. My joints pop, releasing the pressure and tension of this cramped metal ball. My muscles stretch as I move, as I sway and step and jump.

The Humans around me scream out in delight and amazement, voices blending with the music. It all melts together, pulling the tension from me as a new song begins.

"She is Young, She is Beautiful, She is Next by Perturbator. 2014."

I don't glance at my Link to see what it is, don't care. The foreign music steals me away, transports me to somewhere comfortable, somewhere free. It pulses steadily, evening out, and I follow its lead. I become fluid and gentle despite the pressure the song begs for.

The crowd fills in around me, moving in the same trancelike state they were in before, the state the music lulls me to now. We move together, and for a moment, one single moment, we're the same.

Eyes still closed, I marvel at the million auroras floating across my eyelids. The lights morph and flow together, undoubtedly painting masterpieces across my white dress.

But I don't look.

I don't care.

The music fills me, drowning out everything. The song changes a few times, but I don't bother to check the titles.

I drift from this place, from the harsh music and the flashing lights. Time disappears, crushed by hard, brutal sound.

Until the music softens.

Finally, I open my eyes, looking for something, *someone*, familiar.

But all I see are Humans.

Nico, Lachlan, and Olivia dance near the counter. Maria and Matteo stand behind it, serving drinks.

But it isn't them I seek.

Nearly a hundred strangers mill about, brushing against me.

But they aren't the one my heart calls for in this moment of freedom.

I go still, pushing my hands through my long hair. My heart hammers, and I stare out at the crowd. A heavy weight settles over me.

I push my way through the crowd, eyes alighting on the sign for the bathroom at the back of the bar, a chance at sanctuary. Ominous sounds swirl around me, and suddenly, I just want to get away from it, to get a bit of privacy.

Maybe I should just leave.

I don't belong here with these aliens. I belong... somewhere else.

But where?

The thick, black walls in my mind hold firm, and exhaustion settles over me. My stomach drops.

I'm so tired of not remembering, so tired of failing my family by losing them.

I drag myself through the crowd, all the while beating at the walls in my mind, desperate for something, anything.

But I know it won't help, won't bring my home back.

There's no home for me anymore. There's nowhere I truly belong.

My legs move faster, propelling me out of the crowd. A few people mill about near the wall, but they pay me no mind.

A small sign glows above the entrance to a little hallway exclaiming "RESTROOMS" in bright red letters. Tucked just behind it, in the corner where no Human could see it without a ladder, a tiny elephant figurine hides.

A new song begins. "Turtle Ship by Ghasper. 2016."

I try to move forward, try to escape into the restrooms, but a strange barrier holds me back. Before me, the fabric of space splits open, and from nowhere, perfect green eyes appear, set in a beautiful, pale grey face. Shocks of long black hair fall around chiseled cheek bones and a strong jaw.

My heart stops. It swells, and my lungs struggle for air. I bring a hand to my chest, eyes fluttering in disbelief.

It's him.

I don't know who he is, but I know him. I know those eyes.

A brilliant blue tattoo glides over his collarbones, disappears beneath natural-looking clothes, the type of clothes I *should* be wearing. Dark leather hardened with special sap from the Juno tree, washed and treated over and again, until it becomes durable yet flexible.

That tiny fact brings a smile to my face. Just a scrap of memory about clothes and armor, a scrap of my life. A piece of me.

He smiles, eyes warm, and the face in the air says, "Finally," just as a sinister laugh reaches from the speakers of the bar.

My jaw hangs open, and I stare. Questions flit through my mind, but my mouth refuses to form the words.

A touch on my arm, gentle and soft, draws my attention. I stare down at the skin above my elbow where fingers caress me, but there's nothing there.

Panic filters through, and for a gut-wrenching moment, I wonder if I've lost my mind.

But there's that voice again, whispering so close to my ear, "Can we go somewhere more private to talk?"

That voice tugs at a brick in the walls of my mind, trying so hard to pull it free, to let a memory loose. But nothing comes.

Staring at perfect, vibrant green eyes, I nod.

The face disappears, and my mouth goes dry. But that unseen hand lingers on my arm.

My heart races as I doubt my mind, my sanity, but I turn, making my way to the door. I glance at Olivia, meeting her gaze, and mouth, "Sorry."

As an extra apology, I send her a message containing the location of the little elephant figurine, hoping that'll make it up to her. But Olivia isn't alone at the bar and doesn't look particularly upset.

A man I've never seen, with smooth olive skin and amber eyes, leans close, speaking with her. Lachlan looms, grimacing from a distance, but Maria keeps a watchful eye on it all.

Olivia will be fine.

I take a deep breath, vowing not to worry about Olivia. She has her friends after all, Nico and Maria and Matteo and maybe Lachlan.

Seeing faces in mid-air, hearing voices I thought lost to the darkness of my mind, feeling invisible things touching me...

Those things worry me.

And set my soul on fire.

I walk onward, compelled to go wherever that voice might ask, to search again for those magnificent eyes.

I duck through the Human-sized door to the hall with the music wafting out to follow me. The sinister laugh of the song bursts through the air, the last thing I hear as the music fades behind me. It taunts me, telling me that I've finally gone crazy.

But I focus on the touch at my arm, soft and so familiar. Something inside screams to be let out, to be remembered, but the walls in my mind loom, thick and dark. Inwardly, I scream in frustration, aching to break the walls down, to learn something, *anything*, about my life before.

Who is he?

Why can't I remember him? I should *remember* him.

My hands shake as I lead my phantom through the station, and my heart quivers unsteadily. My lips beg to open, and my arms ache to reach out for him.

But I only plod along, swallowing nervously.

At my door, I scan my Link and pass through, urging the door open for a few extra seconds. His hand presses against the small of my back, and my heart leaps into my throat.

I let the door close.

Full lips brush against the pointed tip of my ear, sending a shiver over my spine as he whispers, "Turn on some music so we can talk."

How will music help us talk?

"And leave the lights off so I can turn this Belt off. We'll still be able to see each other, but if they have cameras in here, they won't see me."

My brows furrow.

Cameras?

They?

My heart races, but I cross the room, settling on the bench beneath the window as I've done many nights since waking here. But the distance from him leaves me cold.

With a thought, I urge my Link to play music, giving it my emotions to sort the songs by. The speaker by my bed fills the dark room with, "Home, Acoustic Version, by Schwarz. 2017."

My eyes see clearly in the darkness, and again, space is torn asunder. That marvelous face appears, quickly followed by the body of someone whose name I know I should remember.

He's strong and... perfect.

I know every move he makes, know the way his skin moves over his muscles.

But I can't find a single memory of him.

I clench my jaw, trying to remember his name, to remember how I know him, to remember anything about him.

But nothing comes.

He places a strange metal block with a glowing center on my bed and sits beside me. Clasping his hands on his lap, he lets out a slow breath.

"Do you remember my name?" he asks, voice deep and gentle.

It tugs at something deep inside me, pulling my heart into my throat. My eyes flutter.

A lance of pain spears my chest as I shake my head. My voice breaks beneath the weight of betrayal as I whisper, "I don't."

His face falls, and my heart breaks.

"My name is Krona," he says.

He opens his mouth to speak again, but nothing comes out. The muscles around his eyes grow tense, and his brows knit together.

Finally, he asks, "What have they told you?"

Hoping not to disappoint him again, I say, "They said that my planet... *our* planet was destroyed by a solar flare." I drop my gaze to my hands, fidgeting in my lap. "They said they knew the flare was coming, and when they saw life on the planet, they came to save as many of us as they could. They just didn't have enough ships for a mass evacuation."

I sigh, then continue, "There are five of us here. I'm the only one awake though."

I force myself to look at him.

Voice thin and quiet, I say, "There were six. They said my partner was on the ship with us, but he died before I woke up. Everyone left back on the planet..." Pain slices through me at the thought of such loss. "They all died."

Krona's hands ball into fists. "Well," he hisses. "That's not true, or I wouldn't be here."

He forces his hands open, grinding his teeth. Taking a deep breath, he rubs a hand over his face.

His voice softens and he says, "And what they told me isn't true or you wouldn't be here."

"So," I begin, hopeful that maybe I can get some answers, "what *is* true?"

Krona shakes his head and sighs. "I'm not really sure where to begin. It's such a mess."

Start with telling me why you're so familiar, why I want to wrap my arms around you, why I want to hear you sing...

"Start at the beginning?" I suggest. "Maybe it'll help me remember."

I lean forward, eager for anything he can tell me. He nods, and I wait, breath caught in my throat.

The song changes to, "Closer by Kings of Leon. 2008."

But still I wait.

"Please..." I whisper.

So, he tells me of the Drennar reaching beyond their limits in space and contracting a terrible disease. He says that none were spared, save our ancestors. Still young, they slept in cryo-pods on a ship, left untouched until the spread of the disease could be contained.

"They were brought to Regonia, where the few remaining Drennar helped them build a settlement. The

Drennar were battling mutations and fatigue, right up until they left us. They told us to live within the means of our planet and to honor them with our voices and our strength. Then, they died, drifting on their spaceship," Krona says, spitting the words as if they carried a foul taste.

But in my mind, a single brick falls from the massive wall. I peer through the tiny hole left in its wake to find a cozy room with a magnificent stone fireplace, a chair made of wood and broad, flat antlers.

And a woman.

Grandmother...

Long white hair held back with a single string, she sips a mug of something warm. Suede clothes her, but I see tattoos. All the ones I have and many more, brilliant blue shining against her dark skin.

On the red woven rug before her, a younger version of me, only 8 summers old, listens as she retells our history. The Drennar, the disease from the stars, the building of the settlement.

"Grandmother had a fondness for one Drennar in particular," I whisper. "Norvin. She said he spent more time with the ancestors."

I smile, beaming at Krona. "It's helping."

Hope plays tentatively in his eyes, and he breathes a sigh of relief. And for some reason, that small gesture threatens to split my heart wide open, for I see the pain that lingers behind the hope, hear the desperation playing just beneath the relief.

I claw at the walls in my mind, trying to widen the gap, to find more memories. But it won't budge, won't crumble. I peer closer at this one piece of my life, straining for details, but nothing more comes.

I groan in frustration, resigning myself to wait for him to tell me more.

At least that's an option now. It's more than I had this morning.

Another song, slow and somber, rolls over us as Krona considers his words. "Genocide by Link Wray. 1969."

I close my eyes, letting the drums and guitar sink into me while I wait.

Krona speaks, walking me through the splintering of the original clan in the early years. "Roon and Vaerkin are our enemies, but we've allied ourselves with Taron Tribe in the mountains. We trade with them. Our food for their weapons and Bellona flowers. The little blooms help with sleep but only grow on high peaks."

They appear in my mind, tiny white petals fluttering as a gentle breeze slips over them. My heart skips a beat.

But now that I can get answers, I ask, "Okay, but what about that's different now? You said it's messy?"

Eyes solemn, Krona whispers, "They lied. The Drennar lied to us."

I frown. "What?"

"The Drennar are alive, and they've been watching us." He runs a hand through his hair, eyes downcast. "Who's to say what else is a lie? They're the reason we sing, the reason we dance. But why would that matter to them if they lied?"

He meets my gaze, brows furrowed with the uncertainty that weighs on his voice. Even in the darkness, I see the sadness etched into the lines of his pale grey face.

"But what does that have to do with the humans?" I ask. And then, I remember the conversation with Matteo and Nico in the cafeteria while Olivia was gone. "They're *taking* Humans."

Krona nods. Bitterness seeps into his tone, and his eyes scrunch up as he says, "I don't know how many, but it was enough for some of the Humans to think it was okay to take our entire Tribe and experiment on us."

Shock spreads through me, flowing through my veins in icy waves. My jaw falls open, and I whisper, "Why?"

"We're close enough to the Drennar that the Humans think they can learn about them by studying us," Krona spits.

My blood boils at the hypocrisy, and my hands curl into fists. "What makes them think they have a right to do that?"

"I don't know," Krona says with a shake of his head. "It's only a select group of them that are in on this. The man who brought me here is looking for someone named Olivia. He thinks she'll help us. Apparently, she doesn't like the Coalition."

I smile. "Not really. She never said why though."

Another song, even slower than the previous ones, "We Were Never Young by Raised by Swans. 2010." The tones reach out, threatening to haunt us through our dreams.

"Does your friend have yellow eyes?" I ask quietly.

Krona nods. He grimaces at the word *friend*, though that expression softens within seconds.

"He already found her, then. He was with her at the bar," I say.

"Do you think she'll help?" Krona asks, voice tinged with desperation.

"Yeah, I think so."

"Would you trust your life to her? That's exactly what this comes down to, and I'm not sure I trust your life to anyone outside this room," Krona says. "I had to balance it on fragile trust in Ricardo, but even that feels like a stretch."

My heart leaps into my throat at his earnest expression, his fervent tone. But I force myself to focus, considering Olivia.

"Yes, I trust her," I decide. "And anyway, it seems I have to."

My mind spins, but here and there, a few pieces fall into place.

Antar's worry that I might remember suddenly makes sense.

She feared me, feared that I would seek vengeance. As well she should.

My teeth grind together, and my hands shake with fury. I finally have answers, but they're all terrible, somehow even worse than what I thought before.

Tension builds in my muscles, and I ache to move. Resorting to the one thing that always helps, I stand up as a new song starts.

"Precious by Depeche Mode. 2005." slips through the air, and I turn the volume up, thankful for the soundproof room.

I dance in the middle of my room, moving without any Human eyes upon me. Only the eyes I've been searching for shine up at me in the darkness, grounding me. Suddenly, I don't feel lost like I did back in the bar.

This is how it's supposed to be.

Or at least, as close as I can get any time soon.

Krona watches me from the bench, swaying gently. He seems to know the steps, and I can't help but wonder if this is a common dance for our people. I stare at him as my feet carry me one direction, then the other. I trace the lines of his brow, the bobbing of his throat as he swallows.

I don't remember him, and yet, I do. I don't know him, but here I am, arms stretching out for comfort.

He hesitates, and my heart spasms.

I spin, facing away, swaying side to side. My thoughts whirl about, a maelstrom of questions. The little room in my head, just on the other side of the wall, grows hazy.

The Drennar... are alive.

The thought clouds my memory, covering it from view, ripping away the tenuous link I'd found to my past.

Achingly slow, Krona rises from the bench, stars twinkling brilliantly behind him. My heart flutters, calling out for this man who holds all the answers.

I close my eyes as he approaches, terrified of what he may say, hoping for things I fear I shouldn't hope for.

I reach upward, and hands slide along my sides, drifting up the bare skin of my arms until our fingers lace together over my head. My breath catches, and heat slips through me. Krona joins me in this dance, this strange set of moves that I know, that he apparently knows.

His hands fall to my waist, and suddenly, I'm grateful for the thin fabric of my dress. The heat of him seeps through, and gentle brushes of his chest against my back, his hip against mine, pique my nerves.

We move together, bodies bending and swaying in time. This strange music flows around us, unlike anything I've ever heard before, but somehow, the dance fits.

"Do you remember the Marking Ceremony after the battle with Roon Tribe?" Krona asks, voice low and close to my ear.

But like so much of my life before, that too lies behind the wall. I clench my jaw, pulling in a deep breath.

I shake my head, repeating his words in my mind over and again.

The Marking Ceremony after the battle with Roon Tribe. The Marking Ceremony after the battle with Roon Tribe.

The Marking Ceremony after the battle with Roon Tribe.

Tiny fissures form in the walls, and light tries so hard to pass through, to show me something.

But nothing comes to mind.

Krona nuzzles his face into my hair and whispers, "You danced like this that night."

My heart flutters.

"How often have you danced like this since coming here?"

Every time I've been overwhelmed. Every time I've been sad or angry or lost.

"Too many times," I say.

His hand tightens on my waist. My skin buzzes, and I grow warm. So many nights alone, so much time wondering what's happened...

But he's here with me.

My heart quickens.

The familiar presence moving with me in the dark eases the tension of my life on Odyssey. Time falls away, and I turn to face Krona. I stare up at him, watching those piercing eyes as we dance.

His hands rise with mine, reaching slowly toward the ceiling, then out to the side. We move together, and when I spin again, I step closer as I come back to him, nearly pressing against him.

His scent drifts to my nose, tickling my senses. A slew of memories spring to the tip of my tongue, press against the walls in my mind. I feel them, hear them, clamoring for my attention, crowding my mind, just out of reach.

And all the while, we dance.

The air fills with a new song. "Sunny Delights by I Monster. 2003."

Krona's eyelids droop, heavy with the same emotions, the same heat that stirs within me. My hand deserts his, moving up his arms to rest on firm shoulders. He touches my waist, slides his hands around to the small of my back, throat bobbing as he swallows.

Our steps slow, adjusting to the beat of this new song as the singer breathes out the words.

But my heart hammers in my chest.

Floating on the notes of the music, I spin once more. He pulls me in, holding me firmly against him when I come back. Our bodies meld, and our lips almost touch.

And that beautiful green shines in the darkness, just as vibrant as I remember.

Krona's heart beats frantically, throat pulsing beneath my hand. He leans in, and my breath catches.

But he closes his eyes, presses his forehead against mine.

My breath comes hard and fast. Our feet stop moving, leaving us stock still amidst the thrumming sounds.

Brow furrowed against mine, breathing roughly, Krona sucks his lips in. "What do you remember?" he whispers desperately, painfully.

My heart splinters, hating the answer I have for him. "Bits and pieces, mostly. I remember riding a horse, but it wasn't a horse."

"No, they're Vyrtons," Krona says, voice a hoarse whisper of disappointment.

"I remember running through a field with tall, blue grasses whispering against my legs. Someone was running with me, just behind me," I say. "We were laughing, but I don't know why."

The words tremble on the tip of my tongue, and I can almost hear them. I *know* what happened that day, it's all there, but it's all locked away.

Krona holds stock still, breathing hard. He clenches his jaw.

"I remember your eyes," I whisper, hand gentle on his cheek.

And finally, he looks at me. His arms tighten around me, and my heart thrills at the sensation.

But his gaze is guarded.

Swallowing, I say, "The Humans call that color mint. Which is odd because the leaves of mint are actually quite a bit darker. But the Humans don't exactly make sense. Not all the time, anyway." My heart hammers my lungs, stealing my breath and stopping the torrent of words.

"You're babbling," Krona says with a gentle smile. "You babble when you're nervous, which doesn't happen often. Not even when facing the blades of Roon warriors. So," he wonders aloud, "what has you so nervous?"

Heat rushes to my face, and I drop my gaze. My answer hangs unspoken on my lips.

Can I tell him how badly I want to move into him, to press my lips to his and dig my hands into that thick black hair?

Is this right?

Yet again, I can't remember enough to know, can't remember if he was my partner, my secret lover, a friend.

Is this sort of closeness normal among our kind?

Is this a betrayal to someone I should be mourning?

Or was that a lie from the Humans, too?

A knock at the door, barely heard over the soft music, stills my tongue before I speak a word, before I embarrass myself. We stare at the door, and I shut the music off.

The knock sounds again.

I snatch up the thing Krona called a Belt and hand it to him. When he disappears beneath its concealing embrace, I turn on the lights.

I cast a glance at Krona, or the air where he used to be, and my heart stutters. For a moment, I wonder if I imagined it all, if my mind has fractured under the strain of this strange circumstance.

Then, I cross the room and open the door.

Chapter 20
Odyssey Space Research Station

Olivia

I sip my drink, staring at Tenna as she dances. She moves and sways gracefully, twisting and jumping when the music calls for it, somehow expecting the turns the songs take.

Who knew she could dance like that.

As she dances, I finish my first drink, the first of many for the night, but decide to wait to get another. I rise to my feet, joining Nico and Lachlan where they dance nearby. The music guides me, but not the way it seems to pulse through Tenna.

Frustration burns my veins when Lachlan presses close, trying to make this more than it is, more than just friends dancing in a bar. I grit my teeth, taking a step back, a step away from him.

Can't he just take a hint? How many times do I have to tell him he isn't my type?

His dark eyes narrow, and I shake my head. My hands curl into fists. Forcing them to unfurl, I turn from him and head back to the bar, slipping through the crowd.

I'll dance some other time. It isn't worth dealing with him.

A song I've never heard comes on, and I glance at my Link. "Turtle Ship by Ghasper. 2016."

A hand on my arm stills me, turns me in place. Lachlan stares down at me.

"Do you really need another drink?" he asks, voice heavy with disapproval.

I purse my lips and raise a brow. Pulling my arm from his grip, I move away before he can carry on. This time, he doesn't follow, and I breathe a sigh of relief.

I just want a buzz, to let go. I want my brain to slow down. He just doesn't get it.

The lights swirl overhead as I lean on the bar. Maria doesn't ask, doesn't say a word. She pours the drink she knows I want and does the credit transfer. In less than a minute, she's back to serving other patrons.

Simple and smooth.

I sip my whiskey, closing my eyes and relishing the burn, the gentle fog that slows my racing thoughts.

Maria gets it.

She doesn't judge. If she did, owning a bar would be a mistake.

The thought of Lachlan owning a bar makes me laugh. I turn to face the crowd, chuckling at how quickly he'd go out of business as he lectured his patrons on the evils of drinking too much. Or at all, really.

My eyes drift to Tenna, but this time, she isn't dancing. She stares at the people around her in horror, then moves quickly from the dance floor.

My brows furrow, and I lower my glass. A strange laugh seeps through the speakers as she stops in front of the bathroom, shrouded in darkness.

What is she doing?

But someone I've never seen before steps in front of me, blocking my view. He meets my gaze, liquid gold eyes shining. Curly black hair falls to his shoulders, swaying as he leans on the bar next to me. My heart flutters at rich olive-tan skin, and I smile at him.

Where did you come from?

I cast my mind back over the flight schedules, wondering if someone was meant to visit the station. I certainly wasn't supposed to pick anyone up.

In the crowd, visible over this man's shoulders, Lachlan flushes beet red, watching me. I barely contain a smirk.

Maybe he'll get the hint now.

But far behind him, Tenna's leaving, towering over the crowd as she retreats to the exit. She mouths, "Sorry."

My Link flashes with a message from her, but I can check that later.

Pulling in a deep breath, I smile up at the man next to me. My eyes slide over him, drifting over the muscles beneath his tight white t-shirt.

"Hi," I say.

"Hi." He smiles back, eyes sparkling.

The world lights up, and my mouth goes dry. My heart skips a beat.

Maybe I'm more buzzed than I thought.

In the corner of my eye, I can just see Lachlan and Nico arguing, doubtless over whether Lachlan should come over here. I barely contain the eyeroll that wants to slip out as a new song begins, "Roller by Yellow Claw and Eyelar. 2015."

The man with golden eyes leans close. His lips almost brush my ear as he says, "I'm Ricardo. You're Olivia, right?"

I pull back, looking at him with furrowed brows. My eyes flit from his molten eyes to his full lips and back again.

But I nod. "How do you know who I am?"

"I was looking for you," he says with a shrug. "Can we talk? Maybe... somewhere private?"

A surprised laugh bursts from me. "You're awfully forward."

Suddenly stricken, he blushes. "That's not quite what I meant."

A shame…

I sip my whiskey, eyeing his physique over the rim of my glass. Turning away from the crowd, I face him full on. My free hand reaches out, lightly touching his on the bar.

I lean forward, speaking into his ear. "What *did* you mean, then?"

What am I doing?

I don't know this man. Why am I flirting with him? To spite Lachlan?

Ricardo takes a deep breath. His free hand finds my waist, sending a little thrill through me. Heavy breaths brush over my ear. "Maybe we could talk somewhere without cameras or people who could listen in."

I tip my head to the side, watching him. His tone, his movements, his hand on my waist… He's flirting. Butterflies build in my stomach, surprising me.

But there's something else going on.

"It's rather important," Ricardo adds.

"Well, if it's so important," I tease, "what's it about?" I ask, baiting him with a smile.

Ricardo pauses, expression changing. The teasing tone falls from him as weight settles onto his shoulders.

Dread builds within me.

A new song comes on, its peppy beat at odds with the look on his face and the sick feeling in my gut. "Young and Proud by Ace of Base. 1992."

Sighing, Ricardo leans forward again, hand clutching my waist. "It's about Tenna. And your mother."

I stare into space for a moment, chewing the inside of my cheek, and a deep, sick feeling fills me. I drain the rest of my glass, throat burning all the while, but I have a feeling I'll need it.

So much for a relaxing evening.

Slamming the glass down on the bar, I take Ricardo's hand and lead him toward the exit. Behind me, Lachlan yells out my name, but I don't look back.

Was he really watching that whole time?

I scoff inwardly, pushing through the crowd and the shifting lights.

I guess I should've assumed as much.

Out in the hall, the lights hold themselves steady, dim as they may be. Echoes of music follow us out, quiet thanks to the soundproofing of the station.

"That guy seemed pretty mad," Ricardo says. "Was he your boyfriend?"

"No," I say, a little too forceful. Softening my tone, I add, "He's an overprotective friend... who wishes he was my boyfriend."

Ricardo goes quiet. He laces our fingers together, hand warm in mine, and a wave of heat moves through me, oddly comforting.

I lead him through the station, heading to the only place I know without a doubt has no cameras.

My room.

I really shouldn't take him there.

After all, I don't know him. And no one will be expecting me tonight.

But my gut says to trust him.

Or maybe it's somewhere lower in my anatomy that wants to trust him.

I chuckle inwardly.

No... It's both places. My stomach and my... not stomach.

The halls blur together, and I scan my Link at my door, trying my best not to let my eyes linger over him too long as he passes through the door ahead of me. I close the door firmly, locking it and breathing out a sigh of relief. Gesturing for him to sit in my wingback chair, I settle onto my bed.

He sits, eyes travelling over the soft fabrics, the shelves of books and trinkets. His chest puffs out as he breathes in the rich scent of so many old things.

I take a fortifying breath myself and ask, "What did *mommy dearest* do now?" I shake my head, then mutter, "If that bitch hurts Tenna, she'll have hell to pay."

Ricardo gulps.

Everyone knows about the tension between my mother and I, it's been all over the net a few times, but he still stares at me, shocked.

Finally, he speaks, spilling stories of my mother's treachery, and every word he says sends my stomach plummeting. My heart twists as he tells me of the kidnapping of an entire tribe of aliens, and anger and disappointment war within me as he speaks of horrendous experiments.

"I hate, *hate*, having to tell you this. I wish it weren't happening, believe me," he clamors. "I wish there were someone else I could've gone to with this, but ... there isn't. After all the times you've hacked her, none of which could be proven beyond her suspicions, we need you. No one else could do this."

Apologies fall from his lips, running far more freely than the revelations of my mother's wrongdoings.

But fury roils within me. My heart hammers, and my mind races.

I need a drink.

I rise from my bed and make my way to a small trunk at the foot of my bed. Tapestries hang on the wall behind it, draped over the top of it, and I brush them aside. I signal my Link to begin a song and let it fill the room.

"The Best of Me by The Used. 2009." beats the air.

I crouch, opening the trunk and pulling out a dark brown glass bottle. My old friend shines in my hand, sloshing in its container.

I open it up, inhaling deeply of the rich and smoky scent. Pulling a glass from the trunk, I look to Ricardo.

"Would you like some?" I offer.

He shakes his head. "I've still got a lot to tell you. We'll see how badly I need it afterward."

How much worse can it get?

I pull in a deep breath, close the trunk, and stand. After pouring a generous amount into my glass, I set the bottle aside and settle back onto my bed. Eyes closed, I sip at the fiery liquid, letting the music pull some of the rage, some of the hurt, from my soul.

"I should've known she wouldn't let it go," I whisper. My voice quivers, and my fingers tremble on the glass. Every muscle in my body grows tense, and I grit my teeth.

How many times in the past months, the past year, have I thought about checking in? I should've gotten into her files again.

But I was busy with Atlantis. And I spent so much time in The Little Elephant, just trying to stay sane.

"What did you say?" Ricardo asks quietly.

"I said, I should've known she wouldn't let it go," I reiterate. "When they took dad…"

My fingers tighten on the glass as anger and sorrow sweep through me. I force my grip to loosen lest it shatter before I can drink it, then I continue.

"She threw herself into work, trying to find anything, any possible advantage she could. She left me at home to fend for myself," I say, voice tinged with bitterness. "She didn't care. I was only twelve, but it meant so much to her to find some way to get him back, to get back at them, that it didn't matter that I was struggling too. Dad was gone. Mom might as well have been."

I take a long, slow drink, watching over the rim as Ricardo's face twists with sympathy. Broken families leave scars that never quite go away, and briefly, I wonder if he knows this pain, if he lost someone to the Drennar.

Grip tightening on my glass again, I say, "She put all her time into finding something to improve us, working with the Minister of Defense to bolster security, doing everything she could. All well and good for the species, so I really shouldn't be so pissed off, I guess. But she never did a damn thing for her daughter."

I grit my teeth, forcing my tongue to still.

He doesn't need my life story. He doesn't care. He doesn't need justifications for her behavior any more than I do.

"She's crossed so many lines in her research over the years, I *shouldn't* be surprised by this," I say, mind filling with years of watching over her.

The experiments on people and animals, the things she wanted built, all of it. Ethics never really played a role in her decisions.

But to go this far? To kidnap thousands, then experiment on them?

Bile churns in my stomach, and I shake my head. "How the fuck does she sleep at night?"

I take another long drink. It burns my throat, giving me something other than the atrocity of my mother to focus on for one measly second.

The song switches, "Sound Effects and Overdramatics by The Used. 2004." I listen for a moment, then drain the remainder of my drink in one long pull, savoring the fire in my belly.

"What now?" I ask.

"Well," Ricardo begins, "Krona came with me, and I'm pretty sure he found Tenna in the club back there. She stands out." He pauses, then asks, "What does she remember? Did they wipe everything?"

My heart drops, and I nod. My gaze falls to the floor as I say, "She's getting bits and pieces back, but I don't know how much. Not enough to worry Dr. Antar. She clearly doesn't remember all of it, or she probably would've ripped the bitch in half by now."

With a sigh, I add, "Maybe all of us. She's a freaking alien warrior. What the hell were they thinking, bringing them here? An entire tribe of super warriors, and they brought them here, then pissed them off?"

Ricardo sits quietly for a moment, then says, "We have Dr. Jackson unconscious on Ulysses Station. We used his Link to request Dr. Antar's assistance with his portion of their little project. We're supposed to pick her up. She'll be out after that."

I close my eyes, nodding slowly.

"We wanted her to go immediately, but she insisted she had one thing to try, one test to perform on the Regonians here," he says.

I clench my jaw. "What kind of tests is she doing on them?"

"I don't know," Ricardo says, quiet voice full of disgust. "But they'll be safe once we get her out of here. We brought a doctor with us to take her place, one we can trust. He helped us take Jackson out. But for the rest of it... We're going to need a lot of help from you. If you're willing."

I suck in a deep breath. For half a heartbeat, I wonder if I should do this, if I should turn against my own mother.

But my blood boils at the thought of what she's done, and a sardonic laugh seeps from me at the idea of owing her loyalty.

What do I owe her for? Neglect?

I push myself to my feet. "Come with me."

Ricardo stands, watching me carefully with arms raised as if to brace me as I walk. But it takes a lot more alcohol than this to make me unsteady.

He follows me into the hall without question, and I leave my door open behind us. My music drifts into the otherwise silent hall, covering the sound of our footsteps.

I raise a hand and knock on Tenna's door. Anger surges through me, and my fist hits a little harder than intended.

But no one answers.

I knock again.

Music seeps through the door despite the soundproofed walls and doors. I shut off my own music, trying to make out what it is, but it doesn't help. The other side of the door goes silent, then slides open.

Tenna stands before me, skin flushed and eyes wild. A hint of rose blooms beneath the grey of her cheeks, and I furrow my brows at her. My eyes dart over her shoulder, looking for a second Regonian, fully prepared to scrub him from the surveillance footage from the hall.

But I find nothing.

Maybe he's hiding in the bathroom?

"You should come with us," I say before turning back to my room.

Chapter 21
Odyssey Space Research Station

Krona

Tenna's shoulders relax as she leads me into Olivia's room, and as soon as I cross the threshold, I see why. The place seems to live and breathe.

Warm light caresses the tapestries on the walls, and the tomes on the shelves fill the air with a rich, earthy scent. It tugs at my shoulders, trying to bring them down from my ears, but I still eye the little Human woman cautiously.

I hope Tenna's right about her.

If Ricardo is to be believed, we have to get Olivia to help us. Nothing else will work, according to his explanations of this strange place. If she refuses, she could turn us in, and then what would become of us, of our Tribe?

My stomach clenches.

But Ricardo brought me to Tenna. He stuck his neck out in doing so. And Tenna's never given me reason not to trust her instincts before.

She trusts this Human woman.

That has to be enough.

Memories of false memories, the impressions of a story told in bits and pieces, flash through my mind. The idea of her with Mourgam. The thought of her beneath him.

I ignore it all, thankful that the actual images, the implanted memories, have been erased with some concoction of chemicals.

Staring at Tenna, Ricardo, and Olivia, I consider simply turning the Belt off, revealing my presence. But these Humans seem frail, and I wonder briefly if they could actually be scared to death.

But Ricardo spares me the decision. He reaches out to shake Tenna's hand, amber eyes sparkling in the soft light. I marvel at the strange custom, watching Tenna take care not to crush brittle Human bones in her grasp, and a smile tugs at my lips.

"Has Krona found you?" Ricardo asks, getting right to the point.

Tenna replies, nodding, "He's with me."

Olivia's brows furrow, and I don't keep her waiting. I switch the Belt off, and Tenna watches me reappear. My heart gallops as her eyes trace over my form, eyes softening, then smoldering. A smile like coming home perches on her lips, but a haze of uncertainty clouds her gaze.

My heart twists.

Should I have just told her?

I want so badly for her to know me, to reach for me as she has so many times before.

But would she think I was forcing her hand?

Would she think I was taking advantage of her lack of memory?

She doesn't know me, doesn't know our Tribe or how much we value integrity.

Her mossy eyes hold nothing but questions, and my chest tightens. I tear my eyes away, placing the Belt on Olivia's chair. I say nothing as the Human woman stares at me, then raises a glass to her lips with raised brows. She eyes the Belt, tipping her head to the side as her eyes narrow.

Ricardo glances at me, then turns to Tenna. "What did he tell you?"

I breathe a sigh of relief, grateful that he honored his promise to let me tell her.

"He told me what we really are and what's being done to our Tribe," she answers.

Ricardo's eyes meet mine, and I give a small shake of my head. But Tenna sees.

Pain flashes briefly in her eyes as she realizes I've held something back, and a lance shoots through my heart.

Olivia considers me, staring at the magically appearing Regonian. But she recovers quickly, gesturing to the Belt and asking, "What is that thing?"

"Some sort of light refracting device," Ricardo says with a shrug. "We found it in the lab on Ulysses. They were studying it there."

Olivia merely shakes her head, as if to say, "Why not?" After a moment, she says, "Okay. Let's figure this out."

Ricardo smiles, falling into the chair. Tenna and I settle in the floor, eye to eye with our strange Human allies.

Olivia stands near her shelves, restless and sipping from her ever present glass of foul-smelling liquid. She fidgets with tiny instruments as we speak, perching on her bed at intervals as we lay out plans to liberate the other 6,000 members of Daen Tribe.

Ideas form, but the burden weighs heavily upon us all. Shoulders slump as we realize how little we really know.

Olivia slides an innocent footlocker from under her bed and sets it atop the mattress. From within it, she retrieves an exceptionally slim device. Putting the case back on the floor, she settles on her bed and somehow unfolds the strange little device so that one half is vertical and the other horizontal.

I stare at the thing, marveling at the paper-thin pieces. My heart quickens, trying to guess at its purpose.

Does Tenna know? Has she used one since she's been here?

My stomach drops at the gap between us.

What if she's different now? What if she doesn't want our life back?

Ricardo breaks me free of the prison of my thoughts with an approving nod at the little device. "Guess I should've expected top of the line," he says.

Olivia's fingers whir over tiny buttons on the horizontal section of the folding device. Ricardo tilts his head, staring at her in disbelief. She looks up at him, fingers still moving madly.

"What?" she says.

"You're actually typing?" he asks.

"Yeah," she says. "I like the feel of it. And the sound of the keys."

"It has an actual keyboard?" he exclaims, standing to peer at it.

"It's one of very few that have it," the Human woman tells him, though her tone isn't boastful, merely matter of fact.

But even I know her actions are strange. The other Humans use their damnable Links to do nearly everything. Sometimes they tap flat surfaces.

But they never move their fingers over little springy platforms like she's doing.

It gives me a bit of hope.

Maybe she isn't like the ones who kidnapped us.

Silence falls over us as Olivia's fingers work at the things she calls keys. Numbers and letters and symbols appear on the vertical side, things that I'm glad to find make as little sense to Tenna and Ricardo as they do to me.

"Just have to sift through some things," she mutters, but each time I lean to peer at the thing that might be a screen, the symbols flash by too quickly for me to even see them.

Time stretches out as I wait, casting glances at Tenna. She sits, tapping one finger on her leg.

After ten excruciating minutes, a time frame that seems to impress Ricardo for its brevity, Olivia says, "I'm in. Now to look for the files we want."

She searches quickly, face falling with every heartbeat. Her brows furrow, and a frown tugs at her lips.

Bile rises in my throat, putting a foul taste in my mouth. "How bad is it?" I ask.

Olivia's eyes fill with disgust and disappointment, only to soften when she looks at us. My heart stops, and my chest tightens around it. My palms sweat, but still she doesn't speak.

She stares at the device in her lap, eyes moving hurriedly over the screen. After what feels like an eternity, she gasps, and the last bits of hope fade from her.

"She approved this," Olivia whispers. "She had to. She's the freaking Minister." She covers her mouth, and a few tears desert her eyes, leaving them lonely.

Forcing myself to be calm, to keep my tone level, I ask again, "How bad is it?"

Olivia drags her eyes from the screen, face haunted with whatever she's seen there. "They're trying to kill them," she says. "They're trying drugs and all kinds of stuff, probing for weakness."

Her brows furrow, carving deep lines in her face. "Or at least, they were. They found it. Electricity."

I shiver.

Beside me, Tenna cringes, and I wonder if maybe she remembers this. Lightning strikes fear into all our hearts, burns through our veins.

Surely, that must've stuck with her.

Memories of white flashes in the sky and running for the relative safety of home flood my mind. My veins ignite with adrenaline, even now, so far from the clouds which rumble and shake as they cast their angry bolts down to the earth.

"They killed one of them today," Olivia whispers, eyes vacant. "Just before Antar left. They *murdered* him. He was still unconscious. He couldn't even defend himself." She stares blankly, slowly shaking her head.

My stomach churns, and fury boils my blood. Tenna's hands ball into fists on her lap.

Silence falls over us, heavy and tense. I close my eyes, heart breaking for the man they murdered today.

"That's what she had to do before leaving?" Ricardo asks in a hush.

Fingers working at the keys again, Olivia says, "They were pretty sure it would work. They found something on the 'farms' that made them think it would."

My blood runs cold.

"The farms?" Tenna and I ask in unison.

Such an innocent word, but hearing it here, knowing it brought the death of one of our people... I shudder. Some small part of me doesn't want the answer Olivia searches for, even now.

But we can't go into this blind.

She shakes her head, fingers dancing on that strange device. "I don't know yet." Her eyes flutter, brows creasing as the screen flickers repeatedly. Letters and numbers appear and disappear in quick succession.

My nerves wind tight as I wait, desperate for an answer. Every part of me aches to reach for Tenna, to touch her hand, to feel the warmth of her, just to slow my frantic heart.

But what would she think?

Even the possibility of her thinking me an opportunist, using the situation to get close to her, pins my arms to my sides. But my eyes dip to her hands, clenched tightly on her folded legs.

Olivia's face falls further. She sets the device beside her on the bed, burying her head in her hands. With elbows braced on knees, she mutters into her palms, "How far have you fallen, Mother?"

Her mother?

Dread washes over me.

We're counting on her to go to war against her own mother?

My stomach plummets as my hopes shatter. The expression on the Human woman's face twists my heart because I've unwittingly informed her of her mother's treachery.

And asked her to betray her blood.

We sit in silence, letting her grieve. But every heartbeat without answers means my people suffer longer. Every breath I draw sitting in relative safety, they might be dying.

I need answers. I need to help my people.

If only I could look at that screen...

But even if I could, some of the words still wouldn't make sense. Proficiency with reading their language still lingers just beyond my grasp.

And if even the Humans can't all 'hack' the way Olivia does, why would I understand what I see any better than they would?

"May I?" Ricardo asks, indicating the device.

With a sigh, Olivia nods, face still pressed into her hands.

Ricardo's feet thud heavily across the floor. A tear rolls down Olivia's wrist as he leans to retrieve the little thing, and my heart twists.

Sitting next to Olivia with the slim device on his lap, Ricardo reads. His face falls, and he blows out a long breath. Silence hangs over us, weighing me down.

Frustration boils within me, and Tenna clenches her hands. We stare at Ricardo, at Olivia, waiting, and I grit my teeth to keep from screaming at them to read the words aloud. Every muscle burns with impatience.

Finally, Ricardo says, "All 6,000 of your Tribemates are here, on other stations. They're..."

He closes his eyes, swallowing, and my nerves wind tight.

"They're unconscious. The lab techs are taking... samples," he says. "Bone, tissue, blood... It's all being gathered, in small amounts, to be analyzed and catalogued."

My stomach churns, and rage surges through me. Beside me, Tenna's face rearranges into a snarl.

But Ricardo isn't done.

"They're testing the samples, then gathering more for new tests. They're looking for a weakness, something to exploit in the Drennar."

Tenna growls, "And with us?"

Ricardo takes a deep breath, face paling before Tenna's fury. "Whichever memory experiment works best with you two will be implemented on your entire tribe, only... They'll tell them that the Drennar destroyed your planet."

Dread washes over me, cold and heavy, and my nails dig into my palms. My body aches with the need to tear these vile people limb from limb, to cut their tongues out and rip out the very devices that connect them to their horrible equipment.

"After that, they'll either... modify your memories accordingly," Ricardo says, hesitantly, "or kill you. They'd probably keep you alive, send you with your tribe to fight the Drennar. Arm you with weapons that are just as deadly to you as they are to the Drennar."

My heart constricts. "How could they do this? Have they no honor?" I cry out.

But I already know the answer.

My muscles tense, and every part of me begs for war. My palms itch to wrap around frail Human necks, to smash them to pieces for what they've done, what they intend to do.

Heat radiates off Tenna, and a muscle twitches in her jaw. Her eyes spark with the promise of blood.

Ricardo watches us warily, having seen exactly what I can do when angered, what I can do without even trying.

But for now, I grit my teeth, holding myself in check.

I sit beside my partner who doesn't know she's my partner, doesn't know she's my Warrior Queen, in the quarters of my enemy's daughter somewhere in the Realm of Stars.

And I do nothing.

My heart races. My lungs rasp short, harsh breaths through my throat, and my hands clench.

But I sit.

Motionless.

Silence settles over us, suffocating and stifling, broken only by Olivia's racking sobs. Ricardo stares into space, shaking his head every so often.

The lives at stake, the treachery we suffer, the violence I wish to bring upon the vile creatures who could abduct 6,000 sentient beings to be used like tools all flit through my mind. Thoughts run together, chasing each other, chasing their own tails, and chaos spreads through me.

But Tenna rises to her feet beside me, reaches down to help me up. Her hand is warm in mine, rough callouses matching my own so perfectly that it makes my heart twist.

Because she doesn't even remember me, doesn't know we've sparred with each other for years, doesn't know we both favor the same weapons, doesn't know we've lain together, gone to battle together, sang together.

My chest constricts.

"Let's sleep on this," she says. Looking at me, she adds, "You can sleep in my room. I'll spread blankets out or something."

The Human tongue rolls from her lips too easily, and though I know I shouldn't, know it's just a product of her living among them, I wince inwardly.

The feel of her fingers laced with mine threatens to shatter my composure, to make me scream and rail against the injustice. She squeezes my hand, and I exhale softly.

But all I say is, "To." *Yes*.

Olivia looks up, eyes puffy and rimmed in red. Nodding, she says, "Ricardo can sleep on the floor here."

I release Tenna's hand and slip the Belt back on. She leads me across the hall, and we step into her room, dismal and sterile compared to Olivia's, compared to our stone keep on Regonia.

Even compared to my cell on the other station.

With the lights off, Tenna unfolds a blanket and spreads it on the floor, tossing pillows down as well. I watch her, heart lurching, arms aching to reach for her.

But I set the Belt on the bench beneath the window, tearing my gaze from her to stare into the Realm of Stars. Infinite darkness spreads out before me, punctuated by millions of tiny white dots, dwarfing me.

All my life, I never cared for the stars, never wondered about worlds beyond ours.

I shake my head.

That very curiosity killed our ancestors.

But it didn't, did it?

I run a hand over my face.

Everything I once knew, everything that seemed unshakable... Our beliefs, our ancestors and their intentions, the sanctity of my own mind... Even Tenna.

It's all different now.

Sighing, I turn to face her, my rock, my Queen. She moves the same way. When she speaks our tongue, her voice is the same.

But when her eyes fall on me, they don't shine the way they used to.

My heart spasms as I search her gaze. A spark of familiarity lingers there. She knows something, remembers *something*, about me.

But not enough.

Raw anguish seeps into my bones, eating away at me from the inside.

Music drifts into the air around us. Soft, soothing female vocals mingle with an instrument the Humans call a piano. They whisper through the air, trying so hard to ease my pain.

I glance at my Link, willing the beastly device to be useful in *some* way. It reads, "Compass by Zella Day. 2015." I shake my head, hating how comfortable I've already become with this thing, with their letters.

Raising my eyes to Tenna, I find her watching me. And there's that look, clouding her perfect mossy eyes again, a hint of memory but nothing more.

She knows my eyes.

She partially remembers the day I asked her to be my partner.

Scraps of our life, torn apart and scattered.

That day plays through my mind, and I will her to feel it, to see it in my eyes.

We ran through the grass, laughing about a prank we played on Efsi, her brother. We collided, fell to the ground amidst waving blades of aquamarine. They caressed our skin, bending with the wind to embrace us.

She laid in my arms, smiling, eyes dancing. I rolled up onto my elbow, holding her earnest gaze with my heart in my throat.

The words caught, but I pushed them free, the most important question I could ever ask. "Will you join yourself to me for all eternity?"

A single strand of midnight blue lay over her forehead, and I brushed the hair aside. Her chest rose against me, and a smile sparkled in her eyes. The sun shone on her dusky skin.

"Yes," she whispered, voice tender and reverent.

I remember it all, perfect and beautiful, and my heart twists.

Visions of her flood my mind. Standing beside me in our Keep, addressing our Ullavenans and Ullavekyns, listening to advisors, finding the best course of action for our people.

She was always fair and kind as a Queen, but ruthlessly efficient on the battlefield. In my mind, I see her cut foes down in a single arc of her axe, trying so hard to spare her enemy suffering.

I see her riding at my side, ahead of our Warriors, feel the wind screaming past the antlers of my Vyrto as arrows sail by. I close my eyes, and her smile plays over my eyelids, exhilarated and free, hair tied back in a thick plait that flowed behind her.

Now, my eyes trace that luscious hair, loose about her shoulders, and I burn to run my fingers through it as I used to, long to sweep loose strands behind her ear, to feel her skin beneath my fingertips.

A flash of the hideous memory the Humans imposed assails my senses. Her hair in Mourgam's hands. Her eyes locked on his foul face. His hand caressing the tattoo that marks her as my partner.

A cool blade of despair slices into my chest, twisting within, and I sigh, eyes falling shut once more as I try to make sense of it all. For all Dr. Sullivan's attempts to reverse the process, the memories left impressions, tangled into everything else.

I open my eyes to find Tenna standing close enough to touch, close enough to hold.

Her brows crease, and she takes my hand in hers, weaving our fingers together. My heart skips a beat, and I run my thumb over her skin, trying desperately not to think of my hands around her neck.

How is that not even the worst of what these Humans have done?

The song shifts, filling the air with a mournful guitar, and I glance at the Link in a move that's part compulsion, part avoidance, and three parts self-preservation.

"Things Ain't Like They Used To Be by The Black Keys. 2008."

How appropriate.

"Come," Tenna whispers. "Lay down. It's a lot to take in, I know, but we'll be of little use to anyone if we're exhausted."

I nod, grateful for her strength. I can almost hear her telling our Warriors, our people, to feel their pain, acknowledge it, but keep going.

With brows furrowed and lips drawn down at the edges, with tears falling from her eyes, she shows her pain. But her words are infallible.

This is what makes her a great Queen.

She leads me the few steps to the pallet she's made for me, and I settle in. She curls into herself in the too-small bed, lying on her side to face me.

I tug the blankets up over myself, and silence weighs me down. She watches me, eyes roaming over my face.

"I remember the lightning," she whispers in our tongue.

Her hand slips down from the bed, searching, and I watch her questing fingers with my heart in my throat.

With a deep breath, I reach for her, twining our fingers together.

Our hands fit just like they always have.

I swallow hard.

"I remember being afraid of storms," she says, oblivious to the sweet torment of her touch. "I didn't get to think about it much when it came back to me, and I can't get anything more now, but… I remember taking cover anywhere I could when a storm approached."

I try not to think of the times we took shelter together, ducking into our home or someone else's, staying the night and sharing stories over warm food.

Or the times we were apart, and the fear that paralyzed me as I hoped she was safe.

I squeeze her hand. "We have people who study the skies, looking for storms. Of course, there was always the chance one might sneak up on us."

She nods in the darkness. I find myself thankful that I can see her, having never thought about the ability to do so until I met creatures who can't see in the night.

A few tears slide from her eyes, dripping onto her pillow.

"I remember the Sky Watchers' tattoos. The jagged wavering bolts of lightning near their eyes…" Her eyes drift shut, and she whispers groggily, "What happens if we get struck by lightning?"

Horrifying images of convulsing bodies, blackened and sizzling with hair singed off, flash through my mind. I take a deep breath.

"We die," I say simply. "It flows through every fiber of our bodies, destroys our organs... and we die."

"Is it quick?" she asks.

"It takes as much time as it takes to blink," I whisper, suppressing a shudder.

An entire life wiped out in an instant, even though the body keeps twitching.

"So, the person they killed here..." Tenna chokes on the words. "He didn't suffer?"

"No." I squeeze her hand, torturing myself to comfort her. "Even if he'd been awake, he wouldn't have felt it for more than a breath."

Silence falls over us, and Tenna's eyes don't open. But she grips my hand tight.

My body aches to move up to the bed, to wrap her in my arms, to kiss her lips.

But she doesn't know me.

Would she pull away?

Could I withstand it if she did?

The song shifts again, and my Link glows softly near my face.

"Silver Coin by Angus and Julia Stone. 2007."

"How do we mourn our dead?" she whispers, barely audible beneath the music.

"We build a raft and set the body atop it," I say. "The whole Tribe sings as the body is set aflame and adrift on the river."

My mind fills with Tenna, lying on her pyre, burning in the river as our people sang in the false memory.

She's here. She's alive.

Or I've truly lost my mind.

Swallowing hard, I continue. But my voice cracks beneath its own weight.

"Funerals are always at night so the flame can burn the brightest," I tell her. "The Memory Markers tattoo those closest to the Lost One. No one goes home, no one stops singing, until they're done and the flames burn down."

The Humans' fatal flaw in their trickery.

"After the funeral, loved ones search for the sound of the Lost."

"They'll just cast him out into space," Tenna says, voice laced with disgust. "They'll 'jet' him, as they say. Probably already have, unless they want to study his body." She spits the bitter words out.

I cringe at the idea of a death without song, and fury rises within me.

Who will be Marked for his death?

Who will find his sound?

I sigh, wondering if the Memory Markers will have to invent a new mark for all of this.

"What are our weddings like?" Tenna asks.

The words stick in my heart, twisting like a blade. I close my eyes, breathing deeply, but I can't deny her an answer.

"The two to be joined are separated the day before their Partnering Ceremony, but only after a party with dancing and song," I say, thoughts full of the light that glowed in Tenna's eyes as we sang together.

I try to keep the retelling to the details, straightforward and simple.

"They spend the evening with their families. The day of their ceremony, they dress in long flowing robes of sheer fabric with nothing beneath them. They wear headdresses adorned with vivid flowers the color of fire and the molted antlers of young Vyrtons. Chains of blue beads are draped between the points of the antlers."

But despite my attempts to stay detached, my mind drifts back to the ceremony we shared, the light in her eyes and the way the flowers in her headdress contrasted that beautiful mossy green.

"As the sun sets, in the presence of their families, the two are reunited near a small island in the river."

I go on, telling her all about the ceremony, but I drift back through time, across space. The room around us, all the Human objects and the noise of this place, fade away, and I'm back on Regonia.

Tenna walks toward me, reaching out to take my hands. The fading sunlight glints off the beads on her headdress, and her eyes sparkle. Beneath the sheer robe, I can almost make out the lines of her collarbones, soon to be Marked.

The voices of our kin rise in joy behind us as we approach the Memory Markers, always two of them, always draped in white robes.

We light the torches, arranged in a circle around plush blue pillows, and amber light wraps around us. We take our seats upon the pillows, ankles crossed and knees touching, eyes locked.

We open our palms to the sky, resting them atop our knees as the Memory Markers slide our robes down to expose our shoulders. The warm breeze whispers over my skin, and Tenna smiles at me as the needles bite in.

But we don't wince, don't break eye contact. My heart races, and my body cries out for her.

The Memory Markers give us the bands at the base of our necks, crossing our collarbones. As the last bits of sunlight fade and the torches flicker over us, they place our hands, measuring the lines that will extend from the band to match the length of our middle fingers.

One of my hands rests on her chest, crossed over hers. She touches my chest, crossing my hand, and warmth flows through me. With the first lines done, we lower our hands, twining them in our laps as the Memory Markers match the rest of the lines to those.

All four moons shine overhead as they lay down their needles, and we rise from our pillows. A gentle breeze whispers over us, promising a good harvest and carrying us over the bridge to the island for our first night together.

Tenna tightens her hand on mine, pulling me back to the dreary space station. No music plays, and she watches me, free hand tracing the tattoo at the base of her neck.

I cast my mind back over the words I spoke, breathing a sigh of relief that I generalized everything, told her nothing of our own ceremony.

But does she know?

My thoughts race, and I wait for her to ask, to say something, anything.

But she merely watches me, brows furrowed, until we fall asleep.

Chapter 22
Novay
3018 C. E.

Reginald

Dim light glows through the room, illuminating outlines. I stare out, trying to piece the room together in my mind, but the darkness holds it from my grasp.

I try to sit up, but a restraint around my chest holds me down. My arms and legs struggle against their binds, but the buckles merely jangle.

My heart races, and beads of sweat crawl over my scalp.

What is this?

Something isn't right.

Fear slithers through me.

"You don't have to tie me down," I say, voice too high, too frantic.

The Drennar never tie me down, never have to. If I fight, they might take Olivia.

What're they going to do to me?

My mind fills with all the terrible things old sci-fi movies said aliens did after abductions. Surgeries on conscious patients, experiments, samples.

Sickness sweeps through me.

I pull at my bonds, jerking frantically, but the restraints only slice my skin. Blood coats my wrists, my ankles, and pain radiates through me.

My heart pounds, and blood roars past my eardrums. My breath rattles the air around me, loud and ragged.

Blinding light floods the room, and I slam my eyes shut, reeling from the change.

High heels clack hard against the floor in sharp staccato beats.

The Drennar don't wear heels.

A sick premonition fills me, a terrible impossibility. My heart sinks, and I turn to face the sound, eyes adjusting slowly to reveal my normal experiment room. The same steely blue walls I've seen every day for 12 years surround me.

But there she is.

Stomping across the floor, just as she did in the hangar footage, Eva stares at me every bit as coldly as she eyed the sleeping aliens.

"Eva, what are you doing?" I plead, voice cracking over the words.

Her eyes desert me, glancing briefly at her Link before jumping ship for the wall. She approaches it, heels clicking, and I crane my neck to see the wall above my head.

A panel adorned with a plethora of medical instruments unfolds from the solid surface. The scalpels and clamps gleam in the harsh white light, glittering with malicious intent.

I swallow hard and renew my attempts to escape, jerking at my cuffs. Skin sloughs off my wrists in slick sheets. Blood drips over the edge of the table, and all I hear is the sound of it hitting the floor.

Drip.

Drop.

Drip.

"Eva, please, think about this," I beg.

Drop.

Drip.

She walks toward me with a tray of scalpels, tweezers, and needles in hand. Metal legs sprout from the bottom of the tray, telescoping downward to meet the floor, and she settles it next to my head.

She barely looks at me, hands busy arranging tools on the tray.

Waves of cold fear wash through me, and I beg, "No! Eva, don't do this!"

I jerk and thrash, and the table groans beneath me.

Drop.

Drip.

Drop.

My blood pools in the floor beneath me, spreading outward in dark lakes of crimson.

Eva picks up a scalpel, stepping up beside me. Her black high heel plants itself firmly in the puddle of my blood with a small splash.

Droplets fall, splattering the toe of her shoe.

Tears trickle from my eyes, leaking over my temples to fill my ears, but I still hear it. My blood rings out as it hits the floor, loud and clear.

Drip.

Drop.

Drip.

"Please, don't. This is madness! You *have* to see that!"

I jerk, twisting away from her, straining to lift myself from the table, unable to look at her a moment longer.

But my blood runs cold at what I find.

On a table beside me, Olivia lies still, dark hair limp around her head. Her mouth hangs slightly open, silent, and her eyes are closed.

Blood pools beneath her wrists, beneath the bonds she strained against. A halo of crimson coats the floor beneath her head, and my gaze gets lost in the gaping incision in her neck.

A scream rips through me, and my stomach churns with a deep sickness. I twist and kick, pound my fists against my bed, my exam table.

But the cold metal only groans.

My restraints dig into my wrists and ankles, constrict my chest.

Sorrow falls upon me, crushes the air from my lungs. Sobs tear through me, shaking me as I howl in agony.

She can't be dead.

My baby girl...

"What have you done, Eva?" I choke out. "What did you do to her?"

A chasm opens within me, swallows me whole. I close my eyes, unable to stomach the sight of Olivia savaged by her own mother.

Or the visage of the monster I once loved.

"What did you do to Olivia?" I whisper, voice broken by sobs.

But she says nothing, waiting patiently with a scalpel in hand while blood drains from my wrists. Only when I quiet, when I stop moving, does she speak.

"You're not the same as you were before," she says. But she speaks in my voice, a version of my voice.

Calm and colder than ice.

I stare at her with brows furrowed. I shake my head, but blood loss has left me weak. My head lolls to face Olivia as Eva lifts the scalpel, poised over my neck.

Darkness tugs at me, overtakes me, pulling my eyes shut. And Olivia's broken body disappears from view.

I can't see her like this...

And all I hear is my own blood falling to the floor.

Drip.

Drip.

Drop.

I jolt awake and sit bolt upright, screaming in the darkness of my room on Novay. My heart pounds, nearly drowning out the music that blares from the speakers.

"Love is a Suicide by Nostalghia. 2018."

I howl with rage and despair until my voice grows hoarse, until my lungs burn.

Olivia's broken body rests in my mind, bloody and lifeless. Eva stands over me, poised to end me.

My heart cracks in my chest, and I cry out again.

The door to my room bursts open, and light fills the room as my guard rushes in. I jump, staring at her with tears streaking my face. Her short, black hair flutters behind her as she closes the distance, eyes shining with fear as she runs to my bed.

"What happened?" she asks.

Her soft voice quivers with anxiety, and I gape at her. Dark wings flap restlessly behind her, beating the air with great black feathers.

"A nightmare," I whisper, wondering how I didn't realize it, how it followed me into waking. My gaze drifts, and I shake my head.

But my guard drops to her knees, runs her hands over her face. Her chest expands as she takes a deep breath, visibly trying to steady herself.

But the Drennar are never unsteady...

I stare at her, struggling to understand. After all, this isn't the first time I've woken up screaming. Every other time, she's walked calmly to my room, if she checked on me at all.

Because she doesn't really need to.

She could just as easily check the cameras, check my Link, and see that there's nothing actually wrong with me.

So why did she come to check on me now? Why did she run all the way here?

Realization breaks over me like a wave, and my shoulders fall.

The surgery she had, the reason her hair was shaved from part of her scalp...

They made her feel.

And though I don't know why, I ask her, "What's your name?"

She stares at me, eyes narrowed, fucking narrowed!

But for once, she answers me.

"Rone Vargen."

Chapter 23
Novay

Rone

Standing at my auxiliary pedestal, I review vital signs. Accelerated heartrate, labored breathing. Music blares in his room, yet none of his muscles exhibit the telltale electrical impulses of movement.

Reginald seems to be agitated. Is he not sleeping?

I wince at my own familiarity.

The subject.

Not Reginald.

Lifting my chin, I battle against these strange emotions, determined not to be drawn in. I can't let this experiment alienate me from my people any further.

A pang of loneliness shoots through me, and I recall the strange looks, the sweeping fans of analytical light. Cold, vacant stares fill my mind, and I shrink from them.

Is that really how I want to be?

The treasonous thought slithers up to bite me. I shouldn't have wants or desires. These are unnatural perversions, products of my current experimental condition.

Yet, a human song rises, unbidden, to play within my mind. I register its title, "Blood Sport (from the room below) by Sleep Token. 2019." And despite myself, despite the need to maintain some level of objectivity, I let it play.

I record my reactions to it. My heartrate and the pressure within my veins. The speed of the electrical impulses from one synapse to another within my brain, the various sections that the song activates.

But all those records fall into the background, automatic monitoring processes that I've long since grown accustomed to maintaining.

My mind wanders over old human films filled with warm hugs and smiles. Parents playing with their children, teaching them to walk and talk. Friends laughing together over shared meals. Lovers embracing, touching.

My skin warms at the thought, at the images flooding me, but my heart shrivels painfully within my chest.

On my pedestal, I bring up the security footage of the center of Facility 15983 and watch the same Drennar I've been walking these halls with for years. But I feel no pull toward them, no warmth from them. If I cried in their presence, they wouldn't rub my back or wrap their arms around me.

I never thought I'd want them to.

And I don't, not them.

Just... someone. Someone who feels.

I draw in a deep breath, steadying myself. I record all of this. Every thought and the corresponding palpitations.

But I don't sync the information to the network.

I hold it fast within me, knowing I'll have to submit it soon but needing to keep my own council for a while.

The logical part of me knows this makes no sense, acknowledges that this may be a maladaptive response, even among those prone to emotions.

But that doesn't prompt me to upload my information.

They'll be recording my bodily functions and all my work with my experiments, comparing my findings to those of other Drennar who haven't been altered this way. They'll have all their own findings to measure me and the viability of this experiment.

I sigh, turning my attention back to the pedestal before me. With a thought, I eliminate the view of the Facility Center, replacing it with a view of Reginald's room.

The subject's room.

Not Reginald.

He lays on his side, and sweat glistens on his forehead despite the low light. Impossibly, his heart beats faster. His breathing grows shallow.

Twitching, kicking out, Reginald thrashes in his sleep. The blanket tangles around him as he flips onto his back. Music blares in his room, and his lips move. Turning off my own music, I separate the various pieces of the audio recording, pulling his words up from the depths.

He mutters, "You're not the same as you were before."

His words, though clearly not meant for me, hit like a punch to the gut. My brows furrow, and my mouth falls open because even though this human doesn't know me, doesn't understand me...

Somehow, he does.

Another violent thrash shakes his body, flinging the blanket free of him. My hand goes to my chest, clutching at the fabric of my shirt as a strange pain lances through me.

Jolting awake, Reginald sits up straight and screams. My blood curdles, and my heart lurches at the sound.

And suddenly, I'm running.

Cries of despair ring in my ears, and I sprint down the hall. My blood roars through me, heart pounding in my chest.

The wall parts before me, and I rush through, lighting the room with a thought. A strand of short black hair falls before my gaze as I reach Reginald's bedside, eyes wide and lungs faltering beneath the weight of my panic.

The music in his room comes to an abrupt halt, and he stares at me with his mouth hanging open. Rubbing a hand over his face, he shakes his head.

"What happened?" I ask, nerves drawn tight. My voice shakes with the words, and my wings beat a restless rhythm behind me.

"A nightmare," Reginald whispers, shaking his head yet again.

I fall to my knees, collapsing beneath the relief that the one person who could understand me isn't dying or collapsing mentally.

He won't be taken elsewhere for a different experiment.

I run my hands over my face and pull in a deep breath.

Reginald stares at me, and I start to flinch away from him. But where the other Drennar stare with cold, distant analysis, he stares with furrowed brows and soft, warm eyes, if eyes can really be soft and warm.

He closes his mouth, gaze drifting to stare into thin air for half a breath, and then he looks at me anew. Deep lines etch themselves in his face, and he studies me.

My stomach clenches, and my breathing hitches.

"What's your name?" Reginald asks.

I jolt at the question, but only for an instant.

He might understand me. He feels. He knows what this is like.

So, I say, "Rone Vargen."

He nods, blinking a few too many times, a bit too rapidly. Habit forces me to measure all of it, to try to glean his motivations from his bodily functions, but I *feel* the answers that the data can't give me.

He knows me, now.

I swallow hard, lungs faltering at the prospect of being known, truly known, in a way that no data or experiment could ever allow.

Chapter 24
Odyssey Space Research Station

Ricardo

On the bed beside me, Olivia mumbles something about getting me a blanket, but she doesn't get up, doesn't move at all. She pulls in one shaky breath after another. Eyes that sparkled in the bar now appear lusterless and barren as she stares at her room.

I struggle, at a loss for what to do. My mind searches for something to say, some way to tell her I didn't *want* to destroy what little good opinion of her mother she may have held, didn't want to hurt her. I scramble for any way to apologize, to say that I had to, that no one else would be able to do what needs to be done.

But when I glance at her, when I see the tears streaking over her cheek, I close my mouth. Picking at a hang nail, I wait for her to speak, but she merely shakes her head.

Piano and violin call out from speakers around the room, followed by haunting vocals as, "Lovely by Billie Eilish and Khalid. 2018." begins to play.

Olivia hunches forward, burying her face in her hands. Her shoulders shake as sobs tear through her.

But I wonder how she isn't worse than this.

Sure, my parents were no picnic.

I could've done without the beatings, could've used a father that stuck around for more than booze and punching bags, could've used a mother that didn't follow him into the bottle.

I swallow.

But they never signed off on kidnapping and experimenting on 6,000 living, breathing people.

I glance at the bottle of alcohol perched on the floor at her feet, shocked that it still holds half its contents after all of this.

Palms still pressed to her eyes, tears roll down her wrists. I reach out, hand moving back and forth over her shoulders, slow and awkward.

But she looks up at me.

Her face shines with tears, transforming her alluring nature to a forlorn beauty, and my breath catches in my throat. Bloodshot eyes show off streaks of green in hazel irises, so much prettier than I remember them from what was essentially a mugshot a few years ago.

Stunning eyes stared out, framed by silky hair, almost daring the world to find a scrap of evidence that she hacked her mother's files.

I smile, despite everything.

And she throws her arms around me, nearly knocking me back onto her bed. I maintain my balance, though only just, and wrap my arms around her as she weeps against my chest. Her tears soak my shirt, and I move my hand in slow circles on her back.

But it doesn't feel like enough to make up for what her mother has done.

She sobs, shaking the both of us, and I hold her tight, cradling her head against my chest. The music crests around us, crashes over us, and she slowly cries herself out. She pulls away, sniffling and wiping my hair from the tear tracks that glisten on her face.

"I'm sorry," she chokes out, blushing. She doesn't even meet my gaze, and I wonder how long it's been since she cried in front of someone.

Why is that what I'm thinking of?

Exhaling, I say, "It's okay. This can't be easy for you."

Olivia's head moves in a slow nod, then she leans against me once more, hair tickling my neck as her head comes to rest on my shoulder.

Still uncertain, I wrap my arms around her, comforting the woman I always thought was such a badass. The rebel hacker who took shit from no one, who even told the Coalition what she was going to do with her life instead of following their suggestion.

But she's human, just like me.

Her warmth soaks into me, and I hug her tighter. She leans against me, content with the meager comfort I offer. I hold myself steady, desperate not to disturb her.

The same song repeats, swirling around us over and again, blurring time.

Eventually, she pulls back, just far enough to meet my gaze. Blue striations chase shades of brown and green through her eyes, darting past flecks of gold. Those beautiful eyes move closer, and her eyelids fall, stealing them from my view. She tips her head, inching closer.

And I almost pull away, almost take the high road.

But her lips brush mine, inviting and soft.

She touches my neck, pulling me in, twining her fingers in my hair, and my body comes alive. Fire burns through me, dragging me into the kiss. I cup her cheeks, pull her close.

And she leans back, pulling me down over her.

For a split second, I wonder if this is a good idea, if she's sobered up enough, if she's thinking clearly.

But she nips at my bottom lip, and my thoughts scatter to the four corners of Earth, so far away that they hold no meaning here on Odyssey.

A deep need rises within me, matching the fervor of her kisses. I grip her hips, pulling her against me, and she clutches my hair, lips demanding more.

My breath catches, and my heart races.

Her hands trail down my spine, sending a shiver through me, only to slip beneath my shirt. She tugs the fabric over my head, smiling up at me when it falls to the floor.

And a little voice in the back of my head tells me that I'm done for.

Chapter 25
Odyssey Space Research Station

Tenna

My alarm goes off, bright and early. But today, it catches me unaware, lying on the floor of my room.

Strong arms tighten around me, and I exhale softly. Twisting, careful not to disturb him, I look at the man who holds me.

Pale grey skin stretches over a strong jaw and wide cheek bones. Long dark lashes fan out over his cheeks, shielding those perfect green eyes. A few strands of lush black hair drape over his forehead.

I ache to brush them back, to touch his face, but I hold myself in check, not wanting to wake him.

I cast my mind over the things I need to do today, searching for anything I may have forgotten. But I'm off work today and have no appointments in the medical wing.

Letting out a breath, I turn to lie on my side again, nestling into the familiarity of his embrace. I raise a hand to touch the tattoo at the base of my neck, wondering why I don't feel guilty lying in his arms.

I have a partner.

The Humans said he died. I should be mourning.

But the Humans also said my entire planet was destroyed. They said no one else survived, and Krona is living proof that they lied.

But what does that mean?

Before sleep claimed us last night, my eyes roamed over the circle at the base of his neck, the lines which extend from it, marking him for his partner.

His arms tighten around my waist, and guilt washes over me.

I ache to twist around, to see if my middle finger matches the shorter lines of his tattoo, to move his hand from my waist and line his finger up with the center line of my own mark.

Would he wake?

Would it prove anything?

Krona stirs, pulling me closer, and all my thoughts skitter away. A deep sense of satisfaction swells within me as he nestles his face into my hair, breathing deeply.

Could it be him?

Why else would I remember his eyes?

But doubt eats away at me, filling my head with Human words of a dead man, perhaps with the same eye color, with no one to mourn him, his love deserting his memory for the arms of another.

My stomach clenches, and my mouth goes dry at the thought of such a betrayal.

Closing my eyes, I try to pry my way through the walls in my mind, to remember anything.

The lightning memories from last night are firmly bricked off from anything else, and my prison holds me away from everything. I wander through the darkness of my thoughts, and I give myself over to the memory of running through that field, laughing with someone.

Cracks line the walls around the field in my mind. Tiny fissures decorate the bricks, and hope seeps into me. I tear into them, digging until my fingernails run with blood, screaming until my throat is raw. A few tiny pebbles fall free, tumbling to the ground, but no more light shows through.

Half-crazed, I imagine running straight for it, slamming into the bricks with all my mental might. A shower of pebbles falls. Frustration builds within me, and I grind my teeth together.

But Krona shifts behind me, pulling my attention outward. His arm slides out from under me, and he sits up. Cold air rushes to fill the space he occupied, and I fight to suppress a shiver.

He stops short of leaving me completely, cradling my shoulders, moving his other arm from my waist to slip beneath my knees. He lifts me easily, settling me upon my bed.

Disappointment settles over me, heavy and stifling. It clouds my thoughts, my memories. My heart twists.

What good am I to the other Regonians like this?

Krona rests a hand on my waist, caresses my face with the thumb of his other hand. He draws close, leans his head on mine.

His voice breaks as he whispers, "I can't do this without you."

Something in me fractures, but I lie still, cherishing the comfort of him.

My chest collapses when he pulls away. I swallow hard, listening as he settles on the floor, but I dare not move, dare not speak.

Moments pass in tense silence with only the sound of my heartbeat to keep me company. Eternity stretches out around me, sending my thoughts spiraling. Eventually, I force myself to stretch and check the time.

7:08 A.M.

Eight minutes of pure agony since I first woke.

I turn onto my side, looking at Krona. He opens his eyes, offering a smile to greet me, but pain lines his eyes.

"Did we have a system for tracking time on Regonia?" I ask. "The Humans use clocks. Olivia says they kept the old system from Earth. She said something about the day and night cycles of the lights here being forced to match their old planet since there's no rotation here."

Krona sits up, eyes searching my face.

But whatever he's looking for, he doesn't find it.

With a sigh, he says, "No, we don't have clocks. We use the position of our sun in the sky during the day and the position of the stars and our four moons at night. When to plant crops, how much light remains in a day, when to harvest... All determined by the moons and the stars and the sun."

I nod, letting out a deep breath. The good sense of such a system eases my mind. The sunlight on that field in my mind *feels* better than the cold lights of Odyssey.

I roll from the bed. Stepping past Krona, I fight the urge to trail a hand along his shoulders as I move to the bathroom.

Accustomed to the Human things around me, I think the water on, cupping cold water in my hands. I splash it over my face, but the shiver that runs through me isn't from its temperature.

My own adaptations to this place, the things I've learned, the things I still don't know... They weigh heavily on my shoulders, dragging me down.

Krona's reflection appears over my shoulder, and my stomach flutters. "Would you mind if I clean up?" he asks, gesturing to the shower.

A blush creeps up my neck, and I nod.

"I'll get you some breakfast," I whisper, stepping past him.

I almost ask why he moved me back to my bed, though I fear the answer, fear it may crush the hopes I've fostered, daft as they may be.

A small part of me wonders if it would be better to forget having woken up in his arms, but the feel of his embrace, of his body pressed against me, won't leave my thoughts.

He steps into the bathroom, door closing behind him, and I leave for the hall. A chill settles over me in his absence. It claws its way into my bones, clings to me no matter how hard I try to shake it.

But realization settles over me as I meander through barren halls to the general store.

Even if it hurts, even if he isn't my partner, even if it means I'm a terrible person... I never want to forget the feeling of waking up with him. Even if I lost every other memory all over again, I want that one to stay.

Chapter 26
Odyssey Space Research Station

Olivia

I gasp awake, sitting bolt upright. Ricardo's arm flies off me, and I wince at the headache that grips my mind. Sighing, I brace myself as last night washes over me in nauseating waves.

Lachlan's clinginess. Mommy dearest and the insanity of her latest experiment. Tenna and Krona, sitting on my floor with broken hearts.

The sweetness of Ricardo's touch, a bit of relief to end the night.

He sprawls out beside me, hand searching the bed for me, then sliding beneath my pillow. And though heat flashes through me at the thought of what we shared, I sigh.

Because his presence means it was real.

Perched on the edge of the bed, I lean forward, elbows on knees, and drop my head into my hands. My hair falls like a dark curtain, surrounding me, shielding me from the world. My fingers plunge into it, raking it, breaking that lovely curtain into ropes.

With a final breath, I rise and gather what I can find of my clothes from yesterday. I search for my shirt, only to find it on the bed, tangled with the blankets and half under Ricardo's chest. I begin to reach for it, but stop. I don't want to wake him.

I guess that's staying there.

I slip into the bathroom and toss my clothes, sans my shirt, into the hamper. With a thought, I set the water to the perfect temperature and step into the shower, letting the water wash over me.

But it doesn't wash my mind clean, doesn't burn the memory of Tenna's stricken face or Krona's soft gasp as they learned what my mother did from my mind.

I blow out a breath, wash up, and dress quickly. My mind races as I grab my laptop, and the ache in my head builds to a steady pounding. My eyes drift to the bottle of whiskey sitting near the bed.

For a moment, I consider having some, just to ease the pain, to slow my mind, but there's too much to do. And all the tasks ahead of me will put my mind to work.

So, I settle into my chair and crack my knuckles. With my laptop open, I set to work.

First things first.

My fingers tap at the keys, and I slip through a few basic firewalls.

Please, be wrong. Please, be wrong. Please. Be. Wrong.

A sigh of disappointment escapes me when I find a camera in Tenna's room, tucked away in the multi-device on her nightstand, just casually violating about a dozen laws. I rub a hand over my face as revulsion washes over me.

Not anymore.

I disable it with a few clicks, implanting a simple error code within it so anyone who looks will assume it malfunctioning, and chuckle under my breath at how simple it was.

They may as well set all their passwords to "password."

I chuckle again, and Ricardo stirs, turning onto his back. Eyes still firmly shut, one hand scratches idly at his chest, pushing the blanket down to his stomach.

My eyes trace his figure, and my insides flutter and warm. He drapes his arm on the pillow, tucking his hand under his head. My chest rises with a deep breath.

I'm just watching to make sure he doesn't wake up.

I chuff out a laugh.

Who am I kidding?

My earlier agitation at his presence dissipates.

Whether he's a reminder of all this or not... Maybe he isn't so bad.

Sighing, I get back to work, pulling up all the footage from Tenna's room last night. Hating the invasion of her privacy even as I do it, I scan every second since Ricardo and Krona arrived.

I lean forward, eyes close to the screen, when Tenna comes back to her room, silhouetted by the hall light. The door closes quickly, leaving her in darkness.

I wait for the lights to come on, cringing at the thought of seeing what she does by herself, but the room stays dark. The inky blackness of space pours in through the window. Music overrides all other sound on the surveillance footage, and I breathe a sigh of relief.

Krona must've warned her.

I lean in, listening to everything between the door closing and the music coming on, replaying it over and over.

I see nothing, but just before the music comes on, I hear Krona whisper, "Turn on some music so we can talk."

I scrub his voice from the recording quickly, replacing it with the silence of her room before she entered, before he spoke. Then, I listen, trying to separate voices from the song that slips through my mind, courtesy of my cochlear implant.

A pitch black room occupies my screen, no difference, no movement, no changes. So, I close my eyes, listening again, but I hear only the song.

I droop as a single weight falls from me, but many more still rest on my shoulders.

I skip over the part of the recording after Tenna leaves her room to go to mine, knowing that Krona was securely hidden during those hours. But he didn't stay here all night.

My nerves twist when they reenter the room, and I cringe at the thought of listening in.

Again, the lights stay off. Again, the music comes on.

But not as loud as before.

Ah, shit.

I berate myself as I lean closer, straining to hear even though the damn audio is in my cochlear implant, and I don't *need* to lean forward.

A soft whisper moves gently beneath the music. Krona describes their burials, voice cracking beneath the weight of his words.

Ricardo stirs, climbing from the bed, but I don't look up, don't tear my eyes from the dark screen. He slides his underwear on and crosses the room to kneel beside me.

But Krona speaks of weddings and headdresses, tattoos and a night beneath the stars, and my heart spasms in my chest. Dread seeps in, and my mouth goes dry.

No...

Turning to face Ricardo, I ask, "Are they... Are they married?"

Ricardo's long hair sways as he nods.

I swallow hard. "And she doesn't remember?"

Ricardo's mouth moves silently, then he shakes head. His golden eyes soften, and the corners of his mouth turn down.

I cover my mouth with a hand, and tears trickle over my cheeks. "Oh, God..." I whisper.

"I wish that were the worst of it," Ricardo says with a heavy sigh.

I stare at him with wide eyes, dreading his next words.

Ricardo hesitates, looking at the floor before he says, "They're not just partners. They're the Warrior King and Warrior Queen of their tribe."

My brows reach for each other, and I stare at the screen. With eyes closed, I whisper, "Holy shit." My hand comes to rest on my collarbone, and I lay my chin upon it, resuming my watch of the dark screen.

My mind races, flooded with all the terrible things that have been done to them.

And all the terrible things they could do to us.

"How do you become king or queen in a warrior tribe?" I ask.

Ricardo considers me for a moment before answering. "Well, from what Krona said, Tenna was sort-of born into it. She just had to fight her siblings for it."

My head drops back against the chair.

"What, like a fight to the death?"

"Not anymore. It used to be that way, but there were a few... incidents... where they were left without a successor. Now, they fight to submission," Ricardo says. "But to hear Krona tell it, she's ruthlessly efficient."

I sigh, trying to reconcile the thought of Tenna on a battlefield with the woman I saw dancing in the bar. And it isn't difficult. The dexterity, the comfort in her own movements, the stamina...

It makes sense.

"And Krona?" I ask.

"He was apparently one hell of a fighter, made quite a name for himself in their army. He and Tenna started courting or dating or whatever, and no one objected his ascension to the throne," he says. "Partly because he was known to be able to fight anyone and win. Partly because they knew he'd be a good King."

"So... cruel experiments that also risk *our* lives by bringing *fucking Warrior aliens* to literally the only place in the universe that we're safe?"

"Pretty much," he says.

I shake my head. "Awesome."

With a sigh, I set to work, erasing his voice from the audio. Silence fills the room, and Ricardo shifts a few times beside me before rising. He gathers his clothes from around the room, moving quietly.

But neither of us mention what happened last night.

"You can take a shower if you want," I say.

I lean over the side of my chair, retrieving one of his socks, and hand it to him without another word.

"Thanks," he says, taking it and disappearing into the bathroom.

"Alright," I say. "Time to tidy up."

I bend my fingers to the keys, wishing it were more of a challenge to hide Krona's departure from Ulysses and subsequent journey through Odyssey, just to occupy my mind. I hunt down all the location sensors that detected his signature and smile at the attempts made by the tech people on Ulysses.

But they left a mess.

I clean up their attempts at subterfuge, polishing the edges.

The water runs in the bathroom, and for half a breath, I consider joining him. My mind fills with the scent of him, the feel of his hand gripping my hip, the sweet taste of his kiss.

Focus!

I weave through routers and hubs aboard Odyssey. In seconds, I install and activate Ghost Mode on Krona's Link. All of my mother's locks and restrictions fade away with a few taps of the keys, opening the net to him.

As a gift, I download all the free music to it.

Not that that'll make up for being abducted, lied to, and experimented on...

I purse my lips.

Carefully, I back out of everything I've done, checking to make sure no one will ever find a trace. And then, the real work begins.

I open the locked folder containing my little side project, the project that's occupied all my free time, the project that motivated me to push for a job that *allowed* for free time.

But also the project that kept me too busy to dig through confidential files in recent years.

Has it really been years?

But I know it has.

Countless late nights, days where exhaustion was played off as a hangover, evenings of actual drinking because I couldn't figure this shit out... They all flicker through my mind in quick succession, and I sigh.

I guess Mom isn't the only one who can't let it go.

I shudder at the comparison and set my fingers to work again. But finally, after all these years, Atlantis is almost done.

Chapter 27
Odyssey Space Research Station

Ricardo

When I exit the bathroom, Olivia is still tapping away at the keys of her laptop. She stops for but a moment, rubbing a hand over her forehead.

I perch on the edge of her bed, toweling my hair dry, and send a message to Francis back on Ulysses. "How are things with that shitty doctor?"

A reply flashes across my Link almost instantly. "Not too bad. He's much more tolerable when he's unconscious and, you know, not tormenting people."

A morbid chuckle crosses my lips, and I send back, "Is Giselle having any trouble keeping him under?"

After all, it's been a while since she trained for medical. She's been a Guard for a long time.

"No problems here. Really. Worry about your own part of this mess." I can almost hear the sarcastic tone in her voice as she thought the message.

Before I can send anything else, another message comes through. "How are things with your dream girl?"

Her question sends my eyes darting to Olivia, then to the tangled sheets beneath me. My mind fills with the previous evening and heat sprawls through me.

But Olivia doesn't look up from the screen of her laptop. I marvel at how quickly her fingers move over the keys.

Another message comes in, and I drape the towel over my lap as I read it.

"You know, I meant it as a joke. I just meant to ask what happened when you told her, how it all went, if you found Tenna, all that. But... I fully expected you to gush about her. You've had this weird crush on her forever. I didn't think I'd have to ask. What happened?"

I blush and block all outgoing messages for the sake of sparing myself an embarrassing ramble. Pulling in a deep breath, I put together something as coherent as I can manage.

"She took it... better than expected. She can certainly drink, but that's to be expected after news like that."

I consider removing the part about Olivia drinking because really, isn't it a reasonable reaction? And hopefully it'll keep Francis from making a joke about me saying, 'she took it.'

Forging ahead, I add, "We found Tenna, but her experiment is pretty bad. She doesn't remember anything. At all. I'm not sure how Krona's going to handle it."

Again, I consider taking out the bit about Olivia's reaction. But I send it.

The response flashes red on my Link, marking it as urgent. "Well, that's shitty for Tenna and Krona. Worse than I thought. But what do you mean, she can certainly drink?"

Regret seeps through me. I quickly gloss over her drink at the bar and the bottle in her room, hoping to ease Francis' mind.

But she only worries further.

"Just... be careful. I know you liked her before you ever even got there, but don't do anything rash. If she's stashing bottles in her room, that's not great. She may handle her liquor well, better than your parents, but that doesn't mean it isn't a problem."

I purse my lips, hand gripping the towel tightly at Francis' reaction. Then, I send, "She drank with friends, then had more after bad news. That hardly constitutes a drinking problem."

But an inkling of worry seeps in beneath my defensiveness.

Chapter 28
Odyssey Space Research Station

Krona

I move along behind Tenna, Ricardo, and Olivia, heart racing. My arm rises, hand invisible before my eyes, as I reassure myself yet again that the Belt is working. My stomach turns at the use of star-sickness, this *technology*.

But it hasn't mutated me, hasn't spread.

The Link, the translator, the Belt, all these things are exactly where they should be. The Belt can even be removed.

But is star-sickness even real?

How many lies did the Drennar tell?

My mind whirls, and I ache to reach for Tenna, to draw from her strength, to offer mine to her. But even that simple gesture has been ripped from me.

The pain of waking this morning slices through me. To feel her yet again, to hold her, to wake thinking our lives were normal... Only to recall that she doesn't remember me.

I flinch, thankful that Tenna can't see it.

Sighing, I refocus my attention, matching my footsteps to Tenna's as we move through the halls of Odyssey toward the hospital wing to mask the noise. I fall into step with her, my body matching her rhythms with ease.

A few Humans approach, walking together. Tenna takes the lead, letting Ricardo and Olivia walk side by side behind her, funneling the Humans further away from me. I duck as I near the curved outer edge of the hall.

Laughter and gentle words float through the air as the other people pass us by, smiling and greeting Tenna as one of their own, waving to Olivia. The woman of the group lets her eyes trail over Ricardo, batting her lashes.

But he looks forward, oblivious or uncaring.

I turn, gazing at them long after they leave us behind. I trace their forms, commit the shades of their hair, their skin, their eyes, the shapes of their faces, to memory.

Just in case they're in league with this Doctor Antar, this horrible woman who monitored Tenna and experimented on our tribemates.

This woman who killed one of our people.

My hands ball into fists, and anger roils in my gut. I try to stuff the fury down, forcing my hands to unclench.

A few more halls pass us by, and I monitor my breathing, slowing my lungs to slow my heart. By the time we reach the hospital, only sorrow courses through me.

For the man who died.

For the loss we've suffered.

For Tenna's blocked memories.

I take a deep breath and follow Tenna into the hospital. Dr. Sullivan, the man who came to take Dr. Antar's place, stands off to the side of the room. White clothes gleam against his dark skin, and the glaring lights shine in his near-black eyes.

He leans over a patient, smiling softly at the young girl as he injects fluid into her arm. She winces, but he wins her over, eliciting a laugh as he speaks something low and soft. A mountain of bushy brown curls tumble from behind her ear as she giggles, and she brushes them away from her freckled face with her free arm.

But I shudder at the invasive medicine, the barbaric nature of their technology, however sophisticated they may think it.

Have they no respect for anything?

Bits and pieces of Human history slip through my mind from my conversations with Ricardo. Bombs that killed millions and rendered entire stretches of land unusable for centuries. Prison camps where hundreds of thousands were enslaved, starved, and murdered.

I shudder.

They haven't learned much from their past.

But I remind myself to be fair, to remember that this plot against us was kept secret because most Humans wouldn't go along with it.

The young girl looks up from her doctor, eyes drifting over Olivia, Ricardo, and Tenna. Keenly aware of his patient, Dr. Sullivan smiles at us.

"Ah, yes," he says. "Just the people I wanted to see. I have a question for you, Tenna, if you don't mind."

"Not at all," Tenna answers, voice contorting over the Human language.

"Would you mind waiting for me in my office?" Sullivan asks, gesturing around the corner.

Tenna nods, and we move through the medical facility. She sinks into a chair that makes even my hips hurt at the idea of squeezing into it, and I cram myself into the space behind her. Olivia sits beside her, looking far more comfortable, and Ricardo smiles as he settles in beside me.

I rest a hand on Tenna's shoulder, tearing myself away from her far too quickly, wishing I could let the touch linger. I swallow hard.

She has to remember me on her own. If she thought I was manipulating her...

My stomach roils at the thought.

And yet, my head fills with the impressions of those memories, impressions of her in Mourgam's arms, her dying by my hands, burning atop her pyre, and I ache to reach for her yet again.

Just to reassure myself that she's here, that she's alive.

She's safe and alive.

I silently vow to do everything I can to keep her that way as Dr. Sullivan walks in. I allow myself just a hint of reassurance, offer her a bit more of my strength, and rest my hand on her shoulder for a few heartbeats, then pull it away again.

But does she even need my strength?

Does she need me?

Does she want me?

Sullivan closes the door behind him, skirting around us to sit behind the desk. "I'm Dr. Sullivan," he says, shaking hands with Olivia and Tenna.

His dark eyes soften, and his lips fall at the corners. He gazes at Tenna for a moment before saying, "I'm afraid I have some bad news."

Lines etch themselves into his face, clawing at my heart. Guilt slithers through me that I might have thought him like Eva Dobovich, written him off in my rage for what others did.

"Is this about the tests that have been done on the Regonians here? Or about the one they killed yesterday?" Olivia asks.

I wince.

Dr. Sullivan blinks a few times, staring at her. "Well, both. But how did you..."

"I told you she was good," Ricardo says.

Dr. Sullivan lightens, shoulders easing at the relief of not bearing such awful tidings. But Olivia and Ricardo glance at each other, then pull their eyes away too quickly.

I tip my head to the side, considering them, noting how stiffly Olivia sits, how careful Ricardo is not to bump her chair.

What happened between them?

But Dr. Sullivan laughs softly, drawing my attention away. "Yes, you did, Ricardo."

He sighs, turning to Tenna, eyes darting to where he knows I should be for the briefest moment. "Well, that saves me some time. But I was curious how funerals are handled on Regonia. It feels... disrespectful to handle it as we do without even consulting you. Has that memory come back to you yet, Tenna?"

I smile, surprised by his thoughtfulness.

"Sort of," she whispers. "It isn't exactly feasible here."

"How so? Perhaps we can adapt it?"

Tenna relays my account of our funerals, and Sullivan's face falls with every passing word. No one here will let us burn a body in their water source.

"Do you remember the songs?" Sullivan asks. "You could sing them as we jettison him."

"I don't," Tenna says, "But I'll try to remember."

Again, I touch her shoulder for a few heartbeats. An ember of hope burns within me, despite the terrible topic.

Maybe if she sings the songs, she'll get something of our life back. Maybe she'll remember more.

***

After a morning of re-teaching Tenna the songs and sounds of our passing ritual, sans the traditional instruments, we join Olivia, Ricardo, and Dr. Sullivan in the airlock. With assurances that the surveillance footage will be fixed, I ditch the Belt as soon as the metal doors slide into place behind us.

My heart races at the vast emptiness of space, so close, just beyond the walls.

What would happen if I went out there?

A shiver rolls through me at the thought.

But it's time.

I take Tenna's hand in mine, marveling at Olivia's promise to remove my voice.

Does she know how our tones will blend and mingle?

Tenna begins the low hum, and I join her, letting the notes buzz in my throat. She squeezes my hand as we harmonize perfectly, just like we used to. Heat seeps into my skin at her touch.

Our voices rise from a hum to a gentle susurration, ebbing and flowing hauntingly. Tenna returns to the low hum, building the atmosphere around us, and I sing.

"Hoo mai taenruta." Your sound will go on. "Joo taeparnam hoo." We will remember you.

Tenna leaves the ambient hum, raising her voice to join with mine in the words as Dr. Sullivan loads the body of our Lost One into a small chamber on the side of the vestibule.

"Joo taeka coom joo." We will carry you with us. "Ar joo maiverns, hoo darten taenruta." In our voices, your life will go on.

But we don't sing anymore than just the most basic song. It barely crosses our lips before this cruel world cuts us off. With the press of a button, Dr. Sullivan sends our Lost One flying into the abyss, and my heart twists.

I long for a window to watch our comrade, our subject, our tribemate. And though the image of him floating for the rest of his life would haunt me, not seeing feels like shirking my duties.

A King should never turn from the suffering of his people.

Tenna turns to face me. Her arms wrap around my waist, and she buries her face in my chest. I suck in a breath, enveloping her in my arms, savoring the feel of her. My head dips to rest atop hers, and the scent of her, buried beneath the smell of Human soap, fills me. My eyes fall shut as a deep sense of peace fills me.

I ache to kiss her, to stay like this, to hold her tighter and never move.

But Ricardo clears his throat, albeit gently.

I take a deep breath, gritting my teeth. Slowly, I release Tenna, turning to face the tiny Humans. Anger seethes within me. Anger at the way things have gone, at the time constraints that limit our mourning.

My face shifts into a glare, and Ricardo flinches. Regret stings me, and I soften.

"Sorry," I whisper. "I'm not angry at you, just..." I shake my head, looking around this barren airlock, the hole one of my people just disappeared through, the woman I love who doesn't remember me.

"I know," Ricardo says.

His brows furrow, and his lips fall into a frown. Golden eyes go soft.

I nod and put the Belt back on. With the press of a button, I disappear. Turning back to Tenna, I find an expression I know well. She stands with her shoulders squared, her eyes fiercely alert. When Mourgam dammed the river and our crops suffered, she wore this look. Determination and a need for justice, a craving for revenge.

She'll stop at nothing.

The Humans responsible will pay. And the Drennar will answer for themselves.

***

On Tenna's bed, I recline against the wall with knees drawn up and arms propped upon them. My mind whirls, awash with Dr. Sullivan's post-funeral revelations. That he yet advocates for the sedation of my people burns me.

But they need a safe place to wake, to acclimate.

And we need a way to explain why their Queen doesn't remember them, doesn't remember that she's their Queen.

I drop my head into my hands, plunging my fingers through my hair. A deep breath fills my lungs, but it offers little clarity.

Perhaps we should restore Tenna's memories before we wake them?

I sift through my thoughts, trying to be sure that this isn't just my own desires, that reversing her experiment before waking them really is the best course of action.

How much harm would it do to our people? To our Tribe?

If they question their Queen's mind...

Our past holds no comparisons for me to draw upon, but I know it wouldn't be good.

And Dr. Sullivan worked wonders reversing the memories implanted within me. The impressions remain, but the details are hazy, almost forgotten.

The agony of betrayal, the guilt of murder, of slaughter... Those will always remain with me, an aftermath of the tampering, an acute sting as if the stones of my cell bruised my flesh.

But the memories of such atrocities no longer slink through my mind. The best I can hope for, according to Dr. Sullivan's lengthy explanations.

But for Tenna, he holds more hope. Something about no tangled or interwoven memories.

I drop my head back against the wall, rolling his words over in my mind. "Things will simply come back, possibly slowly, but they'll come back."

How I need her to remember...

But she wants to wake the others first, doesn't think her own memory worth more than their continued sedation.

I smile, even though her sense of right and wrong is, perhaps for the first time, counterproductive.

The door eases open, incredibly slowly, giving me all the time I need. I slip the Belt on as Tenna steps in with our lunch, then ditch it as soon as the door closes.

Music flows through the speaker, and I glance at my Link, a habit I hate that I've formed.

"Your Symphony by Dark Moor. 2002."

"During his funeral..." Tenna begins, trailing off.

Her mossy eyes avoid me as she lays out the strange Human food she brought with her. Every fiber of my being begs me to ask her what she was going to say.

But I wait.

She glances at me, eyes quickly falling to the food. "I remembered something," she finally says. "While we were singing."

My heart stops, and I go still. An ember of hope burns within me.

Please, say you remembered me, remembered us and our Tribe.

"My grandmother..." she whispers.

And my hopes fizzle out.

She takes a seat on the floor, and I slide down from the bed to sit with her. Lines etch themselves into her face as she begins eating, and realization hits me.

I know what memory the funeral brought back to her.

My heart plummets.

Tenna swallows another bite, then says, "I remember singing that song... while my grandmother burned."

Tears slip over her cheeks, and despite everything, despite all my good intentions, I reach for her hand.

Chapter 29

Reginald

My eyes drift out of focus yet again, pulling away from the equation I'm supposed to be solving. My thoughts wander to Eva, the woman I loved, the woman who now exists only in my memory.

How did she change so much?

For twelve years, I've had her on a pedestal, cherishing even the thought of her name. I even forgot the horrors of her experiments on Bolivia Station... mostly.

Wrote it off as a fluke, repressed it.

Something.

But now?

I swallow, heart constricting painfully. My guard shifts on her feet, drawing my attention out of the black pit of my mind, and I stare at her.

Restless wings fluttering, brows furrowed, she watches me, watches the other Drennar in the room. Her eyes drop to my desk.

With a sigh, I force my attention to the equations glowing on the screen of my desk, just as I have done for days now. Ever since they showed me...

I shudder at the memory of Eva kidnapping aliens, shoving the thought away for what feels like the millionth time.

Bending over my desk, I scan the equation before me and calculate the time necessary to travel one lightyear at the current top speed of Drennar spacecraft. My heart falters.

6,015 years.

That's less than half the time it would take our best spacecraft to cross such a distance.

I gape at the number, double checking my math. But as I submit my answer, even that startling reality fails to hold my attention. Already, my eyes drift to the wall, seeing the horrors play out there once more. Nothing changes. They don't actually replay the footage.

But I see her there, just like I see her everywhere else, staring down at a living, breathing, sentient being as if it were nothing more than a tissue sample.

A shudder rolls through me.

My eyes refocus as the set of equations before me disappears, and I shake my head, stunned that I only managed four of the ten. A new set appears, replacing the ones that I failed to complete.

I should've done better.

I should've finished them all. What's wrong with me?

Blinking several times, I try to clear my mind and set to work on the new equations. The first two practically solve themselves, but halfway through the third, I look up, brows furrowing as I stare at the blank wall.

Why didn't they show me anything about Olivia?

Did something happen to her?

My mouth goes dry, and my mind drifts through one terrible possibility or another. A sick feeling builds within me as my dream comes back to me, and all I see is my little girl, cut and bled dry like in my nightmare.

No. She has to be okay.

She must have just... They must not have found anything to torture me with.

I swallow, forcing the horrific dream back down, shutting it away. My lungs fill with a deep breath, but it does little to steady me. I bend to my task, hunching forward and solving two more equations.

But with five still remaining, the problems disappear beneath my hands.

I close my eyes, rubbing a hand over my face. My elbows dig into the desk screen, weighed down by my head as it falls into my palms.

Forcing myself to look up, I prepare to set upon the next group of equations. But the nearest Drennar, a three-meter giant with charcoal skin, interrupts me. Twin fans of blue light project from his eyes, sweeping over me, assessing millions of minute details.

The giant looms over me, a silent sentinel. I squirm beneath his scrutiny, gaze shying away from him. Instead, I watch the reflections of light that blink and flicker across the wall behind him, shining through the clear plate of the back of his head.

A single blue light flashes in the tip of each pointed ear, once, twice, three times. Instantly, the points of the ears of the other Drennar in the room blink three times, receiving whatever results his assessment revealed.

But of course, that isn't enough.

Each one in turn scans me, sweeping blue light over me one at a time. My brows furrow, but I sit still, waiting for them to finish, hating that this is what my life has come to. Rone scans me last, though I know not why.

But then, they surprise me.

The four in the corners take turns scanning her, and I stare at them. I glance at each one in turn, but find no answers to what they're doing, why they're treating her like me, like an anomaly to be weighed and measured.

Their ears blink with transmission, and the room goes dark once more. Then, the wall before me glows.

And my heart goes cold.

I grip the edges of my desk, waiting, bracing for impact. My mind paints Eva a million shades of evil, draws out a billion traumas for Olivia.

But instead, I see a slim man in a suit, standing on a stage. His pale skin marks the footage as old, a relic of the days on earth, before dire circumstance and close quarters bred the human race to a people of averages and dominant traits, with the rare exception.

The man walks across the stage as his name is announced. John Mulaney. My mouth hangs open, and I lean back in my chair, trying to relax.

He begins telling stories, walking back and forth, gesturing occasionally, and the audience before him laughs.

My breath catches.

How long has it been since I heard laughter?

At least, the real kind, not my own morbid laughter.

I shake my head, settling in as genuine laughter reaches out from the speakers to bounce around me. My chest grows lighter, and my shoulders slump with relief, even under the scrutiny of the living statues in the corners of the room.

The light of the screen shines on Rone's skin beside me, but I don't tear my eyes from the screen, from my salvation, to see if she watches it... or me.

A story about a jukebox and the torment of an entire restaurant tugs at the corners of my lips, nearly freeing me of the fog I've fallen into.

But Rone laughs freely, beautiful and light. The sound caresses my ears, pulling my attention from the centuries-dead man on the screen.

Her strange green and blue eyes sparkle with a light no technology could ever afford them. Her dark lips spread wide with a smile as magnificent giggles bubble up from her.

Mesmerized, my heart skips a few beats. The Drennar in the corners of the room scan Rone, but their blue fans do nothing to dissuade her from her mirth.

***

The comedian fades from the wall, and I blow out a breath. The world still hangs on my shoulders, but only one world, not all of them.

My desk screen illuminates with new equations on its surface, and I dive into them. My attention drifts slowly, but I manage to finish most of them, a far cry better than earlier but still nowhere near my usual proficiency.

Rone leads me through the same dismal halls, footsteps soft on the grey floor. "There's an old Human saying," she says.

I stop in my tracks, staring after her.

She walks on for another step. "It says that 'laughter is the best medicine.' We were curious if it held true."

She's... talking to me? Initiating the conversation, no less. And telling me what my experiment was meant to prove?

I gape at her, at the smile she offers when she turns to face me.

"It proved to be the most enjoyable test we've put you through thus far," she says.

Swallowing hard, I shake my head, mouth falling open. Finally, I force myself to speak. "Um, yeah. By a long shot."

She walks on, and I push myself forward, following after her. My mind grinds to a halt, wondering why she's talking to me, why she's offering up information, what angle they might be working.

But the Drennar aren't prone to angles or manipulation, opting more often for straightforward tests.

At the wall which borders my room, her ears blink once and the solid surface morphs, sliding back within itself to allow me passage. I walk through, turning on my heel to face her.

Her skin still shines above her ear, shaved clean despite the healed incision. A braid lingers above, holding her hair up.

But why?

Her dark lips lift into a smile, and her eyes soften. As the wall slides slowly closed, she says, "I know it's not enough, but I thought it might help you feel a little better."

The wall fits itself back into place, and I stare at the pale grey surface. The sympathy in her eyes fills my head, and I drop my gaze.

Did she arrange for that test?

I stumble to my bed, dropping onto it. My mind whirls, and then another realization hits me.

She spoke in the Human tongue.

Maybe to eliminate the delay of the translator, maybe to make it easier for me to understand her since I only know some of their language given how little they speak in my presence.

Or was it because my language lends itself better to emotion than hers?

Chapter 30
Odyssey Space Research Station

Ricardo

I sit on Olivia's bed, piecing through what needs done as she clicks away on her laptop. Her eyes focus on the screen, tuning out the rest of the world, and I plop backward onto the bed. My mind drifts back over the feel of her skin, the sight of her moving over me.

But was it just stress and alcohol? Or something more?

She was flirting with me at the bar.

I turn my face into the pillow, trying to suffocate these thoughts. There are more important things to worry about, after all. But the scent of her lingers on the fabric, crisp and warm.

I look back to her, waiting for Francis to respond to my messages. Olivia taps away at the keys, fingers moving far quicker than should be possible as she coordinates accommodations for the sleeping Regonians and cleans up security footage.

And works on something called Atlantis, the thing she mumbled about an hour ago.

I sift through the reports Olivia and Francis forwarded me, read through files from Dr. Sullivan, but they tell me nothing new.

Eva Dobovich is a terrible person, and she's working with other terrible people to torture innocent people. Got it.

When another hour passes without even a glance or a single word from Olivia, with all my responsibilities seen to, I sit up and say, "What are you working on now?"

She doesn't look up, saying only, "Something I should've finished a long time ago."

Well, that's... enlightening.

"Is there anything I can help with?"

She shakes her head, fingers still speeding along.

"There must be *something* I can do."

Regret washes over me as she steeples her hands, pressing them against her face. She sucks in her lips, then blows out a deep breath. I wince at the tension in her face.

"No. I have to do this," she finally says, eyes still locked on the screen of her laptop. "I just... I have to. This falls on me."

Her tone pulls at my heartstrings, and my brows furrow. "Why does it have to be you? Why's it have to be *only* you?" I ask, voice gentle.

"Because it just does," Olivia snaps.

I sit up straighter, staring at her with furrowed brows.

"Sorry." Her eyes close, and she breathes deeply. "For one thing, you don't know computers."

I nod slowly. After all, there's a reason I came to her, a reason I haven't forgotten, but there must be something else I can do to help.

"And for another," Olivia continues, "she's *my* mother. You shouldn't be stuck cleaning up her mess. And like I said, I should've finished this a long time ago."

A sigh billows from her, and she seems to deflate. But her fingers lower to the keys once more, typing madly, calling the conversation to an end.

She can't really feel responsible for this... Can she?

"This isn't your burden to bear. It isn't your fault," I whisper.

"It may as well be. I could've prevented it. If I'd finished this, there would've been no need for any of this."

Her eyes flick to me just in time to see my jaw fall open and my eyes soften. But her fingers never stop buzzing over the keys.

"That doesn't mean it's your fault," I say. Rising to my feet, I cross the room and put a hand on her arm. "*She* chose this path. *She* did this. Not having this, whatever this is," I gesture at the computer, "doesn't justify what she did."

But Olivia only shakes her head, eyes never deserting the screen, fingers never stilling. My heart twists, stung by her rejection, her refusal to move out from under the blame.

"I have to do this," she says. But she gives in, just a little bit. "If you need something to do, take Tenna and Krona to documentary night. Maybe they'll play something that won't make them hate Humans quite so much."

Fine. I'll get out of your hair.

My insides clench, but I nod, fighting the desire to stay and figure out whatever this is, whatever has sprung up between us, whatever has made me feel so attached already.

Whatever has made her feel responsible for so much.

My Link flashes with a message from Olivia. It holds only an attachment, a map of Odyssey with the location of the "theater" highlighted.

I leave her room, telling myself that whatever she's working on is more important than our personal drama. And I know it is.

But my heart still aches.

The mind has little power over the heart, and long past are the days when I could fool myself into believing otherwise.

Chapter 31
Odyssey Space Research Station

Tenna

My heart drags the ground behind me as I walk through dismal, grey halls. My eyes slip out of focus, and I brush past Humans.

He was there.

The memory floats through my head once more, showing me Krona standing beside me at my grandmother's funeral. He squeezed my hand that day to offer strength.

It meant something to both of us that he was there. It meant a lot.

But what did it mean?

And what changed between us in the years since?

He walks behind me, hidden safely by the Belt, but I feel his footsteps, his heartbeat, each and every breath that moves past his lips.

Or maybe that's my imagination. Maybe my heart is just reaching for him, aching for that connection with him.

Is he what the Humans call an ex?

A thousand arrows pierce my chest, chasing the air from my lungs. My blood runs cold as death.

But why?

I pound mental fists against the black walls in my mind, trying to understand the relationship between us, the distance.

But the wall stands firm.

One foot in front of the other, I plod along behind Ricardo, almost bumping into him when he stops moving. Benches fill the alcove in Odyssey's family section, all packed with people sitting shoulder to shoulder for documentary night, just as Olivia said they would be. The window glows softly, illuminated like a screen and blocking the open space beyond.

Ricardo leads us between benches, squeezing into the only remaining seat. I settle on the floor beside him, and Krona fits himself in beside me, pressed close. Our bodies touch from shoulder to feet, and a soothing warmth dances along my skin, eating away at the tension in my shoulders.

Someone turns out the lights, and the window-screen comes to life. Krona gasps softly beside me, the sound drowned out as the crowd around us erupts with applause. The information about the people who made the film scrolls over the screen, all just as lost to humanity as the planet the film features.

But those long-lost people fall away, and a massive body of water appears. Sunlight sparkles over the surface, and the people around us fall silent.

A voice flows from the speakers, extolling the riches of the vast oceans and the need to protect them. The view dips beneath the waves and soars through the water, finally coming to rest on a peculiar animal called an octopus.

My nose wrinkles at the number of arms the thing has, but when it morphs, spreading its skin to envelope its arms and cover its prey, I nod appreciatively.

The narrator speaks of its predators and defenses, and I watch the creature shift in color, moving from brown to red to blue, then back to brown again. It changes shape, mimicking the strange things around it, things called coral reefs.

When all else fails, it emits a cloud of noxious ink and quickly swims away from the disoriented predator.

Such a strange universe.

I marvel at just how big it really is, and my fears grow, nearly overwhelming me, humbling me. My circumstances demand someone big enough to make a change.

Will I be enough?

The narrator shifts his monologue to the octopus' predator, a shark, and what it brings to the table. Endless rows of teeth and super senses.

But Krona's hand slides gently across my thigh, taking my hand in his, and the documentary slips away from me. Rough callouses adorn his hands, and I relish the feel of them.

His chest rises and falls just a little bit faster, and my heart dances.

***

Thoughts spin through my mind like a hurricane, and I step into the shower, seeking refuge. But new thoughts, musings of inviting Krona to join me, flit through my head, spinning along with the maelstrom.

I can almost imagine the feel of his hands on me, can almost see his eyes getting closer, falling shut as our lips meet.

Hot water pours over my dusky skin, and I focus on the way it courses down my back, trying to clear my head.

Music plays beyond the bathroom door. "The End of Heartache by Killswitch Engage. 2004." Guitar and drums pulse through the room, and I wonder if he got restless waiting for his turn in the shower.

Or is he restless with thoughts of joining me?

I shake my head.

Stop thinking like that.

I focus on the music, far heavier than I would have chosen, but it distracts me just fine. The instruments chase the thoughts from my mind, and I drift on the notes as I wash up.

The vocals shift from beautiful to harsh and screaming, and the music turns brutal. Tension flows from me, and I find myself wishing I knew the words so that I might sing along, *scream* along. I need the violence to flow from me, to take the rage with it, and these words just might do the trick.

Before I realize it, I'm done with my shower, stepping out and wrapping a towel around myself. I dry off quickly and grab my clothes from the counter.

But my shirt slips from my hands, landing in the still-wet shower.

The blood drains from me. I close my eyes, drawing in a long, slow breath.

And then, I call out for Krona.

The music quiets, just barely audible, and I call out his name once more. His feet hit the floor, cross the room toward the bathroom door almost eagerly.

No. Don't be silly.

I can't tell that from his footsteps.

But my heart dances erratically in my chest. My skin prickles with anticipation as I wait.

Will he open the door?

My mind fills with images of him bursting through the door, putting a hand on my waist. I can almost feel his hand on the back of my neck, pulling me in for a kiss. A deep blush spreads over my skin as my body warms, and I imagine him pressing against me, pushing my backside against the sink.

I clear my throat, scrambling to get a grip on myself.

The door handle twitches with the weight of his hand. My heart races, beating a frantic, almost painful, pace. My lungs struggle for air, as if it's all been sucked out into space.

Eyes trained on that tiny piece of metal, I wait.

It twitches once more, but the door doesn't slide inward. He doesn't appear in the open doorframe.

My heart stops.

Something thuds against the door, soft and gentle. Krona speaks, almost whispering, so close to the door that his head must be leaning against it. "Is everything alright?"

"I just..." I trail off, trying not to imagine what stopped him, what kept him from walking in. My brain stutters, and I try not to think of ways to invite him in. "I dropped my shirt in the shower. Can you get me another?"

The words feel like betrayal as they drag themselves across my lips.

His footsteps thud across the floor, slow and heavy. I close my eyes, listening as the wardrobe opens and the hangers click together. Muted footsteps, almost covered by the angry music, come back toward the door, and my heart flips.

I grit my teeth against my heart's foolish games, but the same thoughts come back to sting me. My mind floods with images of him pressed against me, backed against the counter, Human instruments of cleanliness scattering across the floor as his lips rove across my skin.

The doorknob twitches again. But he doesn't move, doesn't open the door, doesn't speak.

I take a deep breath and force myself to move. Clutching my towel, I draw myself up, pushing my shoulders back and my chin up.

Resolution fills me.

I'll figure this out.

I'll search my memories as well as I can. I'll do whatever I can to find out why he's staunching the feelings that *must* reside within us both.

Tomorrow morning, I'll go to the doctor to restore my memories.

His part in stopping the experiments on our sleeping fellows is done for now. He may as well do this.

I jerk the door open. Krona stands there, eyes strained, and my heart cracks. But his pain only serves to strengthen my newfound resolve.

His hand still grasps the doorknob, white-knuckled. He opens his mouth but says nothing.

The song changes, "Paradise Lost by Hollywood Undead. 2008."

Krona's eyes rake over me, taking in my face, tracing my neck and shoulders. His gaze slips over the towel I clutch tightly to slide over my legs.

I swallow as a trill of desire sweeps through me. My eyes flutter, but I hold myself still, luxuriating in his gaze and hoping that what I learn about myself tomorrow doesn't taint this.

Krona breathes deeply, then holds out the shirt for me. Something in his eyes pleads for an answer, but I know not what he asks of me.

He unfurls his hand, easing his death grip on my shirt. I reach out, fingers brushing his palm as I take the strange Human fabric, and heat explodes through me.

Deep breaths.

"Thank you," I whisper, eyes still locked on his.

A million questions perch on my lips, begging to be asked. My lips part, but he speaks first.

"You're welcome," he whispers, chest rising in a sharp breath. His eyes fall to the floor. "I should let you get dressed."

He meets my eyes for just a breath before turning away. The door shuts behind him, and he turns the music up as he disappears from view.

I turn, falling back against the door and heaving a great sigh.

All the problems that the Doctor has to deal with race through my head, but a weight falls from me now that he's sitting idle. Krona's insistence that I get my memories restored before we do anything else echoes through me, and now that the Doctor isn't doing anything else...

I'll see why Krona wants nothing to do with me.

I pull my clothes on and rein in my thoughts, a slightly easier task now that I've made a decision. I slip into the bedroom, crawling beneath the covers as Krona showers. My eyes fix on the window, staring out at the vastness of space, and the music flows around me, easing my tension even in this strange language.

Chapter 32
Odyssey Space Research Station

Ricardo

Music pulses through the air in the bar, sending ripples over the surface of my drink. My Link flashes the name of the song, "Mission by Beats Antique. 2009."

But it skips past my notice.

I sit at the bar, perched on a stool that barely lets even my long legs reach the floor. My eyes slip out of focus as my fingers tap the glass, and my mind wanders.

"Not quite where I thought I'd end up," I mutter, voice disappearing beneath the loud music.

As a kid, all I ever wanted was to keep a low profile, to keep my head down, to stay away from Dad's fists. And the habit stuck.

I stare into the glass, just as Mom and Dad would after a long night of drinking, just before they'd pass out or fight.

But my mind is a mass of chaos, far from the stupor that ruled them in those moments.

I did what I always wanted. I got a good job, but one that doesn't draw attention. Got a good assignment, far from Termana and its bustle, far away from them.

My hand plunges into my hair, and I shake my head.

I got what I wanted, and I was fine. I've been fine.

No more getting knocked down anytime I stood up. I've been fine. I got by, and no one fucking saw me.

But now?

I sigh. My free hand goes to the glass, turning it in place.

How did I end up a rebel? A fucking revolutionary, depending on how deep this all goes.

Jesus, I busted a prisoner out of the cell I was supposed to guard, went against orders from the Minister, sedated one doctor and sent another to the same fate, sought out a renowned hacker...

A sour chuckle escapes me.

I lift the glass to my lips but take only a small sip. All I can think of is Dad's breath as he screamed in my face, telling me to mind my own business so he could punish my brother, only to hit me instead.

And I set the glass down.

I know exactly how I got here.

Because I can't just stand by, cowering in some corner, while someone else gets hurt.

Every scar seems to pulse, reminding me of the beatings I took on behalf of my brother. Not that it did any good.

Ferdinand Bourdeau, the famous doctor and brilliant scientist, never realized the price I paid to spare him, never learned empathy, never saw how much it hurt to keep him safe.

I close my eyes as a deep, sick feeling washes over me.

Because after all his unethical experiment proposals in school, there's a good chance my baby brother is wrapped up in all of this. Glancing at the glass, I briefly wonder if I would change it, if I'd let him take a beating, knowing how he turned out.

I shake my head.

I'd do it again.

Maybe not for the man he turned into. Hell, I'd love to punch him myself if he's involved in all this, but... for the little boy he used to be...

I'd take the beatings again.

I rake a hand through my hair, turning to watch the crowd of dancers, though my eyes never focus. My mind drifts, wondering how much backlash will fall on me for doing the right thing this time.

But even so, I wouldn't change it.

Sighing, I let my head hang back, staring at the ceiling. But my Link lights up, flashing red.

A message from Olivia sends my heart skipping.

Is she actually going to talk to me now?

But when I open the message, I go still. All the blood drains from me.

"Please. Help me. Quick."

My heart freezes, and a chill seeps into my bones.

I leave my drink on the bar and push through the crowd. Angry strangers glare at me as I pass, but they'll forget I was here soon enough.

My feet pound the cold floor as I sprint through the halls to Olivia's room, and the pulsing music fades with each step.

Chapter 33
Odyssey Space Research Station

Olivia

I shift, struggling to get comfortable. Hours hunched in my chair have not been kind to me. I need to get Atlantis operational, need to finish this program.

But my fingers ache, and my eyes blur.

Frustration simmers in my gut, and I rub my temples. Closing my eyes, I try to ease the strain of staring at a screen, try to relax the muscles of my back.

I don't have time for a break.

All the nights I wasted in The Little Elephant rise to bite me, and the knots draw tighter in my shoulders, the irritation burns hotter.

I just need to get this done already.

I bend my fingers to the keys once more, but three numbers into a line of code, my hands cramp again. Gritting my teeth, I shake my hands out.

"Fuck," I hiss.

Saving my work, then resaving it, I close my laptop just a little too hard and place it on a shelf. My bones creak, and my joints pop as I stand, stretching my arms overhead. My back aches as I arch.

Silence rings too loud in my ears, and I turn music on, desperate to break the air, to distract myself, if only for a moment. "Pretty Visitors by Arctic Monkeys. 2009." fills the air, and I pace restlessly, stretching my fingers and wrists to work out the cramps.

Vaguely, I wonder where Ricardo might be.

Surely the documentary didn't run this long. Did he not want to come back here?

The morning rolls through my mind, and I wince at how I acted.

I guess I can't blame him.

And yet, my heart twists at the rejection.

But with everything I have to do... Maybe it's better this way.

And it does have to be me.

I sweep my hair back, resting my hands atop my head as I pace, trying to rein in my thoughts and prepare to get back to work. Guilt slithers through me for even taking this much time, especially to walk around mooning over a one night stand that... didn't quite feel like a one night stand.

I sigh, lamenting the distraction Ricardo could offer, the distraction I can't afford.

Maybe it's best if he goes back to Ulysses with the sleepers.

For more reasons than I originally thought.

Ignoring the stupid spasm of my heart at the thought of saying goodbye to him, I stretch one last time and ease back into my chair, pulling the laptop down with me as I go. Giving my hands a break, I try thinking the digits of the codes, allowing my Link to do the work for me as everyone else does.

But tension builds within me, and my hands itch to move, to type, to do anything.

Trying not to think of my dad's archaic journals and handwriting or the affinity for typing that we share, I resume my work, hands speeding along.

But a knock at the door interrupts me.

My head drops back against the chair, and I blow out a breath. All the while, some small part of me hopes to open the door and find Ricardo, having come for a talk.

Or a... *talk.*

Get a hold of yourself.

I rise to my feet, stowing my laptop away on a shelf, but when I open the door, my brows furrow. Lachlan stares at me, fist poised to knock again.

My stomach flips as disappointment and unease war in the pit of my stomach. His dark eyes burn with a strange intensity, and his inky hair falls in disarray about his face. My gaze roams over flushed skin and bloodshot eyes, and though it makes no sense on Lachlan, I know what I'm seeing.

Has he been drinking?

I stand straighter, staring at him. The hairs on the back of my neck stand on end as he tips a little to one side.

He doesn't drink, not like this. What happened?

"May I come in?" Lachlan asks, and the scent of alcohol pours off him. "I need to talk to you."

I move aside to let him pass, concern etching itself into me. Stress turns my stomach, but I push the worries of my mother's crimes, crimes I could've prevented, away.

"What's up?" I ask.

But Lachlan doesn't answer. He stands in the middle of my room, eyes drifting over my things.

My hands hang awkwardly at my sides, and I wipe my palms, suddenly sweaty, on my pants. Taking a step toward my bed, I ask again, "What's up, Lachlan?'

A hint of worry seeps into my words, betraying the calm I wanted to project.

Finally, Lachlan turns to face me. "Why?" he asks.

I shake my head, brows coming down. "Why what?"

But something tells me I don't actually want to know why he's acting this way.

"You know what I mean," he whispers, voice an icy hiss.

I take a step back, silent as I stare at him. My eyes dart to the door, now far from my reach with him between me and my exit. Swallowing nervously, I wait for him to go on.

The silence drags out, and the song changes, morphing around us.

"Familiar Taste of Poison by Halestorm. 2009."

A song I know well.

Lachlan takes a step forward, face falling. "Why *him*? Why not me?"

A flicker of sadness crosses his face, overshadowing the rage for just a moment.

But rage? That can't be right.

This is Lachlan, after all.

I meet his gaze, searching for the friend I've known for years, but the look in his eyes sends a chill over my spine. And hasn't he been too close, too possessive, too much, for far too long?

I stammer, trying to answer a question that doesn't make sense.

Lachlan's face contorts into a scowl, and he screams, "Why?!"

I jump back, and cold fear slips down my spine, slimy and disgusting.

He leans in, eyes burning. "I've been there. I've *always* been there." His hands ball into fists at his sides, the movement drawing my gaze. He speaks again, volume rising to a shout as the words cross his lips. "But it wasn't *good enough! Why?*"

Panic races through me, and my heart gallops. I swallow but force myself to speak.

And the truth comes out.

"You're too closed-minded. Rules are rules to you, and that's it. Stepping beyond them condemns a person, regardless of their reasons. But rules aren't always right."

Not to mention the levels of crazy that you're reaching right now...

I wince as he scoffs. "Rules?" he spits. "He's a Guard! He *is* the goddamn rules."

He lurches forward another step, inching in close, and again, my eyes dart to the door. And though I've never been one for the old religions, I pray for a way out of this.

The sudden appearance of an almighty savior would be pretty fucking handy right now.

Realization sweeps through me, and I let out a breath. My heart races as I send a clipped message to Ricardo. Though not a God of old, he'll do well enough.

If he answers.

If he gets here in time to stop whatever Lachlan has planned.

My throat goes dry as Lachlan stares me down.

"How is he different?" he snarls. "How is he *better?*"

I freeze, startled by the ugly mask that has replaced the kind face I've known for years. Suddenly, the strong arms built up by fixing spaceships seem a little too much like weapons.

Just stall him. Keep him talking.

I open my mouth to speak, but my tongue feels like sandpaper.

Lachlan surges forward, grabbing me roughly by the arms. "HOW. IS. HE. BETTER?"

Ice fills my veins, and I stutter, "Because he does what's right, not what the rules say."

"That's BULLSHIT! The rules *are* what's right..." Lachlan whispers, seemingly uncertain, if only for a hairsbreadth of a second. Reaffirming his belief, he repeats it, grip tightening as his volume increases, "The rules are Right. The *rules* are RIGHT!"

He releases my arms and stomps to the door. My heart soars.

Maybe he'll leave.

Maybe this is done.

But he turns on his heel, facing me once more, and my heart plummets.

"What has he done to impress you so much? Buy you a fucking drink? He's just a nothing Guard from a tiny station."

Insanity peeks out from behind his eyes, bright and rabid.

Please don't ignore my message, Ricardo.

Please get here.

Gulping in a breath, I stall. "He isn't a 'nothing' Guard."

Lachlan closes the distance in an instant, shouting in my face, "Goddamnit, Olivia!"

He shoves me, and I topple back onto my bed. Tears prick at the corners of my eyes, and I fight to hold them in.

But Lachlan vaults atop me, straddling my waist, pinning my shoulders with strong hands. "You've always thought the rules don't apply to you," he begins, trailing off into incoherent mumbling, breath filling the air above my face with the reek of cheap alcohol.

All this time, this is what's been hiding underneath?

Shock spreads through me, but I struggle, bucking beneath his bulk. I flail and try to pull my arms free, but my efforts are wasted. My blood runs cold.

He's too strong.

Beyond our struggle the song changes. "Suspended in Dusk by Type O Negative. 1993."

It's one thing too many to focus on, one too many abrupt shifts for me to handle.

Above me, chaos lurks in Lachlan's eyes, begging to be set free. He leans in, hands gripping my shoulders and scowl deepening.

So, I give in, I answer him, hoping it'll spare me.

"Ricardo's helping me with my mother." Tears prick at my eyes, and my throat tightens, but I force the words out. "Tenna's planet wasn't destroyed. The Regonians are close to Drennar, biologically. My mom kidnapped the whole tribe. She kidnapped all of them. She's been experimenting on them."

My voice cracks, and my words stop.

But Lachlan's hands grip my shoulders tighter, digging fingers into my flesh as he mutters, "*No*. No, no, no, no, no!"

Just stall. Just keep him busy until Ricardo gets here.

"It's true. He found out and told me. We're trying to fix it," I say, hoping to get my point across.

But he lifts me, slams my shoulders back down into the bed. Leaning close, he screams in my face. "No! You just don't get it. She has a reason. *I know* she has a reason. The rules are right, and she makes the rules. She *has* to be right."

I kick and flail, trying to throw him off, but he doesn't budge. My heart races as my blood turns to ice, and I squirm desperately.

Lachlan's voice falls to a sinister whisper. "If she's wrong, if the Coalition is wrong, then how would we know what to do?"

Tears stream over my cheeks as I struggle beneath him. A pitiful whimper rises from me as his fingers claw my collarbone.

My knees slam up toward his back, but I can't get leverage. I claw at him, arms flailing uselessly, still pinned. Terror and tears conspire against me, blurring my vision, and I fight back a scream.

No one will hear me.

Dear God, no one will hear me.

A thousand images flood my mind, a thousand terrible things Lachlan could do to me, and I shudder to the tune of a thousand mutterings of, "No." Our voices mingle into a cacophony of pain and fear and anger and madness.

I draw my head back, then slam it upward. My forehead crushes his nose with a terrible crunch, and a torrent of blood gushes forth.

And hysteria claims him.

He screams, "God fucking damn it!"

Thick hands wrap around my throat, grip as hard as diamonds, and I gasp, bucking beneath him.

"You just don't *get it*! You don't get it!" he shouts. "You never have. Never. And now, you never will."

A chill sweeps through me.

His hands tighten, sending sparks flying across my vision. He leans forward, putting his weight onto my neck, and the world begins to fade.

But I pull my arms free, clawing at his fingers, his wrists, his arms. I dig in, trying to loosen his hold, heart racing, lungs screaming out for air. My body begs for relief, for help.

His blood drips a steady beat across my forehead and nose, mixing with my tears as it rolls down the sides of my face. But he only tightens his hold, squeezing my neck, leaning into it.

Still more sparks fly across my vision as I gasp, lungs aching with their efforts. My muscles burn, crying out for oxygen.

Darkness closes in, and a sad little voice in the back of my mind whispers, "Who knew it would end like this?"

How many years have I longed for death, thought about it, craved it?

My lungs fold in on themselves, and my heart shatters into irregular beats as I stare up into crazed eyes. My chest collapses, and pain spreads through me.

A burst of light fills the room as the door flies open, crashing into its pocket and shaking the shelves. Books topple, and trinkets rattle, a cacophony of noise and sound.

But Lachlan looks up, and the hands around my throat loosen.

Eyes bulging, I gasp in a breath, hoping it isn't my last. My hands claw at Lachlan, prying his fingers away.

Some small part of me wants to look at the door, to see what happened, but I can't move. A faint hope flickers within me.

But all I know is air and the darkness that won't leave the edges of my sight.

Words float through the air, incomprehensible, just before Ricardo plows into Lachlan, a blur of dark hair and obscenities. The two men fly over the end of the bed, and sweet precious air rushes into my lungs.

I gasp and cough as the sound of fists hitting flesh crashes into the air. Rolling onto my side, I draw my knees up to my chest, dragging in one rasping breath after another. Tears roll over the bridge of my nose, somehow falling into the other eye.

The commotion at the end of the bed swims in and out of focus as my brain struggles to piece my life back together. But gradually, the room falls into place. The darkness recedes from my sight, and I see Ricardo.

He came to save me.

Fresh tears spring forth, and I barely contain them. My lungs falter as a sob rises to throttle them.

Then, I see what Ricardo's doing.

His fist slams into Lachlan's face, over and again. The rhythmic thuds ring out, horrifying and all too satisfying.

He's going to kill him.

Panic moves in again.

They'll take him away if he kills him.

Coughing, sputtering, I try to speak. Words scratch their way up my throat. "Stop. Wait, please."

But my voice is barely audible, and Ricardo doesn't stop.

Another punch, and Lachlan's head flies to the side, lolling limply. Then, another.

"Please, Ricardo," I beg, pulling myself up to sitting. The world spins around me, and my throat throbs. But I try again, a little louder. "Ricardo! Please!"

He stops, fist raised for another strike, and turns to face me. Scrambling up, he rushes to my side.

"God, are you okay?"

But he doesn't give me time to answer before he scoops me into his arms, cradling me on his lap.

Tears well up, and my head falls onto his shoulder. Lachlan moans on the floor, barely conscious, and whispers fill the hall as a crowd forms beyond my open door.

But I can still feel Lachlan's hands around my neck, feel the bruises that are already forming, feel the droplets of Lachlan's blood on my forehead.

And my sobs grow rough and harsh, battering my poor lungs.

Ricardo rubs my back, cradles my head against his shoulder. He whispers soothing words, but I barely hear them over the pounding of my own heart.

Guards bustle into my room, blurred shapes parting the sea of bystanders as I weep.

And amidst the wreckage of my mind, a bomb goes off.

Everyone will know, now.

Even the Coalition.

I quickly hack through my Link, hopping around to find Lachlan's in the network, only to find a mostly coherent message sent to my mother, filled with just enough to incriminate us.

And more than enough to endanger us.

I dig a little deeper, suddenly still on Ricardo's lap.

She's already notified the Minister of Defense.

Soldiers are coming.

My blood runs cold as realization spreads through me like frost.

Everyone here, all the Regonians spread across the other stations, they're all in danger...

Because of me.

A sob wracks my body, shaking me in Ricardo's embrace. He holds me to his chest, rocking me gently back and forth.

But in the depths of my soul, I know.

I was tested...

And I was found wanting.

Chapter 34
Odyssey Space Research Station

Krona

A knock at the door breaks the tense silence, ringing out in the darkness, and I roll to my feet. Taking the Belt in hand, I conceal myself as Tenna moves to the door.

She glances my way, eyes glowing softly as she searches the darkness for me, then turns on the light. My heart skips a beat, begs me to reach for her.

But she opens the door.

Yet again, I wonder how Humans can stand to see nothing in the night.

I glance beyond Tenna, and my stomach drops.

Olivia stands in the hall, neck purple with angry bruises. Tears and blood streak her face, and Ricardo holds her close as he stares in at Tenna, searching the space behind her for me.

My pulse quickens, and thoughts of Human inferiority go out the window into the darkness of space. My fingers curl, aching for revenge upon whoever did this to her.

I hold myself still, waiting for them to speak, to explain, to tell me who did this to my friend. I ignore the implications of my change of heart, that realization, eyeing the crowd that mills about in the hall.

And finally, Ricardo speaks. "We have to tell them. Come with us." His brows raise, but his voice lowers. "Both of you."

My heart hammers in my chest, but this strange Human has yet to steer me wrong. After all, he got me back to Tenna. Taking a deep breath, I press the button on the Belt and lay it on the bench seat by the window.

But my mind fills with questions.

How will we talk to them all? What will we tell them?

My heart clenches.

We can't tell them who we really are. Tenna doesn't even know yet.

"Shouldn't you go to the doctor first?" Tenna asks, eyes tight.

But Olivia doesn't speak.

My own throat aches with sympathy, recalling times where similar bruises adorned my own flesh in my training days.

"That's where we're going first," Ricardo says, sparing Olivia the painful task of speaking. With a nod in the direction of the hall, he adds, "Anyone who wants to hear what we have to say will be waiting for us in the cafeteria. Olivia's already arranged it."

She holds up her Link to show her method of doing so, hand shaking as she does, then tucks it against Ricardo's chest once more.

Now's my chance.

I swallow, preparing all my arguments to convince Tenna to restore her memories now. I go over them in my head as I turn to her, shouldering them all like weapons for the battle of overcoming her need to protect others before herself.

"Tenna, we need to have Dr. Sullivan restore your memories while we're there," I say, heart pounding. "Someone else can see to Olivia. We'll need him there when we talk to the Humans anyway, so we'll have to wake him up no matter what. He may as well do this while Olivia's taken care of."

She opens her mouth to speak, but I need her to hear me.

"I promise," I beg, humbling myself before her. "You'll understand why it's so important when it's done. Trust me, please. Do you trust me?"

My heart stops, gripped by the real problem, the idea that, given a blank slate, she won't want me anymore, won't trust me. My blood runs cold, stricken by the words that hang over my head as I search her gaze.

My heart fractures as I wait. Big green eyes stare up at me, inscrutable.

And then, she smiles.

I dare to hope, waiting as time stretches out before me. She lays a hand on my arm, and my heart jumps. My lungs catch.

"I trust you," she says.

I let out a breath and throw my arms around her. My head falls to rest on her shoulder, face buried in her hair, hand cupping the back of her head. My stomach flips.

Her arms slide up to my shoulders, then her hands are on the sides of my face, burning my skin with her touch. She pulls back, stares into my eyes, gaze still unreadable.

But she leans her forehead against mine, lending me her strength without even realizing the meaning of the gesture.

"We should go," she whispers.

"Okay," I say, nodding, and we make our way to the hospital wing.

She grips my hand tightly, and my stomach flutters with the wings of hundreds of Molans. But a new fear grips me.

When she remembers, will she wish she didn't? Will she miss the freedom of not knowing?

***

I blink against the glaring lights as we step from dim halls into the too-bright hospital. A passing nurse, short even for a Human, stops to greet us. Her jaw drops as she takes in Olivia's bruised neck and blood smudged face, and she immediately rushes the Human woman to a bed.

Ricardo follows, requesting Dr. Sullivan for a different matter as Olivia settles onto her new resting place.

Finally, the nurse looks at the rest of us. Her impossibly large eyes widen further as she takes in the fact that *two* Regonians stand before her. She glances at the beds where our people lie sleeping. She even counts them twice, shaking her head.

All accounted for.

"That's what we need to see Doctor Sullivan about," Ricardo says.

The nurse nods, brows furrowed in confusion even as she wraps a cuff around Olivia's upper arm. "I called for him. If you could just have a seat outside his office, I'll see to Olivia."

I stare at her, wondering how she called for him so quickly, how she knew Olivia's name. But the Link on her arm glows with the strange Human letters that make Olivia's name.

I glance down at the alien technology firmly planted in my own arm, and wonder how I could've forgotten its existence, how I could've gotten so used to the thing that I'd overlook it. With a frown, I tear my eyes from the thing and move toward the office.

Olivia whimpers behind us, voice raspy and thin as it tears through her bruised throat. "Ricardo?"

We all stop, turning to face her, and she asks him, "Will you stay with me?"

"Of course," he says, rushing to her side.

Tenna and I proceed alone. We lower ourselves into chairs far too small for our frames and wait. Time stretches out, spiraling into what feels like infinity before quick, soft footsteps draw my attention.

Doctor Sullivan's hushed words reach around the corner as he greets Olivia and Ricardo, asking the nurse a few questions. But she sends him our way. My heart jumps as his steps draw near, and I close my eyes for a moment.

This is real.

She's going to remember me again.

With a deep breath, I rise to greet the doctor, and Tenna stands with me. He smiles up at us, affable as ever.

"Sorry to do this so late," she says, voice contorting around the Human language. "I was going to come see you about this in the morning, but it suddenly became urgent." She smiles at him, then adds, "I need you to restore my memories. You've found the way to do it, correct?"

Sullivan nods, but he frowns. "How urgent is it?" Concern edges his voice, filling his words with unspoken questions.

"Extremely," I answer, watching as the weight of that one words settles onto his shoulders.

Sullivan nods, then ushers us to a crisp white hallway tucked behind his office. On one side, a pair of shining doors slide open, revealing a tiny box of a room. I eye it suspiciously, but we follow him in, hunching over to fit into the low-ceilinged room.

Dr. Sullivan reaches for the panel of buttons beside the doors. "This may feel strange," he warns, pressing the button that reads, "Laboratory." He scans his Link, and the doors slide shut.

Everything about this Human world has been strange.

We've been imprisoned and experimented on. My mind has been made unsafe. I've flown through the Realm of Stars in a craft that bucked like an unbroken Vyrto.

How much weirder can it get?

Then, the tiny room moves.

It breaks loose from the hospital wing, floor, shifting upward beneath my feet. I brace myself, knees bent, and Tenna grabs my arm, unsteady for just a moment.

The floor settles back into place, and the doors open, revealing a whole new set of rooms filled to the brim with the instruments of Human experimentation. They shine in glass and silver, perched on tables throughout the main room, so much like the lab on Ulysses that a shiver rolls down my spine.

And though my only real memory of that lab are of my experiment's reversal, my stomach still churns.

"Sorry about the elevator," Sullivan says. "It was closer than the stairs."

We step out, unfolding to our full heights, and Dr. Sullivan leads us straight ahead. A door lurks in the shadows, likely hidden to Human eyes, and I wonder how well Sullivan has acquainted himself with these rooms in his time here to weave through the tables so well.

The lights snap on, and the good doctor says, "I'm having the others brought up to be woken."

"Good," I say. "I want my people to be able to fight for themselves rather than being cut down in sleep when the Soldiers get here."

Sullivan stares at me, face aghast. His mouth silently forms the word, "Soldiers..."

But he nods.

My heart races as he leads us into another room. A blank wall, cabinets, and a single bed await.

"Lie down, please," he says, opening cabinets and laying things out on little trays.

The wall blinks itself awake, illuminating four rows of five screens, each eagerly waiting to report various bodily functions. I look around, searching for differences between this room and the one from Ulysses, but find none.

Tenna settles onto the bed, bathed in the harsh light of the overhead lamps, highlighted by the soft glow of the screens. Her dusky skin becomes a map of bright white and darkest night beneath its glare, and her chest rises with a deep breath.

I swallow hard, hoping her procedure goes as well as Dr. Sullivan promised days ago.

He wraps a thin band around her arm, then another smaller band around one of her fingers. Several screens flash numbers and letters, conspiring with the little bands to break Tenna down into digits and calculations.

A long thin line stretches across one screen, bumping up and down in a jagged rhythm, measuring her heartbeat with that sharp wave and numbers glowing in the corners.

My heart begins to race, right alongside hers. My breaths speed up, coming in time with the screen that tracks her lungs.

But nothing else on the screens makes sense.

Sullivan sticks circular pads to Tenna's head, one on either temple, and a few more screens jump to life, scrolling data in a constant stream. I stare at the foreign characters, picking out a letter or two here and there.

My heart clogs my throat, and I tell myself to breathe.

He did as he promised on Ulysses. He afforded us a funeral for our fallen. There's no reason not to trust him.

But this is different.

I gulp in a breath.

This time, Tenna's life could be on the line.

I reach for her, place a hand on her arm. My thumb moves back and forth over her skin, but she puts her hand over mine. Tearing my eyes from the wall of screens, I look down at her. She smiles, dark green eyes burning with intensity.

Sullivan places another small circular pad on her chest, and the final two screens glow, pulling numbers from thin air.

I take a deep breath as the doctor pulls out a needle, and a chill sweeps through me. The little pinch of it when one bit my skin on Ulysses was nothing compared to the tattoos I bear.

But I knew what would happen with those needles.

This Human needle does unspeakable things.

Tenna squeezes my hand as Dr. Sullivan breaks the needle trying to push it in at the crook of her elbow. He breaks two more, winding my nerves tight with every attempt, then finally succeeds with the fourth.

Hooking it up to a bag of fluid via a long tube, he says, "This is just some diluted Bellona, from a plant on your world. You'll start to feel groggy soon."

His deep voice is soft and kind. Just as it was when he did this to me.

And sure enough, Tenna's eyes begin to droop.

"It's okay to fall asleep," the doctor assures her.

I squeeze her hand, and she looks to me, mossy gaze half hidden beneath her lids.

"It's okay," I tell her. "I'll protect you."

Her chest rises with a deep breath, and her eyes close.

Picking up a small syringe, Doctor Sullivan explains, "Now, it won't be instantaneous. The drug has to circulate through her system. Her heart rate may become erratic, and we'll handle it if that happens. We'll monitor her closely."

His words wash over me, and I nod my understanding, having heard most of this before. All except for the delay.

My heart drops, wondering how long it'll take, wishing she would just open her eyes and know me again.

"Why must she be asleep?" I ask. "Is it the same as mine?"

Dr. Sullivan nods. "If she were awake, it'd feel like her veins were on fire. A rather unpleasant side effect," he says with a grimace. "That'll wear off after about ten minutes, just like yours. We'll start waking her up then."

He approaches the wall of screens, tapping one, then another, bringing up further data. Dissecting Tenna into numbers.

My fingers lace themselves through Tenna's. I cradle her hand in both of mine, stomach fluttering as I wait.

"Once she's okay to move around," Doctor Sullivan says without turning, "light exercise will help get the remainder of it flowing through her a bit quicker."

He pauses, thinking for a moment as he considers the screens before him. Then, voice suddenly a shade darker, he adds, "Given the impending attack, I doubt physical activity will be hard to come by."

A few select numbers change in apparently just the right way, and he turns to face us. "She's ready."

Approaching Tenna, he inserts the syringe into a port on the clear tube attached to her arm. He pushes the plunger of the syringe, sending chemicals to float in her bloodstream.

And the elevator opens with the arrival of the first yet-to-be-woken Regonian.

Chapter 35
Odyssey Space Research Station

Tenna

My life filters in, bits and pieces falling into place.

I stand in a paddock, sent by Mother to break in a new Vyrto. I smile at the praise she offered, the knowledge that no one connects with these lovely creatures the way I do.

I marvel at the massive beast, a great black steed with antlers larger than any I've seen in my fourteen summers.

"Where did they find you?" I whisper.

Vague thoughts of short Human years float through me, but I shun them for now, reveling in the memory that consumes me.

Approaching the steed, I measure my footsteps, keeping them slow, my movements fluid. I hum a low soothing tone, all the while. My hand rises, and I place it over my heart for just a moment.

One more step, and I reach out, likening my movements to a more gradual version of our harvest dance. Blowing out a long breath, I take another step, watching the posture of the Vyrto for any subtle changes.

Its nostrils flare, and its black eyes are wide with fright, as they always are at first. I stare up at the beast, humbled before it.

Slowing my pace, I try to accommodate it as well as I can. And it relaxes, just a bit, lowering its head to my level, no longer trying to seem big or intimidating. Curiosity gets the better of it, and it takes one furtive step forward.

My heart leaps, but I hold myself steady, keep my movements small and slow. A gentle breeze flicks blue-green grass against my legs, blows my scent toward the Vyrto. It tests the air, nostrils flaring as it takes me in.

Another step forward, heavy hoof making a solid thud as it hits the ground. And finally, it presses its massive nose into my hand, muzzle warm against my palm.

With my heart in my throat, I spread my fingers out, slide them up the animal's face. Large antlers dwarf me, spread wide like plates with spikes ringing the edges. They cast shadows over the ground, over me, easing the heat of the midday sun.

Its fluffy tail swishes easily behind it, brushing the tall grass, and it snuffles my hand. The breeze catches its long, black mane, sending it flowing outward, and my breath catches at the sight. The animal steps forward, less tentative, nudging my hand happily, and I stroke its neck.

A few more moments, and I'll introduce the saddle, let it sniff it.

Eager to recall more, I wander out of that memory, only to find myself in a large stone keep. I sit in the floor, waiting for the Healer to come down and announce the outcome. I drum my fingers in impatience but force myself to sit still.

But only nine summers old, my excitement nearly bubbles over.

Finally, the Healer finally meanders down the stairs, white robes billowing, just like the robes of the Memory Markers to come. A smile dances in her eyes when she looks at me.

Mother must be okay.

And the baby, too!

I shoot to my feet, and words tumble out of me. "Is it a boy or a girl?"

Grinning ear to ear, the Healer says, "A healthy baby boy."

Giggling, I vault up the stairs, taking them two and three at a time. Excitement bubbles through me, sending me sprinting down the hall, past beautiful tapestries, careening around the corner.

I burst through the door to my parents' room and rush over to join my sister, Kala, at their bedside. She smiles at me, tucking long strands of silky black hair behind her ears.

Strands of vivid blue hair hang loose from Mother's braid, plastered to her forehead and neck with sweat, but she smiles dreamily, reaching to take my hand for a moment.

Pressed to her dusky breast, our baby brother suckles happily. Barely blue hair, nearly white, shines in the light streaming through the window, and his ash-colored skin looks just like our Father's.

Leaning over the newborn babe, Father whispers, "Bray kur daet, poorumlar Tine." Welcome to the world, cherished Prince. He presses his lips to my brother's forehead, *Efsi's* forehead.

And then it hits me, hard as a kick from a Vyrto, blunt and sudden.

The monarchy.

My family, leading the Tribe.

I fall into the memory of fighting Efsi and Kala for the position of leader, *Inera*, of the Tribe.

Adorned in traditional armor, treated with the purest Juno sap and armed with our weapons of choice, we face each other. My heart races, and I praise the ancestors who changed the rules of this battle, thankful we won't be fighting to the death.

Our Tribe stands around the battleground, watching, chanting. Our parents watch, hands locked together and voices rising with those of our people.

Efsi bows his head, sheaths his sword. His eyes meet mine when he rises, and he nods slowly. The vote of confidence buoys my spirits.

But a long battle lies ahead.

Kala and I fight, my axes clanking against her sword, her shield. I wince with her as I spill droplets of her blood across the dark earth.

She lands a hit here, parries there.

But as the sun dips, she submits, dropping to a knee and sheathing her sword.

All around, our people chant the songs naming me the next Kinera.

Kinera.

The word floats through my mind, a realization in the present.

Queen.

That's what I am. Queen of Daen Tribe.

In that long ago time, I search the crowd, mind reeling, until my eyes find a familiar face. Krona.

He was there, offering me his support.

He smiles at me, and I rush into his arms, aglow with victory and joy and... love. Glorious and open, free and warm, it washes through me.

But where did it go?

If we were so close, why does he now hide his feelings?

Chapter 36
Odyssey Space Research Station

Krona

I grip Tenna's hand, waiting for it to be safe to wake her. She lies motionless, oblivious to the pain.

In the main room of the lab, Olivia and Ricardo rush around with Dr. Sullivan and the nurses, removing the I.V. needles that keep our people unconscious. The lab tables lie in jumbled heaps around the outer edges of the room, pushed aside for the beds.

Ricardo explains the situation to the nurses, his voice floating through the open door. Olivia's raspy tone stumbles along in his wake, tearing through her bruised throat to speak of warnings sent to the residents of Odyssey.

Tenna's hand twitches, and I drop my gaze back to her. I squeeze her hand, trying to come up with something to tell the others when they wake.

Explanations of where we are and what's going on form in my mind, and I hope it'll be enough, hope they won't lash out against the Humans they see first. Our only Human allies.

The station rocks, and metal groans. I shift, knees bending, and brace the table Tenna rests upon. A glance out the door finds Olivia still pulling circular pads from chests and needles from arms, leaning against beds to steady herself.

"They're here," she says. "I couldn't keep them out. Their clearance codes were too high. I didn't have time to block them. They were moving too fast."

"Too fast is right," Ricardo mutters. "It's a wonder they didn't knock this place out of the sky."

I swallow nervously, stomach dropping. The realization that, even as she pulled needles from arms, Olivia was hacking this place lifts my lips into a smile.

The last needle comes out, and Dr. Sullivan comes to stand next to me. With a glance at the screens, he rolls Tenna's bed out into the main room with our people.

I breathe a sigh of relief.

I have to be the first one they see.

"I sent another message to the people here," Olivia says. "I said the soldiers are here, asked them to stay in their rooms to stay safe."

I nod, blowing out a breath. A chill sweeps down my spine at the thought of soldiers unleashed on civilians, and I wonder if the Human leaders would go that far.

My eyes trace the tattoos on the sleeping people here, reading their lives. A leatherworker with three children. A Vyrto herder with children and grandchildren.

I glance at the marks on those farther away but find not a single warrior among them.

My stomach drops, and I fight to keep from gripping Tenna's hand too tightly.

Of course, they would send soldiers against civilians. They already have.

The main lights go out, leaving only emergency lighting, and my heart races. The Humans around me gasp.

"The Guards in the shuttle bay are engaging the Soldiers," Olivia says, eyes unfocused and Link flashing. "Partially by choice. Partially out of self-defense."

I close my eyes in disgust at such dishonorable behavior from the Soldiers.

"One of them must've hit the light controls in the service corridor, must've broken the panels," she goes on. "I can't get them back on."

Music blares over the speakers throughout the station, echoing all around. Even unconscious, Tenna's Link flashes the name of the song. "EAT ME, DRINK ME by Marylin Manson. 2007."

"They must have hit the P.A. system, too," Olivia says with a shrug.

We wait in the dark, and my nerves wind tight. The fight moves through me, races through my veins, begs me to meet them head on.

I'd fare better than the guards, the families.

But one of my people stirs.

And then, another.

Their eyes search the room, wide and frantic, until they land on me, on Tenna lying motionless on a bed just like theirs.

They whisper and turn to each other, questions buried beneath the music that pulses around us, beneath the Human sounds and words that echo off strange metal walls.

"There isn't time for all the details," I say in our tongue, hoping I get time to explain the translator and the voice it will put in their heads. "But here is what I can tell you now. We're under attack. Not everyone here is an enemy, so fight only those who attack first."

I grit my teeth against the disadvantage this puts upon them. The enemy will have the element of surprise.

One of the newly awoken, the older woman who tends Vyrtons, speaks with furrowed brows. "I'm not a warrior, Tinera. I'm not sure I can serve our people well."

My lungs fill with a deep breath. I lower my voice, just quiet enough to escape the Humans present. "These Humans are not as strong as us. Their bodies are not made of the same stuff we are. They're soft."

But I understand her misgivings. Back home, I'd never send her off to fight.

My heart aches to tell her that she'll be fine, begs me to assuage her fears, but I learned long ago never to tell someone heading to battle that they'll make it out alive. Certainty belongs only to fools when the stakes are this high.

Instead, I say, "We are the only hope for Daen Tribe right now. If I had any choice, I'd send only warriors, but circumstances allow us no other options. I must ask you for this."

Shoulders back, she rises from her bed, and her companions follow suit. They steady themselves with deep breaths.

A man several years my junior pushes his light blue braid back over his shoulder. He stands tall as he says, "Where are they?"

"They're coming to us," I say, then step back to Tenna's side, taking her hand in mine again.

The older woman speaks up again, "What happened to Kinera?"

"She's fine," I tell them.

Their shoulders fall with relief.

"She just needs to sleep a little longer." I touch her cheek, then turn back to them. "I'll explain this later, too. Thank you for trusting me on this."

I only hope you're all around for the explanation.

"They're getting close," Olivia says. "Really close."

"Ricardo?" I turn to face him, still clutching Tenna's hand. "Will you show them the way to the hospital? I'll be down with Tenna as soon as she wakes."

Ricardo nods. "But... Shouldn't you come too?"

My people stare at him, mouths agape, and touch their heads, just above their ears where the translators are located. Their brows join together, and they look from Ricardo to me.

"Another explanation for later," I assure them. "The voice will tell you what he said. He has one that tells him what we say."

The young man nods, swallowing hard. But he rubs his temple. They look around, fear and horror playing over their features.

One murmurs, "Sootvali..." Star sickness.

The older woman turns to Ricardo. In starts and stops, she tells him, "Tinera cannot leave Kinera. His partner comes first. Together, they must save our Tribe. We will fight."

I offer her a smile with my heart in my throat.

Turning to Ricardo, I ask, "Are there stairs? The elevator will only disorient them."

He nods, dark hair swaying.

Tenna's hand twitches once more, and my heart clenches. But she doesn't wake, *can't* wake just yet.

Blowing out a breath, I look at the woman who seems to have become their leader. "Trust him," I nod at Ricardo. "He's helped us more than you yet know."

They stand taller, some nodding, some going still, and I thank the ancestral Kings and Queens for not being so corrupt as the Human leaders as to ruin the trust of our people. One by one, they line up before Ricardo, waiting for him to lead them.

My stomach flips as they move toward an alcove near the room Tenna occupied mere moments ago. My heart races as they disappear from view. I squeeze Tenna's hand, swallowing nervously.

On all sides, the doors to the rooms around us latch as nurses lock themselves out of harm's way. My concerns for them ease, even as they stare through windows at us.

But my mouth goes dry at the thought of what my people and my friend will face in the hospital below us. Guard or not, he may not be trained as well as the Soldiers handpicked to end us. Guilt wells within me, and a new fear follows in its wake.

I hope he knows enough to stay out of the way of my people.

Even untrained, especially untrained, they could accidentally hurt him, could hit him with whatever they find to use as a weapon.

I watch Tenna, heart beating too quickly, too shallowly, as I wait for Dr. Sullivan to say we can wake her. My palms sweat, but I don't release her hand from my grip.

Please wake before the soldiers get here... We need to be down there, need to protect them.

With every passing breath, Olivia grows more agitated, drumming her fingers faster and faster on the table nearest her. My heart races along, trying to keep pace with her dancing fingers, and my lungs struggle to drag in enough air.

Olivia goes still, and I stare at her horror-stricken face. Muffled bangs and thuds rise through the floor. Crashes and echoes reverberate through the station.

They're here.

"How many?"

"Too many..." Olivia whispers.

"How many?" I ask again, voice tight, too demanding.

"Station-wide, nearly a hundred to start. The Guards took out... thirty-five. Fifteen are spread out, searching the station. There are fifty downstairs."

Four of our people and one Human. Against fifty.

If it were warriors down there...

But they're farmers and tradesmen.

Turning to Dr. Sullivan, I say, "When can we revive Tenna? She can't be lying here helpless if the Soldiers make it up here."

When the soldiers make it up here.

"We should really give her a few more minutes," he says.

My muscles tense, and my stomach clenches.

The music softens, goes quiet, and a loud boom shakes the floor before the next song begins.

"Relax My Beloved by Alex Clare. 2011." starts up, and seconds later, a scream rises, clawing at my ears.

One of our people.

I picture their faces, searing them into my memory, promising to mourn them if they fall.

"*If* we can wait," Sullivan amends.

The air grows heavy, laden with tension, as the battle wages below us. My heart rips in two, torn between protecting Tenna, preserving our lives to fight for the whole Tribe, and fighting alongside our people downstairs to try and save them.

Another scream rings through the air. Another Regonian.

My blood runs cold, and I grit my teeth. But the scream draws out, shredding my nerves.

"Do it," I tell Sullivan.

"She'll likely be in some pain still," he says with furrowed brows.

"That was half my people down there, screaming, possibly dying." I swallow hard, trying to push the rock out of my throat. "They won't hold them much longer, not at this rate."

What weapons could those puny Humans have?

With a quick nod and steady hands, Dr. Sullivan twists a clamp on the tube feeding into Tenna's arm, then gently removes the needle from her skin. "It should only be a few moments," he says, dark skin marred by worry lines.

I hope we have that long.

Sullivan pulls circular pads from Tenna's head and chest, one by one. The cuff on her arm comes off next, followed by the one on her finger. Her brows crease, and my heart stutters.

But she doesn't wake.

Shouts echo from the elevator shaft and the stairwell, and my head jerks up. My heart pounds as I wait for someone to burst through the doors, wait for the Human soldiers to push my people back, to overrun them. Guilt swirls through me, cloudy and slimy as it slithers over my spine.

Tenna's eyelids flutter, eyes twitching from side to side, and her hands flex. Her fingers wrap tightly around mine. My heart jumps into my throat, and I lift her hand to my chest, cradling it.

She's coming around.

But the elevator buzzes to life, descending toward the hospital, and dread fills me.

A thunderous crash echoes through the elevator shaft, and a grinding sound wrenches the air. The lift-box inside grinds to a halt, screeching noisily.

Sullivan gulps back a breath.

Apparently still tuned into the station, Olivia says, "Ricardo had them smash cabinets and desks through the doors. They'll go for the stairs next." Her voice drops, and she turns to me. "Get her out of here."

I strain my ears, picking the chaos of battle from the music, following it as it trails toward the stairwell. A crash sounds, and my heart twists.

"They won't get past the access scanner," Sullivan says.

I look at him with an ember of hope.

"The Minister of Defense and the Minister of Research sent them. They have clearance," Olivia says, voice flat. Turning to me, she repeats, "Get her out."

Heavy footsteps thud on the stairs, far too heavy to be Human. They stop at the top, but the door doesn't open. Something heavy and solid smashes against the door, landing with a crash on the other side.

This is no retreat.

They're blocking it.

Tenna stirs, opening mossy eyes upon this broken world. "Krona?" she whispers, gaze unfocused.

"I'm here," I say, leaning over her, clutching her hand tightly.

Hope stirs my heart into a frenzy, and a hint of recognition sparkles in her eyes.

But Dr. Sullivan's words float through me like leaves on choppy water, a terrible reminder to be patient.

She won't remember everything instantly.

The music shifts, transforming into, "She Speaks the Language by AFI. 2016." Eerie wails of sound swirl in the air, so at odds with the warmth in my chest, the glow of hope now that she's waking, now that she might finally remember me.

Tenna winces as she sits up, gritting her teeth against the agony racing through her bloodstream. Her free hand slides along my jaw, and she rests her forehead against mine. My breath catches, and questions chase their tails in my head.

Does she know me? Does she remember our life together?

Does she want to erase it all?

My heart soars and plummets, clenches and expands, but the door to the stairway bursts open, leaving us no time for answers. Armored Humans spill out like ants bubbling up out of the ground. Hot on their heels, our people rush them.

Three Regonians grab soldiers, dismantling them in showers of blood or throwing them down the stairs. Rivers of ice flow through my veins.

"Can you walk?" I ask, tearing my eyes from Tenna to sweep my gaze over this misfit army.

Who's missing?

The old woman rips a gun from the hands of a middling-height Human, dislocating his fingers. With practiced ease, she snaps his neck like a farm animal to the slaughter.

She chucks his body down the stairs, and Ricardo ducks, barely missing a foot to the face, as the man flies overhead. An avalanche of bodies rolls back down in a tumult of knees and elbows.

Olivia cries out, but Ricardo comes up swinging, driving a knife into a Soldier's stomach, just beneath a piece of armor. Blood gushes over his hand, and he withdraws the knife, shoving the Soldier back down the stairs. He slips in crimson, sliding into the lab, and relief washes over me.

But it lasts only a moment.

My eyes dance over the crowd, and I find no trace of the man with the vivid braid, the leatherworker with a family waiting on another station. Sorrow washes through me, even as I clench my free hand into a fist.

"I don't think I can walk," Tenna says. "Not yet."

Olivia shouts at us from the wall, gesturing to a broad rectangular opening near the elevator. "This way! Bring her this way!"

I glance at the battle, catch a wave of the older woman as she shoos me away, urging me to save her Queen. Tenna's arms wrap around my neck as I scoop her up, then run to the opening in the wall.

Olivia holds the door open, saying, "Jump in. It'll take you near the shuttle bay. Be careful. There are only a couple Soldiers left there, so you should be fine but... Just be careful."

Only a couple?

We'll be fine.

My muscles tighten with anticipation, eager to finally tear into the creatures responsible for all of this.

"What of you?" I ask, swinging my legs into the opening with Tenna balanced on my lap.

"Dr. Sullivan and I will lock ourselves in. Go!"

She sprints for the nearest room. Sullivan already waits, holding the door for her.

I glance at our people as I slide into the gaping maw of the laundry chute and catch a glimpse of a Soldier jabbing a stick into the older woman's back. Lightning arcs over her skin, pulses through her. She shrieks and convulses, body twisting as screams rip through her throat.

Ricardo steps up, driving a knife into the soldier's neck, slipping into the gap at the base of the man's helmet. The Soldier falls, and the lightning stops flowing.

The old woman stops screaming.

And I let go, freefalling with Tenna in my arms, putting blind faith in the words of a Human.

Last resorts are funny, fickle things.

The world becomes a blur of darkness whizzing past. My stomach leaps into my throat, and Tenna's arms wrap tighter around me.

Chapter 37
Odyssey Space Research Station

Tenna

The air shifts with the laundry-chute-echoes of the newest song, "Synthetic Love by Sarah Jaffe. 2017."

My heart leaps into my throat as we fall, and I hold tightly to Krona. The bottom of the chute comes up to meet us, and we sink into a pile of bedsheets, blankets, and clothes. Krona lets out a soft "umpf" beneath my weight.

I scramble to get my weight off his chest, straddling him. Leaning forward, I put a hand to his face. "I'm so sorry. Are you okay?"

My veins burn with the chemicals Dr. Sullivan injected, but it dulls just a little more with every passing second.

Krona's steady gaze builds a pleasant heat in my core. His hands on my hips send a shiver over my spine. His chest rises and falls quickly, and I struggle to place the look in his eyes.

But another memory rises from the depths, stealing my attention away.

All four moons glow brilliantly overhead, shining on the river, christening the harvest. I glance at Krona, at the sheer robe that hangs off his shoulders. His mark stands out against his pale grey skin. My own still stings, fresh, the Memory Markers having only just left us.

I reach up, trace the edges of the center line that matches his center finger. My skin aches, but the bond between us finally marks my body as it has marked my heart.

Casting a single glance at our ornate headdresses resting safely on the bridge, I sigh contentedly. Then, I step forward, sliding my arms around Krona's waist.

He touches my neck, tips my head back with a thumb on my jaw.

Our lips meet, gingerly.

A breeze caresses freshly marked skin, stinging with a sweet kind of pain. Krona's free hand grasps my waist, pulls me close, and our lips quest for more, parting only to whisper, "Hoo kai voo mai."

You are my sound.

My hands glide over his chest, up to the wide neck of his robe, and I push it down over his shoulders. It falls easily, landing softly on plush grass, revealing the chiseled form of a warrior.

He tugs my robe down quickly, replaces it with his hands, roaming over my skin, cupping me, pulling me against him. Freed by our partnering ceremony, I let my hands trail over him.

We sink down to the lush grass, and I push him onto his back, put one leg on either side of him. I kiss his neck, his chest, his stomach. He gasps, and I kiss his lips again. He stares up at me, eyes hooded.

For half a breath, I snap out of the memory, see the way his eyes mirror that look as he lies beneath me in the tangle of Human bedding.

But now, I see it for what it is.

Desire.

The memory claims me once more, and I see him roll me over, position himself between my legs. Our lips meet, hungry and demanding, and my insides boil. My hands tangle in his hair.

A new memory, another occasion, rises to claim me.

Early spring, with only two moons shining, we stare up at the night sky on our balcony after successfully eradicating a disease from our cattle herds.

Krona turns to me, a smile on his face, and our lips meet. Fire and joy mingle in my belly, and heat pools within me as he touches my neck. I pull him close, and he moves me back, pushes me against the wall.

My hands move of their own accord, ripping his clothes to get through to skin, to feel him.

Now, I look down at him, with Human music echoing around us, with my body burning from Human chemicals.

We're partnered?

Why didn't he say anything?

"You and I..." I begin. Hope and fear beat a frantic pace in my chest, the insecure hoofbeats of a newborn foal. Thump-thump. Thump, thump-thump. Thump. "We've joined?"

Krona chokes out a single word, throat closing over it, "Yes."

My brows furrow. My skin tingles, and the muscles in my face ache with the movement. For some reason, I ask, "How many times?"

Of all the questions, all the things I want to know... That's what comes out.

"Too many times to count." Krona pauses, letting it sink in. "We're not just partners. We're King and Queen of the Warrior Tribe Daen."

But why didn't he say so sooner?

We could've been together, could've curled up together at night. We could've comforted each other and lent each other strength.

But I'm given no more time to consider it.

Footsteps approach. The soldiers from the shuttle bay.

They must've heard us land in here.

Krona stiffens, head turning toward the sound. My heart races, and uncertainty moves through me. Fire still roars through my veins, and every muscle aches with it.

Can I fight like this?

I hate the uncertainty, hate that I can't trust myself to fight alongside him, to defend myself or our people.

But Krona doesn't need an explanation, reads it all on my face. He rolls me onto my back, and countless nights from our past flow through my mind, showing me all the times he's done that, while sparring or joining.

My body aches with the movement but cries out for more.

Leaning close, Krona whispers, lips brushing against my ear, "Stay here. I'll take care of them. As soon as you can move, we have to go back up to the labs."

Beyond the walls of our giant laundry tub, someone shouts, "Who's there? Come out with your hands up."

Krona's hand rests on the side of my neck, eyes full of sincerity and longing and... pain.

But why does he yet hurt?

His thumb trails over my lips, sending shivers down my spine.

Without another word, he pushes himself up, leaving me cold in the absence of his touch, and vaults over the side of the laundry tub. I don't have to look to know that he rolls on the landing to mask as much of the sound as possible.

This is Krona, my best friend, my partner, my King.

I know him.

The voice from before calls out, "I know you're there. Just come out already, and—"

The crack of bones echoes through the air, barely audible over the music. A body falls to the ground with a thud.

A softer voice, a woman, calls out anxiously, "Hideo? Hideo, are you okay?" Furtive footsteps sound as she approaches.

And I can see it all, see the way Krona must stalk her, even now, moving past shuttles, watching the Soldier in the dim light. For all her training, she won't stand a chance against him.

Again, the crack of bones splits the air, quickly followed by the fall of a body.

I listen closely, trying to pick Krona's footsteps out of the darkness, hoping for his swift return. I flex my hands, draws my knees up, feel the fading burn of chemicals.

Almost gone.

I could probably walk, now.

I hope.

The song shifts. "Even While by Approaching Nirvana. 2011."

Out of the darkness, Krona materializes, looking in at me over the edge of the laundry tub. His black hair hangs shaggily, beautifully dark against his pale skin and vivid green eyes.

How could I let them take him from me?

Guilt wraps filthy hands around my heart.

He means so much, but what did I do to fight for him?

"All clear," Krona says. "Do you need help up?"

Frustrated by my own weakness, by how little I've done so far, I push myself up onto my haunches. My body protests, but only vaguely, like a soft, grumbling sigh of disinterest in movement.

I'll make it work.

"I think I can do it." I cringe at the uncertainty, hating that I can't fully trust my own limbs to carry my weight.

I grasp the sides of the tub, easing myself onto my feet. Aches and groans roll through me, begging me for another moment of stillness.

But I have no more time to waste.

Some of my people, my friends, are upstairs, fighting for their lives.

I force my legs to jump and land shakily on the floor. Krona's arms reach out, grasping my waist just in time to keep me from falling. His hands linger, and time stands still.

"Thank you," I say, grateful for his help and grateful that only he is seeing me like this.

If any of our people saw me like this...

I shudder at the rage that would sweep through them, at the innocent Humans that might die before we could explain. Another shudder rolls through me at the prospect of them thinking me weak.

But Krona is here.

"Are you ready?" he asks, words pregnant with meaning.

I nod, and we set off at a brisk walk.

"You set the pace," Krona says.

I nod again, pushing myself almost to a trot despite my body's protests. Krona falls back, letting me lead him through the station I've memorized in my cleaning efforts.

Anger simmers within as we move through one hall after another, passing the fallen bodies of Odyssey Guards and even a few Soldiers. My hands curl into fists, and it builds to a steady rage, carrying me through the lingering tingling in my muscles.

We round another bend, only to find another Guard lying in a pool of blood. I grit my teeth.

These people are innocent. They stood up for what was right, and their leaders cut them down.

Sickness roils within me.

These people died for Daen Tribe, and they will not have died in vain.

I push myself harder. Krona and I fall into a familiar rhythm, jogging alongside each other. Another turn, and we reach the stairs that will lead us to the main level. Taking them three at a time, we launch ourselves into the circular hall that rings the central hub of Odyssey.

The last bits of chemicals fade, and adrenaline sings in my veins. I start to turn, to head for the hospital, but I stop short at voices from the other direction.

Someone begs for mercy, voice hoarse and cracking. A voice I know.

"I'll have a family soon. Please, don't hurt me," Matteo pleads.

"Then, tell me where they are!" A soldier shouts. The sound of flesh against metal echoes toward us.

My skin prickles, and fury roils in my gut. I take off, full speed ahead, aiming for that voice.

He wants to know where we are?

He's about to find out.

I push harder, run faster, and two men come into view. My feet pound the floor, loud and brutal. I don't try to hide.

I need him to step away from Matteo.

The song shifts, fading to silence for a few seconds, as if designed to alert the soldier to my presence, even if it does play, "Silent Running by Hidden Citizens. 2016."

The Soldier falls back, staring at me with wide eyes. Reaching for his holster, fumbling desperately for his gun, he moves away from Matteo.

I smile.

A burst of endorphins flows through me as I push my body to its full potential. For the first time in ages, I delight in the pull and flex of my muscles.

Closing the distance, I drop a shoulder and barrel into the man. We fly through the air, leaving Matteo to shrink into the wall, scuttling out of the way. I pull an arm back, ready to finish the Soldier off, but there's no need.

Blood gushes from his mouth, pooling beneath his head. His chest collapsed in the impact, brittle little ribcage no match for my hard-as-steel shoulder. Landing beneath me was insult to injury.

Springing to my feet, I turn just in time to see Krona pull the arms of another soldier from their sockets, then throw the man down the hall. A crack rings out as the soldier slams into the wall.

"Hey, Matteo," I say calmly.

"Uh... Hello," he says. "Thank you."

Okay, now to the labs.

With a wave to Matteo, I sprint over to Krona. One foot after the other, we catapult ourselves toward the hospital. An unarmed citizen lies in the middle of the hall, arm twisted at a painful angle, unmoving.

I can almost see Matteo lying like that, and I swallow hard, glad that we came through here when we did.

I hope everyone else got to their rooms.

We vault over the pool of blood beneath the nameless woman, and I tell myself that we can mourn the dead later. For now, we must protect the living.

We round the bend and find three Soldiers that my Link doesn't recognize standing sentinel at the hall leading to the residential area. My mind reels as I wonder how many are down there, harassing innocent people for the sake of the hunt. Sickness writhes within me.

But these Soldiers won't hurt anyone else.

They turn our way, too late. Krona and I run in time with each other, footsteps ringing out at the same time, every time.

The Soldiers draw their weapons, and one even gets off a shot. It grazes my arm, ricocheting off my skin. The brush of the bullet pales next to arrows and spears made of Vyrto bones.

I drop into a slide tackle, finally appreciating the smooth floors as I scoop the feet right out from under the woman who shot me. She flies up, and I grab her ankles, slingshot her into the wall. Her head cracks against a beam, and blood gushes out. Her body lands with a series of thuds.

Krona grabs the remaining two by their throats, hands wrapping tightly around their airways, and squeezes until they turn blue, then purple. They go limp in his grasp, collapsing.

Releasing them for a split second, he flips his hands, palms up, and grasps their necks again. In one fluid motion, he swings them up over his head, then slams their limp bodies down.

The floor vibrates with their impact, and the Humans shatter into sacks of blood and bone fragments.

My eyes dart toward the hospital, and my body aches to be off again, to get there in time. We fall into sync once more, running through the dark hall.

Only to find the hospital a ruin.

I stop in my tracks, staring at the wreckage of the once pristine room. Hospital beds lie in haphazard piles, and file cabinets clog the elevator doors. Tiny holes punctuate the walls, and nearly every display screen sports a network of cracks.

And everywhere, bodies.

Two dozen Soldiers lie in pools of blood, some in pieces, scattered around. Crimson stains splatter the walls, the ceilings, the desks. Dim emergency lights cast eerie shadows over the whole scene.

And among the fallen Humans, lies one of our people.

My heart fractures at the sight of so much needless death, all because a few Humans could think of no better plan than stealing us from our homes to experiment on us.

Could they not have tried to broker an alliance? Or just left us alone?

"Kingdom of Peril by Hidden Citizens. 2017." echoes through the abandoned hospital, calling to the dead, begging them to listen.

We pick our way through the blood, and Krona bounds up the stairs, stepping over bodies. Screams and thuds reverberate through the stairwell, pulling us upward. The door hangs open, half off its hinges, showing us the chaos of the labs.

Soldiers try desperately to predict what our people will do, but their markings tell me they aren't trained, have no patterns or strategies to guide them. They move in frenzied self-defense, and my heart shatters at the sight.

Humans stare out from side rooms, Olivia, Dr. Sullivan, and the nurses, unfit for combat. Pale despite their warm skin tones, they stare out through observation windows, aghast.

I square my shoulders, sizing up the ten remaining Soldiers.

I like these odds.

We step forward, and half of them break off to face us.

Even better odds.

On all sides, the screens which line the walls blink to life. The image of a woman who looks a little too much like Olivia appears. Wrinkles edge her eyes, and streaks of grey shoot through her hair.

But the resemblance is there.

"Hello, all," says Eva Dobovich, Minister of Research and Medicine, voice hooked directly into our cochlear implants. "Hello, Olivia."

"It's regrettable that it's come to this," she continues. "I had such hope for these experiments. I had hope for you, too, Olivia."

She stares out with pinched eyes, and her face burns itself into my mind. I stare over the Soldiers, committing her features to memory, highlighting the differences between her and her daughter. Higher cheek bones on the latter, bags beneath the eyes of the former.

Where Olivia has warm, sparkling hazel eyes, Eva's eyes shine the same clear brown as the bottles her daughter drinks from. Her gaze is just as hard as those bottles, though the poison they contain is far more deadly.

I'll find her. I'll destroy her for what she's done to us.

"I'll salvage what I can, though," Dobovich says. "Olivia, you could still have a great career with me. You don't have to die here with these creatures. You can come back with the Soldiers. I'll train you personally."

Through the magic of the Link, I hear Olivia's acidic response, "I'd rather die than be a part of this."

One Soldier steps forward, furtive and uncertain. As he should be.

He swallows hard, Adam's apple bobbing just below his helmet. Lifting his rifle to his shoulder, he aims at my head.

My hand shoots out, grasping the barrel of the gun and pushing it upward. I squeeze until the barrel closes in on itself, then rip it from the armored man's grasp.

Spinning it in my hand, I crash it down on his head like a club. His helmet splits, and the stock of the gun buries itself in his skull.

He falls, leaving a gap in the line of Soldiers. They glance at each other nervously.

My heart races, anticipating the battle to come, the battle that's barely even begun.

"I feared it would be this way. You were always headstrong," Dobovich's voice echoes through my mind. "I tried, though. I tried to save you."

Sickness moves through me as I realize what she's doing.

She's making peace with her daughter's murder.

"Do you really think you'll get away with this?" Olivia asks, voice laden with scorn.

The sounds swirling around our ears shape themselves into "Somewhere a Clock is Ticking by Snow Patrol. 2003."

And the four Soldiers rush us.

Two come for me, throwing punches and jabbing at me with blades that tingle when they touch flesh. A droplet of blood trickles free of one, and the skin around it numbs.

What would it do to a Human?

One pulls a gun, presses it to my stomach. I shove it to the side, sending the bullet into my other attacker, then snap the gunman's wrist.

I reel him in close and break his neck with ease. Lifting him up, I launch him into the group attacking our people. Two of them fall beneath the deadweight, landing in a jumble of knees and elbows.

"Of course, we'll get away with it," the Minister continues, unfazed by the destruction she's wrought. "The massacre on Bolivia Station gave us an explanation. All we have to do is say that the Drennar came to Odyssey. It's just a shame that you told everyone there what's going on.

We've lost so many people to the Drennar, we can't really afford such a high body count."

Cold horror sweeps through me.

They plan to kill everyone here? That's their cover up?

I slam my foot into the Soldier I got shot, driving my heel into the bullet wound weeping from his side. He topples backward, sliding on his own blood, and knocks the legs out from under a woman still fighting our people.

I turn as Krona drives an elbow into the side of the lone remaining attacker, and the man falls like a sack of rocks to land atop his comrade.

More soldiers explode into the hospital below us, and the Minister goes on, justifying her choices in the silence that follows the temporary break in our fight. "This research is worth it, though. It's our only chance to make any headway against the Drennar. It's our only way to get our people back."

She pauses, then, "Besides, the Regonians will be fine. There are three planets full of them, after all."

I go still, staring at the screens in confusion. Krona and our people do, as well.

Eva Dobovich plays coy. "Oh, you didn't know? I'm sorry to be the one to break the news."

But her lips twitch into a small smile.

Three planets full of us?

My world crashes down around me, yet again, collapsing for what feels like the thousandth time in days.

But Soldiers come forth, surging from the bowels of Odyssey, a plague spreading out to destroy everything I love. They spill from the stairs, filling the room around us.

Surrounded, I take one punch after another, endure a stab or two. My ears ring as one fires a shot.

And then, I come alive.

I draw up a knee and send my foot into the face of a nearby Soldier. He soars backward, flying through the air.

A bullet slams into my sternum, splits the skin, but the little piece of metal falls, landing on the hard floor with a plink.

That'll leave a nasty bruise.

Surging forward, I slam my attacker into the wall, and frail Human bones shatter. I drop the Soldier in a heap.

Eva Dobovich's words hiss through my mind. "Now, let's draw all of this to a close. You, all of you, stop this mess."

The screens change, drawing my gaze in furtive glances. No longer do they show Olivia's foul mother, instead switching to show stacks and shapes, vague and dark.

Then, I see it for what it is, and my eyes glue themselves to the screens.

A camera on another Station pans across a large, dimly lit room with impossibly tall ceilings, perhaps once the cafeteria. Metal bunks fill the space, one above the other, arranged five high.

Sleeping Regonians fill row upon row of beds. Wires and tubes hook up to them, and circular pads dot their skin. Tiny patches of gauze decorate their bodies.

Our people... Cut and measured and tested... Lying there, defenseless.

My veins freeze as I stare at the screens.

Three Soldiers jump me from behind, nearly pulling me from my feet. I force myself back into the fight, dropping an elbow to crush a sternum. It crunches, brittle and delicate.

Sharp, clear piano caresses my ears. "End of Innocence (Piano Version) by Kamelot. 2015."

I spin, driving my elbow into one throat, then another, and the other Soldiers fall. Dropping to a knee, I grab their faces, lift them up, and slam their heads into the floor with all my might. Blood pools beneath their broken skulls.

"Your Tribe is spread out on three different stations," Dobovich drones, almost bored. "As you now know, there are more where you came from. You are expendable. Disposable."

My blood boils, and I slam their heads into the floor one more time.

"I'm prepared to dispose of these specimens," Dobovich says, "unless you immediately stop fighting. Allow this research to come to fruition. More of you will survive if you just let us finish this work and move on. No one else even needs to know about this."

I grab another Soldier by the waist and slam her down. I draw a fist back, punch through her helmet, crushing her skull in one blow.

But Olivia's voice fills my mind. "It's too late for that."

I glance at the screens in time to see the Minister's perfect facade fracture. "What do you mean?"

An ember of hope burns within, hope that Olivia will have outsmarted her terrible mother. I grab an ankle, jerk it upward, and a Soldier falls on his back. I drive my fist down on his neck, bursting the soft flesh, scraping my knuckle on the jagged edge of his helmet.

"Everyone knows," Olivia says. "I streamed ALL of this to Termana. I told the rest of the Coalition. You and that bastard, Mulvaney, are going down. They're sending Guards, Soldiers, Specialists, anyone that isn't privy to the disaster the two of you created."

"You couldn't have. We covered all our bases," Eva argues.

Disgusted, Olivia spits out, "You tried. Your people did a decent job of it, too. But not good enough."

A Soldier jumps on my back, and their heft tugs at the seams of my stupid Human garments, nearly splitting them.

Rage boils in my veins, and I grit my teeth. Reaching back, I grab the opportunist and slam her to the floor. The air whooshes out of her in a great gust, and I drive my fist into her face. Once, Twice.

"You lie," the Minister accuses her daughter, voice hissing through me.

"Why would I?" Olivia says. "They'll be at your house soon enough. I don't need to lie."

I look up, assessing the room. Krona tears into three of his four attackers, sending them flying in all directions. But one stands behind him, holding a stick that looks too much like the one they used on the older woman earlier.

The one that shot lightning through her.

My heart drops, and ice flows through my veins. I shout, but Krona doesn't turn, can't tear his eyes from the three Soldiers in front of him.

A sinister whisper oozes into our ears as Eva Dobovich says, "Do it, Ferdinand."

Across every screen, electricity surges through wires and into our people. It arcs over their skin in ripples of purple and white, singeing their hair, ruining their organs.

I stare up at the screens in silent horror, attention ripped away just a heartbeat too long.

Krona screams, and I wrench my eyes from the screens. The lightning stick presses into his back, and white sparks jolt over his skin.

I spring to my feet, launch myself across the room. Leaping over bodies, I plow into the lightning bringer.

He slams back, crashes into the wall. I land before him, down on one knee, and he slumps, falling flat. I drive my fist into his chest, over and again. Raw satisfaction courses through me. I draw back, driving my fist into his chest once more, punching straight through, denting the wall behind him.

I spin as Krona stumbles back, knees wobbling beneath him. He falls, and I scramble forward to catch him in my arms.

The music cuts off, and the air grows still around us, broken only by the sounds of stragglers falling at the hands of our people.

The lights flicker, come back on.

My mind fills with the sounds of Eva arguing with Guards, telling them they can't arrest her.

But I don't look at the screens.

I stare at Krona, motionless in my arms. I pull him against my chest, crooning softly, rocking back and forth.

"No..." I whisper, voice hitching. "I finally have you back, I can't lose you, again."

I kiss his face, his lips, clutching him tight.

Ricardo and the other Regonians close ranks around us as they take down the last Soldiers. Tears fall, and my breaths hitch as my periphery fills with convulsions on a few screens.

I stroke Krona's face, trying not to hear the sounds of Mulvaney's arrest, but the noise of it, his arguments, fill my head.

Screen by screen, the convulsions fall away as Olivia replaces the carnage with the arrests. Before she changes the last screen, their convulsions stop, and they lie still in their beds.

As still as Krona in my arms.

I touch his slack face, rub my thumb over his cheek, but he doesn't reach for me, doesn't smile, doesn't even open his eyes.

"Please..." I beg, voice cracking. "Please, wake up."

Another body falls, the last body.

All around the room, the doors to the observation rooms slide open. Footsteps assault my ears, and I wince as they all see him like this, see him broken in my arms.

Silence fills the room, heavy and stagnant. I rock back and forth, one arm under Krona's shoulders, the other hand tangled in his hair.

I bow over him, press my forehead to his. I touch his cheek, and tears drop from my eyes, landing on his. His eyelid twitches.

My breath catches.

I lean closer, place my ear against his lips, waiting for a breath. My hand goes to his neck, and time stretches out like an abyss.

A tiny gust of air brushes my ear. A miniscule flutter of a heartbeat moves beneath my fingertip.

Relief washes over me, and I break into pieces. I clutch him tighter, crying out.

"Thank you," I whisper, voice hoarse.

But I don't know who I'm thanking. I can't thank the ancestors anymore, not now that I know...

But it doesn't matter.

Krona's here.

I cup his cheeks, kiss his lips, willing more air into his lungs.

"Krona," I plead, tears still streaming over my cheeks. "Please, please, wake up."

My lips find his, press against his cheeks, his jaw. My heart crumples, and I beg him to return to me.

His eyes move beneath his lids, and I choke on my next words, stifling them before they erupt. His hands flex faintly, briefly, and a thousand Molans move within my stomach, fluttering rapidly.

Vivid green opens to the world, perfect eyes gazing up at me, releasing light back into my life. He tries to lift his arm, reaching for my face, but he groans in pain.

Sputtering, I grab his hand and press it to my cheek.

"Tenna," he whispers, voice rough but so sweet.

"Krona," I croon, kissing him softly.

His lips press against mine, feeble at first, but he grows more insistent, slips a hand to the back of my neck. I clutch him tighter, deepen the kiss.

The screens around us flicker in my periphery, and I glance up at a new face. A middle-aged man with silver strands of hair falling to his jaw, draped over his olive-skinned face.

I help Krona sit up, brace him against my body. We watch this stranger sweep his hair back, only for it to fall forward again. His dark brown eyes hang heavy with interrupted sleep.

"Good evening," he says. "To those of you who don't know me, I'm Johnathan Croon, Minister of Human Affairs, though that title may be misleading in this case." His voice drops, and he says, more to himself than to us,

"Housing, roads, jobs. That's more my forte, not... whatever this is."

We stare up at the screens, waiting as the man tells us that all the arrests are being made, that they'll hold a tribunal to decide how to proceed in the coming days. "You'll all be excused from your work details, of course," he says. "We'll need you at the tribunal."

His face softens. "I'm so sorry, for all of this." As he goes on, his voice grows insistent, desperate. "I should've seen it, should've figured this out, should've stopped it somehow."

Krona takes my hand in his.

On the screen, Croon shakes his head, lips pursed. "We're drafting a statement for the public as we speak, and another will be made after we reach a decision at the tribunal."

He pauses, perhaps waiting for an interjection or a question, but he's alone in his home and we wait in the floor of the lab. Leaning forward, Croon steeples his fingers.

"Your injuries will be treated immediately," he says, eyes far away. "The off-duty nurses are on their way, now."

"You can sleep in the side labs for the time being. It's the only place they can treat you." Shaking his head,

Croon apologizes again, then ushers us off for treatment and rest.

"Thank you," I whisper, unsure if Croon hears it through whatever channels Olivia has open.

Rising to my feet, I help Krona up. I ache to carry him off, but I settle him onto a bed before I bustle about, straightening the lab, wheeling beds into side rooms.

My heart spasms as I lift a young woman named Kuna into a bed. Her dark braids fan out on the pillow, and her marks drink in the light.

Blood seeps from a deep gash, an old injury reopened by Human weapons. The dark liquid seeps into bed sheets, and nurses move into place, holding pressure, trying desperately to staunch the bleeding.

The off-duty nurses rush up the stairs, crowding around the young woman. I move away, move to Krona's bedside.

But he and I need only rest.

He rises, pushing himself as we see the rest of our people into beds. He holds himself steady, body recovering far more swiftly than the Human nurses expect.

But things that don't kill us don't last long.

I squeeze his hand, thankful that the lightning didn't move through him even a heartbeat longer.

Ricardo stumbles toward us. He presses one hand to a hole-shaped wound on his upper arm, the other to a stab wound on his side.

I lift him into a bed and press a hand to his shoulder. "Thank you," I whisper.

Olivia comes to us, clutching Ricardo's hand.

***

With everyone settled into beds and the nurses working, Olivia, Krona, and I walk together through the Station. Olivia trails along in our wake, quiet and subdued. I clutch Krona's hand as our footsteps echo through the halls.

At our rooms, we part from Olivia. As her door slides closed, she mutters, "Back to work..."

Krona and I slip into my room, and my heart skips unevenly. But one question lingers in my mind.

Why didn't he say anything?

Uncertainty rolls through me, and I step into the dark room. Music flows through the air, and I dance.

Chapter 38
Odyssey Space Research Station

Olivia

The door shuts firmly, closing me off from everyone. I stand in the center of my room, staring into the darkness, trying not to think, not to see the dead and dying.

But their convulsing bodies flicker through my mind in a strobe of horror and betrayal, and my breath hitches.

2,000 Regonians... Dead.

How many Humans?

How many of my friends and coworkers died tonight?

My Link goes off in search of the answer, but I stop it, unable to bear the weight of that number piled atop the overwhelming loss of 2,000 souls.

And Ricardo...

The blood on his skin, the exhaustion in his face, the sweat plastering his hair to his forehead... It all flashes before my eyes, and my heart falters.

And my mother is to blame.

I'm to blame.

My knees buckle, and I fall to the floor, crumpling into a heap. My brain spirals, and guilt churns in my gut.

"Stop it. Stop, stop, stop, stop, stop!" I mumble, pressing my fists to my eyes, trying to chase the sight of so much death from my mind.

But pools of blood in the hospital and hallways paint themselves across the backs of my eyelids. Regonians writhe in my mind, rattling me to my core.

"I could've stopped it," I whisper.

My insides twist, pushing themselves down to make room for the burden settling within me like a stone.

Tears fall like rain, and as they land, each one seems to whisper, "My fault."

Splash.

Fault.

Splash, splash.

My fault.

"Why did I waste so much time?" I whimper, words choked by the lump in my throat as every useless night of drinking with friends, of sitting in the darkness of the airlock with only music and the stars for comfort, slips through my mind.

I should've spent all that time on Atlantis, on keeping track of what Mother was doing, but now...

Tears rush from my eyes, splattering on the floor in a quiet symphony of guilt.

"They're all dead. Because of me."

I choke on a sob, hunching forward, pressing my forehead to the floor. Quiet, useless words pour from me in mutters and whimpers.

"If I'd finished Atlantis... If I hadn't told Lachlan..."

My throat grows tight, closing on the words I can't speak.

If I hadn't been such a fuck-up.

If I hadn't been so weak, so stupid.

Fault, fault, fault.

All my fault.

The tears fall, singing of my sins as they crash to the floor. They break me, sap my strength, and I curl into myself.

"I'm so STUPID!" I scream, words shattering the silence in my dark, cold room. I jam my fists into my eyes, crying out.

Anger rocks through me, and I pound my fist against the floor. Harsh sobs rack my body, beating me from the inside, threatening to tear me apart.

But guilt settles over me, as thick and oppressive as smoke. It clouds my mind, pollutes my thoughts, until all I can think of is my own worthlessness and all I see are the bodies.

"They're all gone." The words come out a hoarse whisper. "Because of me."

Chapter 39
Novay C. E. 2018

Reginald

Rone's wings flutter restlessly as she escorts me back to my room. The black feathers reach out, brushing my arm, and I jolt. She looks back at me, eyes wide, apparently just as startled as I am by the contact.

I didn't realize I was walking that close. Or that her wings were stretched out quite so far.

I drop my gaze, flushing at the casual reintroduction to physical touch. After all, aside from contact necessary for attaching equipment to me in various tests, no one has touched me in twelve years.

Everything in me cries out for more, and I barely hold back from reaching for her.

Rone's eyes sweep over me, and something in her gaze is different, a far cry from the cold analysis so common for her kind. I tip my head to the side, trying to pick out the meaning of this change in her, but she turns away, resuming her walk to my room. I expect her to step aside when the wall slides open.

But she passes through ahead of me.

My brows furrow.

Strange...

But so is the way her fingers tangle together in front of her, fidgeting.

"Is... something wrong?" I ask, uncertain of the words even as they cross my lips. My voice cracks from disuse.

Nodding, she wills the wall to reassemble itself. Her mouth opens and closes, but she says nothing.

I gesture to the bed, the only seating I have to offer, and she takes me up on it. Swallowing back my shock, I sit down beside her.

The intimacy of the moment strikes me. Or maybe it only seems intimate to me. Either way, with her so close, my skin buzzes with electricity, begging me to reach out.

I plant my hands firmly in my lap.

The gesture doesn't feel right, my posture too closed off, but anything more open feels foolish.

Rone sits quietly, scraping one fingernail over another. I almost ask what's bothering her, almost push, but I shut my lips tight.

Her multi-colored eyes land on me, vivid blue lines shifting over green irises, and she opens her mouth to speak. But again, nothing comes out. Sighing, she drops her gaze to the floor.

My nerves wind tight, and I know I can't hold back much longer. My hands itch to reach for her, and my brain begs me to speak.

So, I choose the lesser of two evils.

"What's wrong?" I ask. "Sometimes it helps to talk about your feelings."

Her head jerks up, and she stares at me, open-mouthed. "You can tell? About the feelings?"

"Of course, I can," I say, chuckling softly. "You aren't exactly acting like the others. And you all experiment on yourselves as much as you do on everyone else."

Her eyes flutter, and she slams her mouth shut.

What did I say wrong?

She looks away from me, staring at her fidgeting hands. "All these experiments..." she mutters. "I can't talk about them though. Not to you."

"Do you have to be somewhere right now?" I ask.

She shakes her head, so I urge my Link to play music. "Deadweight on Velveteen by Jose Gonzalez. 2003." slips through the air. Classical guitar washes over us.

I reach out and take her hand, and my heart races. My fingers lace with hers, and I hope it comforts her the way I mean it to.

Be calm. This is nothing.

It's only been twelve years since I've held anyone's hand.

But the warmth of her skin flows into me, tugging at the knots which have twisted my spine for far too long.

Catching my breath, I lay back on the bed and close my eyes.

The guitar dances around us, stirring a strange energy within me. It builds tension, but not in an unpleasant way, joining forces with the feel of Rone's hand in mine, the knowledge that she's right there, right on the edge of my bed.

It's almost like butterflies, flipping about in my stomach.

My tired soul lets go of some of the pain it's held onto so greedily, hoarding any reminder of home, no matter the cost.

The mattress shifts, pulled down by Rone's weight as she lays down beside me, and I open my eyes to the sterility of my room. Turning from the steely blue ceiling, I seek her out.

She lies on her side, wings unfurled behind her to drape over my pillow. She releases my hand for a moment, drawing her knees up onto the bed, and I turn to face her.

I lay my hand on the bed, fully expecting her to leave it there, all alone, but she laces our fingers together once more, watching me carefully.

A single tear falls from her dark lashes.

And there, in those magnificent green and blue eyes, I find life.

Chapter 40
Odyssey Space Research Station

Krona

"Wicked Game by Ursine Vulpine featuring Annaca. 2016." reaches from the speaker near Tenna's bed, slow and heavy. Clear notes ring out over the atmospheric hush.

My mind spirals, and the events of the night repeat, over and again. Olivia, attacked. The station, invaded. Tenna waking, seeing me, *knowing* me. The jolt of lightning, and the death of a third of our people.

I take a deep breath, heart twisting in my chest.

And before me, stepping in time to this strange Human music, Tenna dances. She spins, moves side to side, reaches out.

For me.

I swallow, stepping forward to take her hands, answering the call I've never been able to resist. We sway together, and I draw comfort from the familiar movements, the feel of her against me.

My hands trail over the bare skin of her arms, then slip to her waist. My breath catches.

I relish the feel of her moving against me and soak in the seductive music as it wraps around us, shutting out the rest of the worlds. Every fiber of my being begs for more, aches to pull her in, to press my lips to her neck.

But my heart lurches, wondering if maybe she regrets me, if she liked the reprieve from our life together, the reprieve from the responsibilities of being Warrior Queen.

After all, leading the Tribe was always her life. Even if her brother or sister had won the battle for Inera, she would've been the next in line.

She never knew a life unburdened by leadership, never got that choice.

She turns to face me, moving in time with the music. She doesn't speak, only holds my gaze. Her breathtaking, moss-colored eyes hold storms of emotion, soft and violent at the same time.

She steps closer, and my heart skips a beat. Her hand glides down my arm, trails over my wrist, and she takes my hand in hers. Raising our joined hands, she presses a kiss to my palm. I suck in a breath. Her lips linger, sweet and delicate, and weight falls from my shoulders with a sigh.

She releases my hand to touch my cheek. Her thumb moves back and forth over my skin, leaving trails of fire in its wake.

Our feet go still, calling the dance to an end, but the music swirls on around us. Swallowing, I stare into her eyes, but she seems nervous. I pull her close, tightening my arms around her waist.

The feel of her, the smell of her... It tears at my willpower. My arms drift lower, hanging at her hips.

She steps closer, eyes dropping to my lips, and my heart skitters into a frenzy. Her nose brushes mine, and my eyes flutter shut.

She touches her lips to mine, tender and soft, and my breath catches. Her perfect lips part, inviting me in, and I taste her. She cups the back of my neck, deepening the kiss.

And my self-control fractures.

I grasp her buttocks, and she moans against my lips. The small sound makes heat pool within me.

But it also brings reality crashing back down onto me. My body aches for her, fighting against my mind, yet I force myself to go still.

"Wait," I say. "What do you remember?"

She considers the question, searching my gaze. Finally, she whispers, "I remember enough."

The soft words brush my heart, but they don't completely assuage my fears.

She leans in to kiss me, and though my body begs for it, I hold her upper arms, stopping her. "This is important," I say. My heart cracks, and I force myself to speak. "I need to know that you remember me. That I told you who I am isn't enough. You have to remember. I..."

My eyes fall, almost closing, and I sigh. "I *need* you to remember me." My voice breaks on the words.

She gazes at me, searching my face. The music changes, filling the space before she answers.

"Tempt You (Evocatio) by Nothing but Thieves. 2015."

She touches my cheek, and her eyes soften with understanding. She smiles, slipping her arms around my waist.

"I remember that all four moons marked the harvest on the night of our partnering ceremony. Our headdresses were especially ornate, befitting the Queen and King of the Tribe." She rests her head on my chest. "I remember our first night together, out on the island."

I take a deep breath as her words sink in, and my eyes close.

She remembers our first joining.

She traces small, agonizing circles on my lower back.

"We put our headdresses on the mantle in the great room of our keep," she whispers, voice carrying over the music. "The blue pearls glisten beautifully in the firelight, almost like they're glowing."

I clutch her tighter, and relief washes over me.

"You were with me at my grandmother's funeral," she goes on. "You held my hand as we sang, and we watched her body burn on the river as sparks drifted into the wind. It was the first public event we attended together."

Her lips brush my chest, sending shivers of excitement through me.

She remembers.

Maybe bits and pieces, but she remembers.

Smiling, I touch her chin, lift her face so that I may stare into her eyes.

"I remember standing side by side in the keep, addressing famine and war," Tenna says. "I remember riding into battle with you, playing jokes on Efsi and Kala, staying up late talking and laughing."

A delicate smile plays over her lips, dances in her eyes. A tear slips over her skin. I cup her cheek and wipe the tear away with my thumb.

"I remember us," she says.

Heat flows through me, and the last vestiges of my restraint melt away. My lips crash down upon hers, tasting her. I kiss her neck, her collarbone, and she moans softly, hands tangling in my hair.

A deep need rocks me, and my body begs to join with her. I need to feel her give way beneath me, need to claim her as mine, even as she claims me.

Her hands slip beneath my shirt, lifting it up and over my head. She tosses it aside, and her lips meet mine, only to leave a trail of tantalizing kisses down my neck, over my collarbone, down to my chest. Her fingers roam over my stomach, and I suck in a breath.

My hands sift through her long, luscious hair, nails trailing over her scalp. She clings to me, and I tilt her head back to feast on the sensitive skin of her neck.

The heady scent of her fills me, and fire rushes through my veins. I rip her shirt open, sending the buttons flying. They plink and skitter across the floor, disappearing beneath the bed, the bench, the wardrobe.

The soft tones of a new song shift around us. "In the Darkness by Dead by Sunrise. 2009."

I push the shirt over her shoulders, let it fall, but some strange Human piece of clothing locks her breasts away from me. I growl in frustration.

Tenna's hands desert my skin, reaching behind her, and the fabric cage falls to the floor. I take a deep breath, reveling in all her perfection. The brilliant blue of her tattoos shines, perched beautifully above her breasts.

My eyes trace the marks, all the ways we're connected. Tribe. Partners. Queen and King.

She traces the mark that rings my neck, and shivers of desire rumble through me like an earthquake. She flattens her hand against my chest, lining her middle finger up with one of the short lines, *her* lines, then lets her hand meander down my torso.

My skin ignites at her touch, and a shiver rolls through me.

My lips find hers once more. I cup and caress her, loving every second of it.

Tenna is here.

Our mouths meld, and I clutch her hip. I kiss her lips, her neck.

This is real.

The feel of her skin, the taste of her lips, the pressure of her body against mine. It's all real.

She's alive, and she's here.

I pull back, searching her gaze, but I see no questions, no uncertainty. Only loyalty, love, desire.

She knows me.

Sliding my hands down her back, over her firm buttocks, I grasp her and lift her up. Long, muscular legs wrap around my waist, and my blood roars through my veins. I carry her to the bed, lower her gently onto the mattress.

The lingering burn of the lightning courses through me, and my muscles protest, but it doesn't matter.

I need this.

She moves against me, and my heart races. Chests heaving, we chase the air from the room. She kisses my ear, and I press against her warmth, delighting in the soft sounds that rush from her.

Fire dances along my skin as her hands reacquaint themselves with my body. Our lips meet, pressed together hungrily, and we tear away the last bits of our clothing. Poised between her legs, I pause for a moment, eyes locked on hers.

"Hoo kai voo mai," I whisper, voice filled with love and awe at the sight of her.

"Hoo kai voo mai," she says.

You are my sound.

The words I've needed from her for so long.

Her eyes shine with pure, unadulterated joy, and she caresses my cheek. I lean down to kiss her lips, her neck, relishing the feel of her heartbeat beneath my lips.

And suddenly, I can't wait any longer.

I plunge into her, reveling in the gasp that bursts from her. She wraps her legs tighter around me, pulling me deeper, moving in time.

Mouths melding, bodies writhing, hands questing, we join together.

***

Tenna's fingers trace lazy patterns on my lower back, sending my stomach fluttering. Lying breathless on the bed, limbs tangled and feet dangling over the end, we relish the sensations of being so close.

From the little speaker beside her bed, soft sounds call out to us in the shape of, "Eric by Mitski. 2012."

Her eyelashes brush my chest, and my skin tingles. I close my eyes, soaking in the feel of her. My arms circle around her, pulling her more firmly against me. She trails her fingernails down my spine, and I shudder.

"What story did they tell you on Ulysses? Not a solar flare," she says.

I shake my head, pulling in a deep breath. "No, not a solar flare." I swallow, reciting the details of their tale, the things I remember only in impressions left in the wake of the removed memories.

"They said you sought out Mourgam…"

She wrinkles her nose, and disgust fills her voice as she says, "For what?"

"For a truce. They said you joined with him, that I found you and killed the both of you," I say, shuddering at the mere thought. "The memories just… appeared. They filled my head with it, but they didn't feel right. They didn't feel like you, like us."

The pain of days past floats through me. Her absence and the cell. The self-doubt and terror. Her inability to remember me and the losses tonight.

But she's here now.

She's here, and she's alive.

And we'll figure this all out. We'll get our people and go home.

I blow out a breath, drawing comfort from her presence.

Her name repeats through my mind, a mantra to fend off the horrors we've endured, a comfort to show me where I've erred in my own judgement.

I was too harsh on my guards.

And Ricardo, Olivia, and Doctor Sullivan...

I shake my head, finally accepting them as friends, not just allies necessary for the survival of my people.

I kiss Tenna's forehead softly, wondering how she can make all feel well, even when so much is left undone. So many hard days lie ahead, but she makes it less overwhelming.

I let out a long sigh.

We can do this. We will do this.

We'll deal with the vile Humans who captured us and experimented on us. We'll get our Tribe back and keep them from killing the innocent among the Humans.

We'll get home, somehow.

I swallow.

Ancestors, lend us strength.

But the thought is an empty habit. Our monstrous ancestors will be of no help to us.

Their treachery against the Humans, their mysterious abandonment of us, their continued monitoring of our lives...

And three planets full of us.

My mind spins, trying to fit the pieces together, to find a way to accomplish all of this without unnecessary death. Tension begins to build within me again, but nothing compared to that which hung over me just hours ago.

The song shifts to heavily distorted guitars and a soothing female voice. "Shame (Jammin' Out Solo Version) by Mitski. 2013."

My heart clamors along with it, agonized and tense, beating raggedly within me. Tenna's palm flattens over my chest, and she looks up at me with beautiful green eyes.

"Our worries will keep for the night," she says. One corner of her lips lifts into a smile, and she slides her hand up to my neck, pulling me in for a kiss.

Gently, she whispers, "This is what we need now."

And then our lips meet once more.

I melt into her, setting it all aside for the moment. She slips her leg over mine, and hunger builds within. Straddling me, she kisses my lips, my neck, my chest.

My body burns at her touch, and I grasp her hips. Her teeth graze my ear. Thankful no clothes or bedsheets separate us, I join with her. We move together, achingly slow, and all the worlds fall away.

Continue reading in *Faltering*, book two of The Regonia Chronicles.

Thank you!

For buying this book. For reading it all the way through.

If you liked it, please leave a review on Amazon, Goodreads, Barnes & Noble, your blog... Anywhere, really. Reviews are the lifeblood of authors, helping books get noticed in the almighty eyes of search engine algorithms. Even if only a few words, a review is incredibly helpful.

Eager to stay up to date on the latest dark fiction from Elexis Bell?

Sign up for her newsletter here.

Other Books by this Author

Literary Fantasy Novels

Soul Bearer

The Gem of Meruna

A Heart of Salt & Silver

Allmother Rising

The Sword and The Savage

Literary Thriller Novellas

Annabelle

Things Left Unsaid

Literary Post-Apocalyptic Novel

World for the Broken

About the Author

Elexis Bell is a quiet nerd with too many hobbies, including everything from gaming to shower-singing and even archery, weather permitting. She specializes in sarcasm and writing stories that make people feel. She's made a home for herself with her husband and a small army of cats.

She writes dark, gritty stories, sprinkling gut-wrenching emotions over high fantasy romance, thrillers, post-apocalyptic romance, and science fiction.

For further information, follow her on Instagram, Twitter, or Facebook, or check out her blog on her website. There, you can sign up for her newsletter to stay up to date on all future book releases, giveaways, and ongoing projects.

www.elexisbell.com